True North

Book Four

of the American Nomads

N. L. Mclaughlin

This is a work of fiction. Copyright © by N.L. McLaughlin

All rights reserved. No part of this book may be reproduced or used in any manner without written permission of the copyright owner.

Printed by:

Twisted Sky, LLC

ISBN: 978-1-7367059-9-5

Proofreading provided by the Hyper-Speller at https://www.wordrefiner.com

Cover art provided by Meagan McLaughlin MeaganEMcLaughlin@gmail.com

N
W
E
S

To every reader who has left a rating or review,
Y'all are the real rock stars.
Thank you for all your enthusiasm and support.

"The past is never where you think you left it."
— Katherine Anne Porter

"Life should not be a journey to the grave with the intention of arriving safely in a pretty and well preserved body, but rather to skid in broadside in a cloud of smoke, thoroughly used up, totally worn out, and loudly proclaiming "Wow! What a Ride!"
— Hunter S. Thompson

Chapter One

The sun was at a low point on the horizon, casting its orange-yellow glow across the sky. Finn rested on the iron beams of what used to be an impressive roller coaster in the ruins that were once the Six Flags amusement park of New Orleans. The old, wooden structure moved and shifted with the gentle breeze. His feet dangled above the murky water of the lake as he watched the fish below gobble the occasional dragonfly that made the unfortunate mistake of getting too close to the surface.

"He's doing good," said Teague, sitting nearby. He was talking on the phone with River.

Finn glanced over at him and smiled when Teague winked. Close to three months had passed since they last saw the others back in Terlingua. When they first set out alone, they intended to sort out their issues and reconnect. Too many horrible things had happened, too much to speak about in one sitting. After a month-long stay at Stoney's with the Nomads, they headed east, aiming for the white, sandy beaches of western Florida.

The ocean was Teague's choice of location, as he wanted to be in a warm and calm place. He had always found the sound of waves crashing to the shore soothing. Finn would have preferred the mountains, mostly because he could guarantee food would be abundant, but, in all honesty, he would have gone anywhere. The only thing that mattered to him was that he was with Teague. The location was irrelevant.

The time alone was exactly what they needed. No drama, no traveling circus, no distractions, and no other people to consider. Just the two of them, with plenty of time to talk and laugh. During the long discussions, he discovered a great deal about Teague and himself.

They spent their nights on the Florida beach with a warm fire, and their days lounging in the sun or relaxing in the cool, ocean water. Food was a challenge, given that they had no means of setting up snares or hunting, not to mention the absence of anything to scavenge. When it came to catching fish off the ocean piers, Teague was much better at it than Finn. This irritated him at first. Finn had a strong aversion to depending on others for his basic needs. But the joy in Teague's face with each catch set those feelings aside quickly.

Finn made a promise to himself to turn over a new leaf. He didn't want to be angry anymore, choosing instead to be more like the people he admired. He yearned for the inner peace that Gunner seemed to have, and the faith in others that Teague possessed, as well as the ability to enjoy the little things like Cash.

When he was living on the streets, alone and desperate, he had been robbed multiple times. He understood all too well the feeling of losing what little you had left in your possession, so part of his new beginning in life was to only take from those who could afford to lose it.

Their money was depleting quickly as the days turned into weeks. They tried their hands at finding work, but no one was willing to give two, homeless campers a chance, so they decided to fly signs. They split up on separate corners, it was the best way to reach out to as many people as possible. That was when Ruth came along; the little, elderly grandma who stole their hearts.

The first time Finn saw the old woman, she had wandered up to Teague. One minute he was alone, holding his sign, the next, tiny, little Ruth was standing in front of him. From his vantage point, Finn couldn't tell what they were talking about, but based on Teague's face, the conversation was pleasant. After perhaps twenty minutes, the old woman gave Teague a slip of paper, then waved goodbye and left.

"What was that all about?" asked Finn, as Teague joined him on his side of the intersection.

"Her name is Ruth," replied Teague. "She asked me if we were interested in earning some money, as opposed to begging."

"Brutally honest I see," said Finn. "Bold." He nodded in approval.

"She's a quick one," said Teague. "Her eyes are crystal clear." He tapped the side of his head. "You can see her intelligence in them."

Teague always had a great admiration for the elderly. Because of his upbringing with his grandparents, he possessed a gift for communicating with them. His face would light up when listening to their stories. And they too seemed to revel in the company of a young person, especially one who was eager to listen. He enjoyed the interactions every bit as much as they did. Finn would tease him, calling him the crone whisperer. But deep down inside, he wished he could be as open as Teague. He just didn't know how.

"So, what's on the paper she gave you?" asked Finn.

"Oh, yeah," said Teague. He pulled a slip of paper from his pocket, unfolded it, and handed it to Finn. "Like I said, she asked if we'd be interested in doing a few odd jobs around her home. She promised to pay us. She also said she'd make us a dinner fit for kings."

Finn studied Teague's face. "You wanna do it. Don't you?"

A bright smile spread across his face. He bobbed his head up and down.

"I guess I don't see why not," replied Finn. He glanced up at the afternoon sky. "We got the whole day left."

Ruth's humble, little home sat nestled in the center of a quaint neighborhood of single-story homes with perfectly manicured lawns. Each one had a large, screened-in patio in the back covering a swimming pool. Tall palm trees swayed in the warm, afternoon breeze, casting little shade.

They rounded the corner and paused, evaluating the amount of work they signed up for. The home itself was well maintained, though there were areas that could use a new coat of paint. A forest of metal bird feeders adorned the overgrown lawn. From his vantage point, Finn noticed a sheet of screen billowing in the breeze as it peeped out from behind the house.

"Looks like we got some work to do," quipped Teague.

Finn didn't reply, he was too busy dividing up the labor based on what he saw needed to be done.

Ruth greeted them at the door with a ready smile. Teague was right, her eyes positively sparkled with life. A sharp contrast to her tired and wrinkled body. With a welcoming smile, she escorted them to the kitchen, where she gestured for them to take a seat at the table.

"I'll make you boys some lunch, then we can get started on what I need you to do," she said.

"Is there someplace to clean up?" asked Teague, holding his hands out to show the grime.

"Oh yes," she replied. "Around that corner is a bathroom."

Teague disappeared, leaving Finn alone with the old woman. The silence was deafening—the discomfort was downright painful. He wasn't very good at small talk. Least of all with old people. Each second may as well have been hours.

"Your friend Teague says your name is Finn," said Ruth. She poured a cold glass of lemonade and handed it to him.

"Yes, Ma'am," he replied.

The old woman studied him and smiled. "I see you're not as conversational as your friend."

"How's everyone doing in here?" asked Teague, as he sauntered back into the kitchen, the floral scent of soap following him. He slapped a firm hand on Finn's shoulder and smiled. "The bathroom's all yours."

Finn needed no prompting, he jumped to his feet and quickly exited the room, thankful for the peace of being away from Ruth's alert eyes.

Photos adorned the walls of the hallway. It always fascinated him how people would hang their life stories like this. A not-so-small part of him yearned for the chance to do the same thing one day. Finn studied a black-and-white image of what appeared to be a much younger Ruth on her wedding day. The young couple beamed at the camera, their faces locked in perpetual smiles.

The next image was Ruth, cradling a baby in her arms. Her husband standing close with one protective arm around her.

Usually, images like these triggered anger in Finn, but for some reason, this one made him sad. He strolled down the hall, taking the time to study each photograph.

The boy grew into a tall, young man while the couple shrunk and aged. It was almost as though his life drained theirs away. Their love for one another was obvious. So much so, Finn could almost feel it.

As far as he could tell, there were no other children, just the one. He wondered what it would have been like if he had parents who actually loved him the way Ruth and her husband seemed to adore their son.

The young man married a pretty woman. The family photo was now four. A photo of the young couple holding twins swaddled in blankets told their own story.

The family portrait was now six.

The next group of images were of the twins. From toddlerhood to school age, the images chronicled their lives. Sprinkled here and there were framed notes and cards from the children to their savta and saba.

Finn wasn't quite sure what those words meant, or even what language they were in, but he imagined it had something to do with calling the couple grandma and grandpa.

The children grew up, each having a picture of their own on their wedding days.

The family photo was now eight. The old couple grew older, their bodies hunched and weak. However, their faces beamed with vibrancy—with inner peace and joy.

Finn had seen many walls decked out like this over the years. He usually avoided them, but this one set off a flurry of warm emotions. He couldn't quite understand why this one had such an effect on him. Something inside him was definitely different.

The family photo grew by four. A cluster of pictures displayed four children of various ages. Then came the last family portrait. Their numbers were minus one. Gone was the old man. The faces still beamed with love and joy, but Ruth's face was different, there was a deep sadness in her eyes.

Finn stopped and stared at the image. Sorrow washed over him. He wondered how he could feel so sad over the loss of an old man he never even knew. He didn't even know anyone's names in these photos. Why was he so sad? It suddenly occurred to him that one day, he could very well be an old man without Teague. The stabbing pain in his heart just thinking about the possibility was too much for him to bear. He pinched the tears from his eyes and told himself to let it go. With a shake of his head, he ducked into the bathroom to clean up.

When he returned to the kitchen, he found Teague and Ruth in the middle of an animated conversation.

"There you are," said Teague, beaming. "We thought you got lost." He winked and smiled. "Ruth made us sandwiches before we get started."

Finn took his seat. "I was looking at your wall of photos," he said, to the old woman.

A melancholy smile swept across Ruth's face. "My family," she said proudly. "My Yoel and I did well. Wouldn't you agree?" She sat down in a chair. A mournful look spread across her face. "He passed five years ago."

"I'm sorry to hear that," said Teague.

Seeing the deep sorrow on Ruth's face brought the stabbing pain back with a fury. "Are the rest of your family nearby?" asked Finn, desperately hoping to find a happier subject.

Ruth exhaled. "Sadly, no," she replied. "They visit as often as they can, but they all live up north. My Joseph has been after me to sell the house and move up there with him and Aida, but I just can't bring myself to do that." She wiped a tear from her eye. "I held my Yoel's hand for the last time in this house. I'm not ready to leave it just yet."

There was a time in Finn's life when he didn't believe love could last for a decade, let alone beyond death, but the past several months had changed his opinion on that. That kind of love was available for everyone—including himself. He glanced over at Teague to find him staring back with a sublime smile.

"Well," announced Ruth, scooting her chair back. "We should get on with the tasks at hand, shall we?" She collected the plates. "As you have probably seen already, there is much work to do around here."

Over the following weeks, Finn and Teague got busy taming Ruth's landscaping. They removed the old screen from the patio and installed all-new mesh. They even painted every inch of trim on the house and cleaned out the gutters. Every day at lunch time, she would entertain them with stories of her youth, while they devoured the hearty meal she prepared for them. Her mind was sharp and filled with knowledge despite her aged, fragile, and petite body. Listening to her stories was comparable to having an audio archive of people, places, and historical events that changed the world.

Every day they worked on Ruth's home; at night, they slept on the beach, their bellies and hearts full. Finn found himself awakening every morning, looking forward to Ruth's amazing stories and snippets of wisdom—the kind you can only get when you take the time to listen to the older generations. He was finally beginning to understand why Teague adored the elderly so much.

Ruth treated them like they were her own grandchildren,

insisting on being called savta, which Finn found out was a grand-mother in Hebrew.

It struck him that he never had anyone in his life he could call grandmother or grandfather. He couldn't help but wonder what that would have been like. Would things have been different? Or would the old people have been every bit as bitter and vile as Daniel and Tricia were?

One day, when they arrived at Ruth's home for another day of work, one of her neighbors met them at the curb. He ran up to them, waving his arms.

"Ruth isn't home," he said. "She had a nasty fall last night, so they rushed her to the hospital. When they were wheeling her out, she asked me to come and let you know there won't be any work today."

A pang of sadness jabbed Finn's heart upon hearing of Ruth's injury.

"Is she okay?" asked Teague.

"Her son's on his way," replied the old man. "Between you and me, it's time for her to move in with him and his wife. She's too old to be on her own." He sighed. "It's doubtful she'll be out of the hospital soon. At her age, she'll be lucky if she can walk after this."

Words defied Finn as he struggled with a range of emotions over someone he just met a few weeks ago.

The neighbor handed Teague a roll of money. "She asked me to give this to you fellas for all the work you've done around here." He gestured to the house. "You boys did a good job."

Before leaving the old man, they found out which hospital the old woman was taken to. Outside of the neighborhood, they caught the city bus. Riding in silence, Finn struggled to process how it was that he could feel such deep feelings about someone he hardly knew. The world was a different place for him now, a shift had happened. He wasn't quite sure if he liked it or not.

They arrived at the hospital in time for lunch. As they entered her room, Ruth's eyes lit up upon seeing them. She smiled and greeted them with open arms. Teague encouraged her to eat her lunch, while Finn set up the television so she could watch her shows. They stayed with her until visiting hours were over. When it was time to leave, they said their goodbyes to the old woman and wished her a long and happy life.

Their stay in Florida had ended. It was time to work their way back to their friends. That night, after connecting with Porter, they hopped a train heading west. There was one more stop that Teague wanted to make before rejoining the others, so they traveled to New Orleans.

Chapter Two

"Okay, come on, here comes another one," said Finn. "Do it right this time."

Thanks to Porter, the first leg of their trip was done via train. He even hooked them up with a ride from New Orleans to the town of Schriever. From there it was at least another four-hour walk to Houma, followed by yet another two hours before they reached their destination. It was already midafternoon, and they had been walking for an hour and a half, Teague was ready to catch a ride and let a vehicle do the hard work for a while.

He moved forward to the edge of the road, ignoring Finn's taunts. With his thumb out, he waited for the vehicle to come near.

The car approached; he could see the face of the driver, a clean-shaved man in his midthirties. He made eye contact with Teague and then averted his gaze. Without another glance, he drove past.

"Well, shit," said Finn. "I really thought he'd stop."

Teague peered up at the cloudless sky. Resigning himself to the task of completing the journey on foot, he said, "At least it ain't summer." Early spring was the perfect time to visit southern

Louisiana. It was warm, without the oppressive heat and humidity that would settle on the area in another month or so.

Another vehicle appeared on the horizon. Finn flashed a bright smile. "Move over, Imma show you how it's done." He pushed Teague aside, then took off his shirt.

"What exactly are you doin'?" asked Teague.

"Gettin' us a ride." He winked and put his thumb in the air.

The vehicle rolled close enough for Teague to see the driver—an elderly woman with a head full of gray hair. He chuckled. "You might wanna put your shirt back on," he teased. "Mawmaw ain't gonna be swayed by your masculine physique."

Finn squinted his eyes so he could see the driver. His shoulders slumped as he let his hand drop to his side. "Well, shit," he muttered.

The vehicle slowed and came to a stop alongside him. The old woman rolled down her window and peered out at the young duo. She turned her focus to Finn and grinned. "Son," she said. "Why you out here with no shirt on? Have you lost your mind?"

A deep, red hue spread across Finn's face. "I was hoping to entice someone into givin' us a ride," he confessed, with a sheepish grin, clearly hoping to play the old woman's heartstrings.

"I know what you were doin', this ain't my first rodeo." She studied them with a cautious eye. "Where y'all going'?"

"Houma," replied Teague. "Well, technically Presquile. But we'd settle for a ride to Houma if you're willin'."

"Presquile, you say," she replied. "Who're your people, son?"

"Leveaux, ma'am."

The old woman tapped her chin. "I used to know a Leveaux, way back when I was young. Etienne was his name. He was a real ladies' man. Any relation?"

Teague couldn't recall ever hearing the name. He shook his head. "Sorry, ma'am. I don't know. I left here when I was a kid, so I didn't get much of a chance to meet many members of the Leveaux line."

The old woman scoffed. "When you were a kid, eh? Son, you

ain't much more than a kid right now." She laughed heartily. "Well, I ain't got all day, hop in, I'll take you where you're goin'."

They tossed their packs into the back seat, and then climbed in. What would have been a six-hour walk suddenly became a less-than-thirty-minute drive.

As they drove through Houma, Teague's stomach twisted and turned into knots. He hadn't been home since he walked away; that was years ago. A whole lifetime had passed since then. He stared out at the scenery scrolling by, wondering how many things had changed. Was Grace still living in the old house? Had she sold it? Her life used to revolve around partying and drugs, she could have fallen on hard times. For the first time in years, he wondered if she was still alive.

They rolled down tree-lined streets, past old houses and small, shotgun shacks; a sign that read Presquile came into view. Teague fidgeted in his seat as the clammy hands of anxiety wrapped around his gut. He tried to distract his mind by listening to the banter between Finn and Dorothy; it didn't work.

They rolled up to the end of the long driveway. Dorothy said her goodbyes and wished them well, then drove away.

Standing at the edge of the road, Teague's legs refused to move. He stared at the old house, allowing some of his most precious memories to wash forward. He closed his eyes and could hear the sound of his mawmaw humming while she worked in her garden, while in the barn, the old man cursed under his breath, as he toiled away on the old pickup truck.

He opened his eyes to find Finn staring at him. "I'm a little nervous," he said.

Finn nodded but said nothing.

"Well." Teague cleared his throat. "Let's go find out how much has changed around here."

His heartbeat quickened as each step brought him closer to the old house. Memories rushed forward like an old movie that was stored deep inside his soul. From what he could see, not much had changed; that seemed like a good sign. The old tire swing still swayed under the giant oak tree. Someone had been maintaining Mawmaw's garden. His lips curled up into a smile, she would be happy to know that.

He slowly climbed the steps to the front galerie, listening to the soft creak of the old floorboards. His palms sweaty, Teague wiped them off on his pants, then raised his hand to knock. He paused. *What if the person who comes to the door is a stranger? What if it's Grace? What should he say?* He glanced over at Finn, who nodded at him in encouragement.

Before his knuckles touched the wood frame, the door swung open.

"Well, damn!" exclaimed Grace. Her face lit up with the brightest smile he had ever seen, as she wrapped her arms around him and pulled him close for a hug. "It's like seeing a ghost, returned from the dead," she said, as she pulled away and took a good look at him.

They stood in awkward silence for a moment.

"Where are my manners?" sighed Grace, as she wiped her eyes. "Come on inside." She held the door open. "Welcome home."

As Finn introduced himself, Teague took in the hallway. The house still smelled the same as he remembered. Images of his childhood washed over him, flooding his heart with emotions. All the times he walked down the hallway rushed to the front of his mind. His first day of kindergarten, returning home from camp with Pawpaw. Running outside during a rainstorm to play in the rain. The day the old man died, followed not long after by the old woman. The dark cloud that covered everything in a shroud of sorrow and emptiness. The morning he walked away from it all.

"Come on back to the kitchen," prodded Grace. "I'll fix y'all something to eat."

Every step brought another wave of memories. He could almost hear the voices of his grandparents as they bickered lovingly over something ridiculous.

Stepping into the kitchen was like stepping back in time. Nothing had changed. It was all exactly how he remembered it, all the way down to the savory smell of a giant pot of jambalaya cooking on the stove.

Grace pulled out a chair and gestured for them to sit. "I got dinner cookin'. You'd be proud to hear that, after many failed attempts, I managed to master the old woman's recipe." She winked at Teague. "I also made some improvements. It'll be another couple of hours before it's ready. In the meantime, I'll toss together some sandwiches for you both."

Instinctively, Teague sat down in the very same chair he had always sat in. He placed his hand atop the table just to feel if it was real or not. A part of him expected his Pawpaw August to wander into the kitchen at any moment, in a futile attempt to steal a taste of the jambalaya.

Grace placed two sandwiches down in front of them along with tall glasses of sweet tea, then she slid into a chair—the same chair she always sat in.

"You look good," she said.

Teague nodded and swallowed against the lump in his throat. There was so much he wanted to say—so much he wanted to avoid saying. Why the hell did he come here? What was he hoping to do? For the life of him, he couldn't recall what he had in mind when he decided to make this trip.

"You are the spittin' image of him," said Grace.

"Who?"

"Daddy," she cleared her throat. "Your pawpaw." She ran her fingers through her graying hair. "The resemblance is strong. You look just like he did when he was your age."

Grace took a long drink of tea. "Are you planning on staying for a while?" she asked.

Teague shook his head. "I'll be honest," he replied. "I don't really know what I came here for." He shrugged. "I guess I just wanted to see the old place."

"I always hoped you would come back," she said. "I was such a shitty mother. You didn't deserve a mama like me."

Mother. It occurred to Teague that he hadn't ever thought about Grace in that way; at least not since he was a small child. He always considered her more of an older sibling. The family disappointment. "I didn't come back to mend any fences," he replied. "No need for apologies. It is what it is. Tracasse-toi pas."

Finn cleared his throat and climbed to his feet. "I'm just gonna let you two have a minute," he said, his tone showing his discomfort.

Grace nodded and pointed toward the living room. "There're a lot of pictures in that room." She smiled. "Including a bunch of Teague when he was young."

With a curt nod of his head, Finn wandered away, leaving Teague and Grace to themselves.

"I didn't mean to be harsh," he said. "I'm sorry."

"There's no need to apologize," replied Grace. "I deserve a real, good tongue-lashing for what I did." She shook her head slowly. "I was a real piece of shit. I mistreated all the people I should have loved —who loved me." She smiled at him. "You, of all people, have every reason to hate me."

"I don't hate you," he replied. Upon deeper reflection, he shrugged. "I don't know how I feel about you."

Grace took a sip of her sweet tea. "I'm not the same person I used to be. The day you left—the way you left, it woke me up." She locked eyes with him. "It made me realize how awful a person I was. My parents were both dead and my only son walked out on me before he was even old enough to drive."

Teague didn't respond.

"I cried the whole day," she continued. "I'd like to say it was because I was worried about you, but it was more so because I realized how badly I messed up." She took another sip of her tea. "I went to the cabin, looking for you. I was sure that was where you went. It took me a week before I realized you weren't coming back." She sighed. "After that, I got clean, went back to school and got myself a good-paying job at a local dentist's office. It didn't take long for all of my friends to leave once they realized I wasn't partying anymore." She sipped her tea. "I guess you could say I was one of those people who had to learn everything the hard way in life. No one's ever been able to accuse me of being smart."

Teague chuckled. His thoughts turned to Finn, then back to Grace. "I used to hate you for being so selfish," he said. "But I've come to realize that some people have to walk through fire."

"Well," said Grace. She leaned back in her chair. "You're lookin' at one right now." She stared for a moment; her face had a pinkish hue. "I'll tell you what," she said. "If you're willing, I'd like to start new."

Start new. He didn't see how that was possible. They never had much of a relationship to begin with. He couldn't imagine calling her anything but Grace.

As if she heard his thoughts, Grace said, "I don't mean you treat me like your mama. I know I burned that bridge a long time ago. I don't deserve that title."

"So, what are you talking about, then?"

"You and I are all that remains of our family," she replied. "I'm hopin' that there's a way for us to at least come together as such. We're all we got left. In this world, kin is all anyone has."

Teague mulled over the offer. His thoughts went to his grand-pere and grand-mere, they would want him to make an effort. To her credit, Grace wasn't trying to pretend as though their past never happened, she was offering a way to move forward. He nodded at Grace. "I'll give it a try."

A warm smile spread across her face; her eyes filled with tears.

Finn appeared in the door frame, holding a photograph of Teague when he was a child. He held it up and grinned.

Grace wiped her eyes. "Check out that door frame," she said. "Three generations of Leveaux children were measured there."

Finn ran his hand along the door frame, a look of awe on his face. He peered up at Teague. "There you are."

"You wanna see somethin' that'll blow your mind?" asked Grace.

"Always," replied Finn.

"On that wall over there." She pointed. "There's a black-and-white photo of a young man. Go ahead and take a good look at it."

Finn turned and disappeared, only to return holding a framed picture. He held it out in front of him. "He looks just like you," he said to Teague, placing the photo on the table.

"Uh, huh," said Grace. "That's my daddy, August." She beamed at Teague. "Teague here could be his twin. Don't you agree?"

Finn nodded, his eyes moving back and forth from the photograph to Teague.

Teague stared down at the image of August, recalling how many times, as a young boy, he would look at that picture in admiration. He used to think his pawpaw was so handsome, wearing his army uniform. He never noticed the resemblance. Seeing it now was a shock. If someone were to tell him he was looking at a doctored photo of himself right now, he would believe it.

"Got any pictures of August when he was older?" asked Finn. "I gotta see what that looks like."

Grace laughed. "Just follow the wall. There's several."

Finn disappeared into the room again.

"So, how long have you two been together?" asked Grace.

Teague stared at her.

"Pshhh," she scoffed, with a grin and a playful wave of her hand. "I might be gettin' old, but I ain't blind. I know a couple when I see one." She tilted her head. "You forget, I lived in New Orleans for years. I've seen it all." She leaned back in her chair. "Besides, it's good to see you found someone."

Finn returned with another photograph, this one was Teague as an infant, his face serious as he stared disapprovingly at the camera.

"I remember when this one was taken," said Grace. "He always had that look on his face. Like he was judging the world and found it lacking." She chuckled. "Teague came into this world knowing who he was." She stared down at the picture. "He scared the hell out of me. He was so alert. Everyone said he was an old soul." She smiled at Teague. "I think they were right. You've always had your own way of being."

"Old soul," muttered Finn, nodding his head in approval as he walked back into the other room.

"How about you?" asked Teague. "Are you still with what's his name? Jake?"

Grace shook her head. "No," she replied, dragging out the final sound. "That ended about a week or so after you left. I've dated a couple of men since then, but none of them ever stuck. I've made my peace with being single the rest of my days. After all these years, I've finally reached a place where I truly like myself." She smiled. "Besides, I ain't really alone. I've got lots of real friends now, some of whom I've known since I was a child. I also have that mean, old barn cat and her colony of feral offspring."

"She's still around?" asked Teague.

"Hell, yeah," replied Grace. "She and her small army. With the help of a few friends, we spent all last summer catching and fixing the entire colony. No more kittens around here." She laughed.

"Tell you what," said Grace. "Why don't you go and put your things upstairs in your old bedroom. It's exactly how you left it. Y'all can clean up, and then we can have a nice meal together."

His bedroom. Now there was something he hadn't thought about in years. He climbed to his feet and found Finn in the parlor.

He took the steps slowly, one by one, his nerves on edge. Why would he be nervous? His mind reeled back to his childhood. Climbing the old stairs made him feel as though he was ten years old all over again. At the top of the stairs, he paused and stared down the narrow hall. He took a deep breath and walked over to the door, then turned the knob.

The room smelled clean, not musty. Teague didn't know exactly what he expected, but he was happy to see that everything wasn't covered in a layer of dust. Grace must come in and clean up from time to time.

He stood on the threshold and took in the room. Everything was exactly how he remembered, from the knick-knacks and books on the shelves, to the bed and his old, space comforter. Walking into the room, he placed his backpack on the floor.

"It's like it's frozen in time," whispered Finn. "Is this how you remember it?"

"It is," replied Teague. "It's strange."

Finn placed his pack on the floor and wandered over to the bookshelf, where he perused the titles. "We read a lot of the same books when we were kids," he stated.

"That explains a lot," joked Teague.

Finn laughed. He turned and walked over to the bed, where he plopped himself down. "This is nice." He bounced up and down.

Teague ignored him, opting instead to open the closet and see if his secret hiding place was still there. He reached behind the doorjamb, pressing on the loose floorboard. Using his pocketknife, he pried it open to find his box exactly where he left it. He carried it over to the bed and sat down beside Finn, holding the box on his lap.

"What's that?" asked Finn.

Teague chuckled. "The most prized worldly possessions of twelve-year-old me." He flipped open the lid and stared down at the contents. A couple of baseball cards. A gum wrapper from his first baseball game with August. A baby tooth.

"What's that?" asked Finn, pointing at the tooth.

"This?" Teague picked it up. "Aurelie's tooth," he whispered.

"Who?"

"Aurelie, she was a girl in my kindergarten class," replied Teague. "Her tooth fell out one day on the playground. She said that giving it to me meant we would get married one day." A smile spread across his face at the memory.

Finn stared. "Is it a Cajun thing to give your betrothed your baby teeth?"

Teague shoved him playfully.

"Seriously though," said Finn. "Why'd you keep it?"

"I couldn't think of anything else to do with it. It didn't feel right throwing it away." He shrugged. "At first, five-year-old me thought I could stuff it under my pillow for the mouse to come get. But that would've been wrong; it not being my tooth. So, I just put it in here." He glanced over at Finn, who was watching him with an odd look on his face.

"The mouse," said Finn. "Is that some sort of Cajun substitute for a tooth fairy?"

Teague cocked an eyebrow. "Well, it makes a hell of a lot more sense than a fairy."

Finn laughed softly and shook his head. "You really are an old soul."

"What would you have done with it?"

"Thrown it away," replied Finn.

"Come on, there wasn't a little girl who had a crush on five-year-old Finn back in the day?"

Finn shook his head. "There weren't any girls in my kindergarten." He shrugged. "At least, I don't recall ever noticin' one."

"I'm willin' to bet," said Teague, laughing. "That there were plenty of girls in the class and you just ignored them."

"Maybe."

Teague placed the tooth reverently into the box, then pulled out a polished rock. He rolled it over in his hand, remembering the day he brought it home. He thought it was the prettiest rock he had ever seen. In fact, he was convinced it was a precious gemstone. Mawmaw played along and helped him polish it until it shined. Old August just laughed at the two of them.

He picked up the stub of a cigar and sniffed. It still smelled the same as the day he smoked it. August instructed him to ensure that the old lady never discovered it. He was certain that if she ever found out that he allowed a six-year-old to smoke a cigar, she would kill him.

"Is it weird being here?" asked Finn.

Teague nodded, unable to form any words. Too many emotions

threatened to overwhelm him. When he decided to come back and visit, he wasn't sure how it would go. He certainly wasn't prepared for the flood of memories he found himself wading through. He closed the lid of the box and carried it back over to the closet. After returning it into his hiding place, he glanced up at the shelf above his head and spied a large bin. Excited, he pulled it down and carried it to the center of the room.

"What's this?" asked Finn.

"You'll see," he replied, as he flipped open the bin, exposing a sea of bright, colorful building bricks.

"Sweet!" exclaimed Finn, as he slid off the bed and joined Teague, sitting cross-legged on the floor. He shoved his hand inside the bin and pulled out a handful of tiny bricks. "I had these too! I once made a working catapult."

Two hours had passed by in a flash. Grace appeared in the doorway to find both Finn and Teague on the floor, like two school children, a small village erected from the blocks spread out before them.

She leaned against the frame and smiled. "So much for cleaning up. I see you didn't make it past the tub of bricks. Boys will be boys, I suppose," she said. "Are y'all hungry?"

"Always," they replied, in unison.

Dinner was amazing. Teague was happy when the discomfort from earlier dissipated, leaving in its wake a good time. After dinner, both he and Finn cleaned up the kitchen, then joined Grace out on the galerie for a drink. The crickets and frogs were deafening. The company was nice.

They told her about their adventures and she shared stories of her own. Much to his surprise, Teague enjoyed the time together.

"Oh!" said Grace. "Before I forget." She snapped her fingers and went inside, returning a moment later, holding out a set of keys. "Go on," she prodded. "Take 'em."

He took the keys, not sure what was going on.

Grace smiled. "This place is just as much yours as it is mine," she said. "Feel free to come by and visit anytime." She pointed to the keys. "You can get in if I'm not here."

Teague wasn't sure what to say.

"That bronze one is for the cabin," added Grace.

"You still have the old cabin?"

"Of course," she replied. "That little shack is every bit as much a piece of my childhood as it is yours." She lit a cigarette and exhaled a cloud of smoke. "It wouldn't be right to sell off our history."

Teague ran his finger along the ridges of the key. He knew exactly where they were heading tomorrow.

Chapter Three

River pulled out her phone, wondering whether she should call Teague to check up on them or would it be better to call Mara first to find out if there's any news about the baby.

According to the last time she spoke with Mara, it could be any day, or it might be another couple of weeks. How could she be so patient? The anxiety over waiting was killing her, and she wasn't even the one who was pregnant.

After Finn and Teague left Terlingua, River, Cash and Zac stuck around for a couple of months, helping Stoney around the compound. With the added help of Gunner, they built out another unit. Not only would it help Stoney bring in extra income, but it would also make their visits more comfortable.

So many things had changed in such a short period. She was usually quite averse to major changes, but her gut told her these were right; that things were moving in a positive direction.

Mara and Ben had made themselves comfortable in their new life. River enjoyed seeing the photos they would post of their small apartment above the garage. She wondered what it would be like when she and Cash settled down. Would they have a cute, little apartment, too?

Nate was riding with Tanner now. As for Gunner, he appeared to be growing some roots of his own, opting to stay with Stoney, Bella and Spinner. He even got himself a job at one of the local bars. He said it was because Gypsy was getting too old to hop trains all the time, but everyone knew the truth.

Stoney was absolutely thrilled to have the company and the regular help.

As for River, wanderlust had settled deep, and she was ready to hit the road again. She could scarcely recall a period when she spent this much time in one place, and even though she adored Stoney and the older members of their misfit family, she needed to see the scrolling landscape again. Finn and Teague were happy, living on the beach. While she understood the need for them to spend some time alone, it still hurt a little being apart. She missed their banter. She even missed Finn's antics.

Finn. He was so different when he returned to the group. Rail thin, pale and quiet; he was a shadow of his former self. When she first laid eyes on him, River wondered if they would ever get their Finn back. A month with the Nomads had put some meat back on his bones and color in his cheeks, but there was still something different about him. His confidence was nonexistent, and he clung to Teague as though he would drown if he couldn't reach out and touch him. Off and on, he would show signs of his old self working its way to the surface. It didn't happen often, and it never lasted very long. She missed his mischievous smile and impish sense of humor. She hoped that their time alone would help him overcome whatever demons he had left.

From what she could see through their video chats, it appeared as though he was coming out of his shell. In fact, the last time they talked, he was more chatty and ready to smile. Even Cash and Zac were impressed with the change.

Mara and Ben left Terlingua a week after their celebration. River made Mara promise she would keep them updated on their progress until they were settled. Tanner and Nate had gone with them, their plan was to see Ben and Mara settled and then head out again. Tanner wanted to be sure his two best friends were situated before he, too, gave in to the call of the open road.

Even though she knew they were safe and that they had plenty of help, River still found herself worrying. Like a mama bear, as Cash would say. That was his new nickname for her. At first, she didn't much care for it, but it didn't take long to grow on her.

She opened her screen and tapped out a quick message.

River to Mara: Hey lady, how are you feeling today?

Mara: My ankles are swollen, I have to pee every five minutes, and if I eat anything, I get serious heartburn. All in all, I'm great. Ben won't leave me alone, he texts every half hour from work.

River smiled. She knew exactly how he felt, she could see the look on his face, she was sure hers was the same.

River: Are you resting?

Mara: As much as I can. Besides, no one will let me do anything around here, so all I can do is sit around and wait. My little man is kicking up a storm. He gets so excited when daddy comes home.

River: You two are so cute. Keep doing what you're doing. I'll check in later today. Love ya, mama.

Mara: Love you too, mama.

River hovered her thumb over Teague's message thread, ready to check in on them.

"What's Mama Bear up to now?" asked Cash, as he walked up to her. "How are the kids doing?" He sat down and gave her a quick kiss on the side of her head.

"Well, the two in Utah are doing just fine," she replied, without skipping a beat. "I was just gonna text the two in Louisiana."

"What about the two in Louisiana?" asked Zac, walking up with sandwiches in his hands.

"Oh, nice!" exclaimed Cash. "You brought lunch!"

Zac pulled his hands out of reach. "Get your own, these are mine," he said.

"But you got three of them," argued Cash.

"Yeah? I'm a growing boy. I need all the sustenance I can get."
River chuckled.

Zac winked at her. "But I will share with Mom," he said, handing a sandwich over.

"How sweet of you!" said River.

Cash stood and brushed his hands on his pants. "Looks like I'm going to get my own," he said. He turned to River. "You want anything else while I'm there?"

She shook her head.

"Oh!" interjected Zac. "I'll take another sandwich, please." He grinned. "I gave one of mine to Mom."

With both middle fingers in the air, Cash spun around and walked away.

"Heavy on the mayo," shouted Zac. "And don't be afraid to put some meat on it."

"Fuck off," replied Cash.

Zac turned his focus to River. "So, how is everyone?"

"I was just about to text Teague and see," she replied. She tapped Teague's icon.

River: Good morning. How are y'all doing?

There was a long pause with no reply, making River wonder if she should have waited a little longer before texting. Maybe they were sleeping in. Finally, her screen lit up with a response.

Teague: Mornin' Mom. We're all good.
   River: Did I wake you?
   Teague: No worries, I needed to get up, Finn's still sleeping. We were up late last night.
   River: Oh?
   Teague sent a photo of a small city built from tiny plastic bricks.
   Teague: We were building.
   River shook her head and smiled.
   River: You two are adorable. What's on the itinerary for today?
   Teague: We're heading out to a special place.
   River: I'm intrigued. Feel free to tell me about this special place. How was it visiting Grace?
   Teague: Fine. She's changed, in a good way.
   River: So, it was a good visit?
   Teague: Yes, ma'am.

Another image came through, this one was of a sleepy-eyed Finn.

. . .

River: How's our boy doing?
  Teague: He's good.
  River: Give him a hug for me.
  Teague: Will do. He says good morning.

Cash sauntered up with more sandwiches and three bottles of water. He handed a bottle to River and tossed one at Zac, then sat down. "Here," he said gruffly, as he handed a sandwich to Zac.

"Thanks, Dad," he replied, with a smile.

"Is that Teague?" asked Cash.

River nodded. "He says they're going someplace special today."

"Was the trip a good one?"

"He says it was."

"Good."

Teague: Are y'all heading out today?
  River: Yup. We should be at the Renfaire camping grounds tonight to meet up with Bells, D. B., and Max. Are y'all still meeting us there?
  Teague: That's the plan.
  River: Awesome! We'll see you in about a week, then. I can't wait.
  Teague: Neither can we.
  River: I'll call tomorrow, and we can chat.
  Teague: Sounds like a plan. Have a safe trip.

She put her phone away in her pocket and set her focus on the sandwich in front of her. It was good to hear that everyone was doing okay. Finn looked good, a little sleepy, but good. A tender smile appeared on her face as she remembered the photo of the city they built. At least some things haven't changed.

"Mama looks happy," teased Zac.

"I'd say so," added Cash.

"Why wouldn't I be?" asked River. "Everyone's doing fine. Finn looks good and we're all gonna be back together again by the end of the week."

Zac's face grew serious. "Hey," he said. "Since we're passin' by Tyler, would y'all mind if we made a little pit stop along the way?"

Cash nodded in understanding, but River was confused. "What's there?" she asked.

"Cole," replied Zac.

River was stunned, she couldn't recall the last time he mentioned his brother's name.

"He's comin' up on his sixteenth birthday," said Zac. "I'd kinda like to peek in and see how he's doin'."

"Is this gonna be a stealth operation?" asked Cash.

Zac nodded. "I don't wanna disrupt his life. I just wanna see him." He flashed a sad smile. "To make sure he's still doin' good." He turned to River. "Think that's okay?"

"Absolutely!" she blurted. The look on his face made her sad. She shared a knowing glance with Cash. However this played out, she was glad both she and Cash could be there for Zac.

Chapter Four

Finn stood under the old oak tree, waiting patiently as Teague said his goodbyes to Grace. The visit turned out to be a pleasant surprise. He was glad, for Teague's sake, that things turned out the way they did.

He pushed the swing, watching it sway gently back and forth, wondering how different life would have been if he had grown up in such a place. Would he be more like Teague?

All the pictures of August swam to the front of his mind. Teague was almost an exact copy of his grandfather. It was fascinating. He couldn't help but wonder if August shared the same mannerisms. His entire life he never considered family lineage, and now, here he was knee-deep in it, and he couldn't get it out of his mind.

What role does genetics play in the person you become—the decisions you make? Is it a matter of upbringing or is it all the individual's choice? If he was raised by his father—his real father, would he be any different?

His real father.

Finn did his best not to think about the man. After all, he knew nothing about him. A part of him wanted to be satisfied that Daniel wasn't kin, but another part of him couldn't make his mind stop wondering about the man who fathered him.

What was he like? Was he a monster, too? Was he a kind man? He knew they shared their eye color, but he didn't know of any other traits. Did he look like him? Or was there some long-dead grandpa out there who he took after the same way Teague took after August?

For as long as he could recall, all Finn ever wanted to do was get away from his family. For years after running away, the very mention of family was enough to ruin his day. And now, here he was, wondering. He had so many questions—many he wasn't sure he wanted answered. Teague told him he thought it would be a good idea for him to find the man, for no other reason than closure. But Finn wasn't sure he felt the same. What if he went through all the trouble of tracking down the man, only to find out he was worse than Daniel? Would Finn even be able to get over that revelation? What would that say about him—about the man he was supposed to be? What if he was always destined to screw things up the way he almost did? Did he even want to know if his destiny was to die alone, angry and horrible?

After an awkward hug with Grace, Teague turned and walked toward Finn, who pushed the swing one more time, and then wandered to the edge of the driveway.

"Good to see y'all have moved on," said Finn.

Teague nodded. "It's what the old folks would've wanted."

"What do you want?"

"I guess," sighed Teague, contemplating. "I wanted it too. I was just too scared to say it out loud." He glanced back at the house. "It's good to see she's taking care of the place. And it's good that she cleaned herself up. I think she'll be fine."

"You have a home to go back to now," said Finn.

"We," replied Teague. "We have a home to return to whenever we want." He looked at Finn. "What did you think of all this?"

"All what? The house?"

"The house, Grace, my childhood."

Finn shrugged. "I'm happy that it went well. I'm glad you could come to an agreement with her and that the two of you can get along somehow. She seems decent. She's honest, at least about your relationship and how she messed up. That's good." He thought about the photographs on the walls. "After seeing all those pictures everywhere, I'm kinda sad I never got to meet August."

Teague nodded. "He would've liked you."

"Think so? Think he'd be okay with us?"

"I imagine so," replied Teague. "He wasn't really the bigoted kind. He always judged folks by their character, he didn't care much about anything else."

Finn nodded. His mind went back to wondering about his own father. What were the odds he could track the man down? And if he did, would the man even want to know Finn? After all, he walked away. He made a choice years ago that he didn't want anything to do with his son. What makes Finn think he changed his mind?

He forced his thoughts back to Teague and the visit. "All those pictures of you as a kid," said Finn. "I liked seeing that."

"Yeah?"

Finn nodded. "Grace is right, you are an old soul. I like the phrase. It describes you exactly." A subtle smile appeared on his lips. "I mean, who else would hold on to some little girl's baby tooth." He faked a shudder.

Teague shoved him playfully. "What was I supposed to do? I didn't want to hurt her feelings."

"And that is what makes you an old soul," replied Finn. "Any other five-year-old would have tossed the damn thing." He shook his head and chuckled. "But you—you not only kept it; you put it in your secret box. It's still there!"

"Sounds like someone's jealous," jeered Teague.

Finn shook his head. "Nuh-uh. Don't even try to change the subject." He grinned.

"You're not gonna let me live the whole tooth thing down. Are you?"

"Would you?"

Teague laughed. "Hell, naw," he replied.

The walk was pleasant. The giant, live oak trees lining the road had long branches that arched overhead, creating a verdant tunnel, their rustling leaves cast shadows on the blacktop. Spanish moss hung heavy on the limbs, their tendrils swaying gently in the soft breeze.

They stopped in front of a cemetery with an ornate, wrought-iron gate. Finn knew they were coming here, he just wasn't sure how it would make him feel. He glanced over at Teague, who seemed to be somewhere else as he gazed beyond the gate.

Before they left the house, Teague stopped in the rose garden and picked some roses to put on his mawmaw's grave. He wanted to pay his respects to the old couple before moving on.

Finn already knew Teague's story. He knew just about everything there was to know about him. The way he talked about his mawmaw and pawpaw with so much reverence was strange to Finn. He grew up in a world where there were no elder family members, let alone such a strong connection to a particular place. He couldn't help but wonder what his life would have been like had he grown up with those sorts of connections. Would things have turned out differently? Or would it have just been another set of abusive and cruel family members?

Teague stepped through the gate and placed his pack down on the soft grass. He pointed. "They're over there," he said.

They strolled reverently down a shaded path, lined on both sides with large, concrete boxes adorned with heavy crosses or weeping angels. Now and then, one of the boxes would be small—child size. Children and death never seemed right.

Teague stopped in front of a grave. He leaned over and placed the roses atop the box, then rested his hand reverently on the stone cross.

Wanting to give him all the space he needed, Finn stood back and watched from the shade of a giant oak tree.

Teague was speaking, but Finn couldn't hear what he was saying, it didn't matter, the message wasn't for him.

He watched as Teague moved over to the other tomb. He pulled something from his pocket and placed it atop the box, then began speaking in the same fashion as the other grave. Finn was curious as to what the item was, but he chose not to interrupt the moment.

It was nearly half an hour before Teague finally turned away from the graves and took a seat beside Finn under the tree.

They sat in silence, listening to the sound of the birds chirping overhead and the gentle breeze blowing through the leaves.

"Are you done here?" asked Teague suddenly.

Finn stole a glance at him, noticing the tears pooled up in his eyes. "Only if you are," he replied.

Teague nodded, then pinched his eyes and rose to his feet. "Come on, let's go somewhere less sad."

Finn was more than ready for that, he hated to see Teague this way. Not having a connection to any of the souls buried in the cemetery, he found the place rather calming. It was obvious this place had a different effect on Teague. Before they walked away, he stole a glance at the two graves, noticing the cigar stub that was in the box, sitting atop August's grave. A shock of sorrow struck him with such force, he could feel his own tears pooling in his eyes. He swallowed against the feeling, willing his emotions under control, then he followed Teague out of the cemetery and back onto the shaded road.

They walked for another hour before turning off the main road onto one made of gravel. Here the trees grew tall, threatening to swallow everything around them. The road became progressively more slender with each half mile until it was finally nothing more than a narrow path. They walked that until it opened to a small, sandy beach. An old canoe sat along the shore, surrounded by a forest of enormous bald cypress trees covered in Spanish moss.

"Almost there," said Teague, his voice dripping with excitement. He tossed his pack into the canoe, then gestured for Finn to join him.

Floating along the murky water, Teague guided the craft with the oar, while Finn sat up front, taking in the beauty that was the bayou. He placed his hand along the water's surface.

"Careful," warned Teague. "Cocodrie."

"Coco—who?"

"Cocodrie," replied Teague. "Gators. There're lots of gators in these waters."

Finn nodded and kept his hands to himself for the remainder of the ride.

The cabin loomed up ahead, in all its rustic, unremarkable glory. Finn stole a glance behind him at Teague, who was lost in some memory.

With its cedar siding and pitched roof, the cabin was exactly how Finn imagined it would be. Spanish moss clung to everything that was over six feet tall.

Teague guided the boat to the shore. Together, they dragged the canoe onto the soft sand and turned their focus to the tiny cabin.

With keys in hand, Teague slowly climbed the rickety, wooden steps to the front door.

The door was built from the same cedar that constructed the rest of the house. Finn wondered if a key was even necessary. "How old do you think you were when you came here last?" he asked.

Teague sighed. "I think maybe eleven." He said nothing more as he unlocked the door and let it swing wide. The rush of fresh air sent a swirl of dust twirling in the sunbeams that poked through the holes in dirty curtains.

The interior walls were lined with cedar boards, the same used for the floor. The entire structure was a single room with an old, potbelly stove in the center. A wooden countertop divided the kitchen area from the rest of the room. Two old cots sat against the walls on either side of the stove. Aside from the chairs nestled under the countertop, the cots were the only furniture in the cabin.

The air didn't smell the way one would expect. Finn inhaled, the entire cabin smelled like cedar and fresh air.

Teague walked around, opening the three, tiny windows, a steady stream of fresh air burst into the room.

"Well," said Teague, brushing his hands off on his pants. "What do you think?"

Finn nodded. "I approve."

"Wait 'till you see the best part," said Teague, excitedly. He spun around and flung open another door leading outside, then stepped through the wooden screen door, letting it clack closed behind him. "Come on out," he said, peering through the ripped screen.

Finn stepped out onto the dock. The river stretched out on either side, flowing steady and calm. He leaned down to peek under the cabin and noticed, for the first time, that the back half of the building was sitting on top of the water.

Teague pulled a hammock down from the rafters and tested it for strength. It didn't break off in his hands, but the amount of dust and spiders that flew into the air was enough to convince them it would be best to hold off on trying to use it just yet. He chuckled. "We can leave that for later."

Struck by the calm and beauty around him, Finn sat down at the edge of the dock, letting his legs dangle above the water below. All around him bald cypress, shrouded in curtains of green Spanish moss, stood sentinel over lily pads and tall grass. Dragonflies flitted about, diving to the water's surface, then flying into the air. Frogs chirped loudly while a group of turtles sunned themselves on a log. Across the swamp, a nearly three-foot-long water snake swam among the reeds, disappearing from sight.

Finn removed his boots and t-shirt, reveling in the warm sun upon his skin. He watched as a large cottonmouth snake, coiled up with its mouth wide open, floated by on the river's current. There was a subtle splash beneath him. He leaned over the edge of the dock and peered down, finding himself face-to-face with a large alligator. The beast made no effort to move, opting instead to float, its lizard eyes staring directly at him, as though daring him.

He sat up and decided it was probably best to avoid the water, instead opting to sit cross-legged and lean against the post.

The door to the cabin swung open, Teague spilled out holding a tackle box and two poles. He flashed an enthusiastic smile and sat down on the dock.

"We'll clean up later," he said, flipping open the lid on the box. "Gotta catch dinner first." He wiggled two cigars in the air, then held up a jar of moonshine and grinned. After pouring a little into two, small mason jars, he handed one to Finn. "Laissez les bon temps rouler!"

They touched jars and took a sip, Finn gasping at the strength of the liquid as it poured down his throat, then he cast his hook out into the murky water and waited, his mouth watering in anticipation.

Chapter Five

Ever since Finn's return, Zac couldn't get Cole out of his head. He wasn't sure what the connection was, but seeing his family reunited sparked an urge to have that same interaction with his little brother. For months, whenever the idea made its way to the surface, he would push it aside. After all, the odds weren't likely he could even visit with Cole. Who even knew if the kid would remember him? Or that he would even want to see him.

His own words startled him when he blurted out that he would like to make a stop. For a moment, he didn't even know who was talking, his voice sounded foreign to his ears. But both River and Cash were on board. Whether or not they were being honest, their agreement was all the encouragement he needed.

The train whistle blew. One long, one short and one long. They were coming into the town. Anxiety, on a level he'd never experienced before, threatened to overwhelm him. He warned himself that now was not the time to lose himself in fantasies—good or bad. He had to focus; it was time to hop off.

He watched as Cash jumped, followed by River, after one final glance around, to make sure he wasn't forgetting anything, Zac jumped. He landed easily, then gathered his pack and followed the others to a safely hidden space in the middle of a copse of trees.

"It's been a while," said Cash, placing his pack on the ground. "Do you remember the address?"

Zac scratched his head. Truth was, he couldn't recall. Luckily, he wrote it down a long time ago. He dug through his pack, pulling out his oldest sketch pad, then flipped through the pages to the very back.

"Let me," said Cash. He snapped an image of the address, then pulled it up on his map app.

"You okay?" asked River, staring up at him with worried eyes.

Unable to speak, Zac nodded. His stomach was in knots, for once he was glad they hadn't had anything to eat yet.

"Got it," announced Cash. He peered up at Zac. "You sure you wanna do this?" He smiled. "You're looking a little green."

"I am," replied Zac.

Leaving their gear behind, they cut through the trees, coming out onto a two-lane road. From there, they made their way to the center of town. The whole time, Zac's emotions spiraled from excitement to apprehension to downright fearful. His imagination conjured up an image of his little brother. What did he look like now? What sort of person was he? Was he the same Cole? For a brief moment, he allowed himself to imagine what it would be like to speak to him, but he quickly shoved that aside, Cole didn't need the trouble of a visit from his past. He was just here to peek.

The town, as small as it was, was bustling with activity. They stood at the lone traffic light and waited for the opportunity to cross.

A horn blasted, followed by someone shouting. "Watch where you're going!" It took Zac a minute to realize he heard his name.

"Zac!"

He locked eyes with Cash, who stared back at him, reflecting the same confusion he was grappling with. He turned to River just in time to hear her gasp and then point.

Zac turned in the direction she indicated, his eyes landing on a teenager, thin, with a head full of curly, auburn hair, riding a bike, heading straight toward them.

The boy skidded to a stop in front of him. "Zac?" he asked, with tears welling up in his eyes.

He didn't need to ask; Zac knew who this was. He reached out and pulled his little brother in for a hug. Tears streaming from his eyes, he pulled back to get a good look at Cole. He was the same as always—the same, little, red-haired boy.

The angry driver sped by, blasting his horn for emphasis.

"What do you say we find a place to sit down and have a visit?" asked Cash.

River bobbed her head up and down. "I'm starving."

"There's a food truck around the corner," offered Cole.

"Perfect!" she exclaimed. "Lead the way, young man."

At the window, Cole tried to pay for Zac, who refused adamantly. There was no way he would let his little brother buy him food. Using the last twenty dollars to his name, Zac splurged and paid for lunch after directing his younger brother to go find them a table.

The sun was warm against his skin with a light breeze. Maybe it was his imagination, but the sun seemed much brighter than ever before. He listened as Cole described his life and his family. Hearing him talk, seeing him so happy and confident, made Zac's heart sing. Maybe leaving was the best thing he could have done for his little brother.

"I still have it," said Cole.

"Have what?"

"Your letter. The one you left for me that day, along with Waffles."

Zac swallowed. He couldn't figure out anything to say.

"You told me to stay, so I did," said Cole. "I ain't gonna lie." He shook his head slowly. "For a while, I hated Mark and Tiffany. I hated them for not wanting to take you too." He stared at Zac. "Sometimes I still feel that way. They ain't family."

Zac sighed. "You can't hold it against them," he said. "After all, they weren't all that wrong." He leaned back against his chair. "I ain't exactly what you would call a model citizen."

"Excuse me?" demanded River. She turned to Cole. "Don't listen to him," she said. "Your brother is one of the most upright, honest men I've ever known."

"Can confirm," added Cash with a nod. "This is true."

"I'm not surprised," said Cole, with a smile. "I wouldn't expect anything else." His face became serious. "Have you been to the cemetery to see them?"

Zac shook his head slowly. Truth was, he never had the inner strength to visit that place. He was afraid if he ever did, he would sink into a pit of despair. Just thinking about it, visualizing the site with his parents' gravestones, made him want to break down and cry. No, that wound was still too fresh. He wondered if there would ever come a time in his life when he could bring himself to go visit.

"I went," said Cole.

"That's gotta be twenty miles from here," said Zac. "Did the Parkers bring you?"

Cole shook his head and peered back at Zac with an impish grin. "I skipped school and hitched a ride."

"You know how dangerous that is?" demanded Zac. His sudden burst of anger surprised even himself.

"Can't be any more dangerous than hopping freight trains," chided Cole.

River and Cash snickered. When Zac glared at them, they quickly turned away, all the while struggling to contain their laughter.

He stared at Cole, who defiantly stared back, unfazed, and unafraid.

"As you can see," said the younger man. "I managed to return home in one piece."

"I can see that," replied Zac.

"It looks the same," said Cole. "At least, the same as I recall." He sighed. "I almost went to the house, but the school called Tiffany and she and Mark used the tracker on my phone to find me. They rolled up right when I was leaving the cemetery. They didn't really scold me, I guess they figured I could've done a lot worse things than to go to the cemetery."

"They sound like good people," said Zac.

Cole nodded. "They are. But they're not kin."

"But they're the people who gave you a home."

"Or took me from one," snapped Cole. "Again," he continued. "Not kin." He took a sip from his drink. "Don't get me wrong, they really are nice, and they do their best. They've never done anything mean or violent. I appreciate all they've done for me, but—" he sighed. "They're not family." He locked eyes with Zac. "Not like you."

Zac smiled. "You got a thick head, boy."

"Seems to be genetic," replied Cole, with a grin.

After lunch, Cole showed them around the small town, or at least the places he liked to go. The pond where he would fish, usually all by himself, since the Parker family didn't much care for fishing. The small coffee shop that he visited from time to time. By his own admission, he didn't care much for coffee, which made Zac wonder why his younger brother would spend time at a coffee shop.

As they walked by the building, a pretty, blonde girl stuck her head out the drive-thru window and shouted, "Hey, Cole." She flashed a sweet smile.

Cole's face went red as he smiled back and, with a crack in his voice, responded, "Hey."

Suddenly, it all made sense to Zac. Not wanting to embarrass his little brother, he simply let it slide.

The afternoon sun hung low on the horizon. Zac didn't want the day to end, but, unfortunately, they both had lives to return to. They walked together as they made their way to the rail yard.

It was time to say goodbye. River and Cash hugged Cole, then disappeared into the woods to wait for Zac.

"Let me go with you," blurted Cole.

Zac shook his head.

"Come on," he begged. "I can hold my own." Tears welled up in his eyes. "I don't wanna go back. What if I don't see you again?"

Fighting back his own desire to bring the kid along, Zac said, "It can't be. Least not now."

"Why not?" demanded Cole tearfully.

"Because you ain't old enough."

"You weren't much older than I am now, when you set out."

"I had no choice!" Zac shook his head. "Besides, I didn't have anyone who would come lookin' for me." He wiped his eyes. "You do."

"I don't want you to leave again," cried Cole.

"And neither do I," replied Zac. "We just don't have any other options right now." He stared at his little brother. "Tell you what. I promise you right now, as soon as you turn eighteen, I will come here and get you myself."

"You promise?"

Zac nodded. "I swear on my life. Nothin' will stop me. But between now and then, you have to promise me you'll stay here and finish high school."

Cole nodded and wiped his face.

"And no more hitch-hiking," admonished Zac. "I mean it."

"I won't," promised Cole.

Zac tapped him on the shoulder. "You got my number. We won't lose touch again. If you ever need me, just text me. I'll come runnin'.'"

"What if I just wanna talk?"

"Anytime," he replied. "You send me a message anytime." He smiled. "And while you're here, you should spend some time getting to know that pretty, little blonde at the coffee shop."

Cole's face went dark red, almost as red as his hair.

As much as he hated it, it was time to head out. He hugged his little brother one more time, and once again, promised to stay in touch. As Cole walked away, Zac's heart ached, he wanted to run after him and have him come along with them, but he knew, that would be a bad idea. They made a plan, one that would work, it was best to stick to it.

Zac turned and weaved his way through the thicket, back to the spot where River and Cash waited.

"You okay?" asked River, after hugging him for a long while.

"I think so."

"You'll see him again," she said softly.

"At least this time, we can stay in touch," he said, trying to convince himself it was a suitable substitute.

"I already added him to the server," said Cash, wiggling his phone in the air. "After all, he is a de facto member of the family." He smiled.

Zac's phone chimed. He pulled it out and saw a message.


```
Cole: Be safe. And don't forget about me.
  Zac: Never
```

Chapter Six

Shards of sunlight sliced through the moth-eaten fabric draped over the windows. Teague lay in silence with his eyes closed, breathing in the scent of some of his most cherished, childhood memories.

Much to his surprise, the whole visit was a positive experience. This trip reminded him of all the wonderful things he grew up with. Sure, they weren't the typical suburban things. There were no trips to amusement parks, no luxury vacations or even video games. In their place was lots of time outdoors, hunting, fishing, and mucking around in the swamp. Time with his pawpaw, listening and learning, committing the old man's stories to memory.

And lots of love. So much, in fact, he hardly noticed any of it—until it was gone.

He was so glad he was able to share some of this with Finn. A tiny part of himself was sad that he would never be able to introduce him to August. He was sure they would have gotten along. His lips curled into a warm smile.

Speaking of Finn. Where was he?

Teague sat up and rubbed the dust from his eyes, then scanned the cabin. There was no sign of him. He must have gone outside to relieve himself. He shrugged, and lay back down and closed his eyes, determined to bask in the cozy feeling for as long as possible.

The door to the dock creaked open, followed by the sound of bare feet softly treading on the wood floor. Something chirped. It was a distinct sound; Teague had heard it plenty of times before. He knew exactly what creature was making it. The chirping continued. "Lawd, please tell me that ain't what I think it is," he said aloud, refusing to open his eyes.

Finn crept close, accompanied by the chirping sound.

Teague opened his eyes and found himself staring at a tiny, baby alligator hovering in the air, inches above his head. Beyond the creature, Finn was positively beaming.

"It's a baby alligator," said Finn.

"I know what it is," replied Teague. "Why are you holding it so close to my face?"

"He's cute," said Finn, defensively. "Don't ya think?"

Teague sat up and rubbed his head. "Why is it inside? And, more importantly, why are you holdin' it?"

"He was swimming in the water off the dock, all alone, making that chirping sound."

"Uh, huh," replied Teague, nodding slowly. "And you just figured you'd scoop him up and bring him inside for what? Breakfast?"

The tiny alligator chirped and wriggled.

A serious look swept across Finn's face. "You wouldn't eat a baby alligator. Would you? I mean, there can't be much meat on his little body."

Teague scoffed. "I'm from Louisiana, I'll eat anything if I can catch it."

Finn pulled the baby gator close. "He looks like a Walter to me." He held the small reptile in the air. "What do you think?"

Before Teague could respond, the alligator squirmed and wiggled its way right out of Finn's grip, dropping to the floor, landing inches away from Teague, who quickly jumped up and moved away from the sleeping bags. "Catch it!" he shouted.

Finn dove for Walter, but the tiny animal was much faster and managed to scurry away, hiding under the blankets, all the while chirping non-stop.

"He's under your blanket there!" shouted Teague, pointing.

"Here, Walter," cooed Finn, as he crept slowly toward the blanket on the floor. "Come on, boy." He made a clicking sound with his tongue.

"He's a reptile," said Teague. "He ain't comin' to you like a dog." The chirping continued unabated.

Preoccupied with hunting Walter, Finn didn't respond.

The little creature darted across the floor, running over Teague's feet as it passed. "Mais la!" he hollered, then leaped onto the counter. "Couillion! Put a little more effort into it."

Finn ran around the room, throwing sleeping bags and blankets, as well as clothing and cushions, into the air as he chased Walter around in circles.

Across the room, Teague's phone rang. There was no way he was going to try to retrieve the device; with all the chaos unfolding, it was best to stay out of the way. "Grab my phone while you're over there," he called out.

Finn paused long enough to retrieve the device and glance at the screen. He shrugged and tossed it over. "It's River." Then, once again, he set his focus on capturing the tiny reptile.

Teague swiped the phone open. The screen lit up with the smiling face of River, hovering close behind her was Cash.

"Good morning!" she shouted. "We just arrived at the Renfaire, so I figured I'd chat face to face." She smiled.

"Mornin'," replied Teague.

A scuffle erupted across the room as Finn dragged a cot away from the wall. "Ah, shit!" he shouted, holding his hand up. "The little fucker just bit me!"

"Cocodrie," replied Teague. "It's what they do."

Finn stepped back. "Alright, you little fucker! Get out here!" he shouted.

A look of concern swept across River's face. Behind her, Zac came into view. "What's going on?" she asked.

Teague chuckled. "Finn's having a little trouble with Walter."

"Who?" asked Cash, leaning closer to the screen.

"Hold up," replied Teague. He flipped the camera, focusing on Finn. "Say hello," said Teague.

Finn gave a quick wave, then flung a sleeping bag in the air, bellowing, "Ah, hah!" followed immediately by, "Shit!"

"I see things are totally back to normal," joked Cash.

"What's our boy doing now?" asked River.

Teague kept the camera on Finn. "He caught himself a baby gator this morning. Named him Walter. The little fella got away from him and now he's loose in the cabin," he explained. "Hear the chirping?"

The others were silent for a moment, the only sound was that of Finn swaying effortlessly between soft calls and cussing.

Zac laughed heartily. "Finn, you dumbass," he said.

"Gotcha!" shouted Finn, as he flipped a cot over. There was a scuffle, followed by more cussing—followed by a shout, "God dammit! The little fucker is fast!" he shook his hand in front of him. "And mean."

Laughter erupted from the phone.

"Hey," said Zac. "Aren't mama gators protective of their young?"

"They are," replied Teague.

"She's gotta be getting' pissed with all the screaming her little one's doin'."

"She's probably on the dock right now," replied Teague. "Lyin' in wait for the dumbass who stole her little one to step outside."

"She'll get him back as soon as I catch him," added Finn.

Walter scurried out from beneath a cot and charged across the room.

Seeing his chance. Finn dove, cupping his hands over the tiny animal. "Gotcha!"

The chirps were more frantic now.

Slowly and with great care, Finn lifted his hand and grasped the little alligator along its body, just under its front legs. He held it aloft and walked closer to Teague, holding the creature in front of the camera. "Say hello to Walter," he said.

"Hello, Walter," said the others in unison.

"Now, give him back to his mama," said River.

"I am," replied Finn. He walked to the back door.

"Be careful openin' that door!" shouted Teague.

"I know, I know," replied Finn, with a wave of his free hand. He turned the handle and slowly opened the door about two inches. He flashed a smile and let it swing wide open, then stepped out onto the dock. "Ya see?" he said, over his shoulder. "She ain't here."

Teague followed as Finn made his way to the edge of the dock. "There she is," he said, pointing.

The mama gator floated close to the edge of the dock. Her fierce eyes stared up at them. When her baby chirped, she glided closer, her giant tail splashing.

Finn crouched down.

The big gator lifted her head from the water and slammed her powerful jaws closed, splashing water in his face.

"Careful!" shouted Teague, in chorus with the trio over the phone.

"I know, I know," scoffed Finn. He held the tiny creature above the water as it wriggled and chirped. "Alright, Walter," he said. "Go swim to mama." He let the little gator plop into the murky water.

The chirping stopped as soon as it reached its mama. The giant alligator made no effort to swim away, she remained in place, studying Finn as the baby climbed atop her head, and settled on her back.

Teague flipped the phone back to his face. "Well, I guess it's a good thing we're headin' out today," he said, with a grin. "Seems as though we've gone and upset the neighbors. She's probably plotting our demise as I speak."

River laughed. "Well, pack your things and make your way over here," she said. "I'm dying to give you both hugs."

"Lookin' forward to it," replied Teague. "We'll see y'all in a couple days." He turned off his phone and studied Finn, who was busy watching Walter hang out with his mama. There was a strange, distant look on his face.

"Whatcha thinkin'?" he asked.

Finn stared out at the gator. "It's weird how she could be so protective." He turned his gaze to Teague. "Bein' a reptile and all."

"Cocodrie are notoriously protective mamas," replied Teague. "Even deadly predators can be good parents."

Finn didn't reply, instead, he returned his gaze to the mama gator.

Teague left him to ponder life as he went back inside to clean up. Thanks to the morning antics, they had much to do before heading out.

Chapter Seven

"Excuse me, fine, sir," said Cash, in his best, renaissance, peasant accent. "Would you like to taste my nuts?"

The man paused and grinned, the metal from his suit of armor glinted in the sunlight. "Well, since you put it that way," he said. "I suppose I ought to." He pulled out a crisp, twenty-dollar bill and handed it to Cash, who promptly made change and handed the man a bag of honey-roasted pecans.

"You will remember this purchase for years to come," said Cash. "There are no tastier nuts than mine."

The man shoved a handful of pecans into his mouth and chewed, all the while nodding in approval.

Cash spun around and, with his arms in the air, he announced, "This man is eating my nuts!"

The crowd that gathered around laughed enthusiastically.

"You, fine sir," said Cash, turning to another man dressed as a pirate. "You appear to have no nuts." He held out the pole that carried multiple bags of pecans. "Might I interest you in purchasing my nuts?"

The crowd roared. The pirate pulled out his wallet and bought every bag Cash had on hand. He then proceeded to hand them out to anyone who walked by.

"Go on," prodded Cash. "I promise you that these are the finest nuts that will ever caress your tongue."

More laughter, followed by cheers.

Cash took a low bow. "I shall return." He waved his arms, then strolled away.

"You were born for this," said River. She handed him a bottle of water.

"A man's gotta do what a man's gotta do," he replied. He downed the bottle in one go, reveling in the cool sensation of the liquid as it poured down his throat. He flashed an impish grin and wrapped his arms around her waist, pulling her close against his body. "How about you?" he asked. "Would you like to taste my nuts?"

River scoffed and shoved playfully against him. "Save the act for later," she said, then planted a kiss firmly on his lips.

"Oh, ew!" said Bells, sauntering up with a tray full of cold beers. "Please, keep it to yourselves, there're children around."

"Ah yes," said Cash. He peered down into River's green eyes. "We must always consider the children." He smiled and pulled away, then bowed. "I shall get on with my day and allow the young lady the freedom to do the same." He took her soft hand in his. "I shall see you later this afternoon, when my shift is over," he said, then placed a kiss on her hand.

River laughed and curtsied. "Thank you, fine sir," she said. "I shall return to my work in earnest, serving cold brew to thirsty revelers." She blew him a kiss over her shoulder, then disappeared inside the pub.

His heart full, Cash spun around, taking note of a group of young men standing nearby. He flashed a crooked grin, then announced, "These men have no nuts!" He waved his arms. "Fear not! I am off to acquire some more to remedy that situation."

He weaved his way through the parade of renaissance fair attendees; a never-ending parade of pirates, knights, noblemen and women. Tight corsets pinched the waists of the women, who were dressed in long, flowing dresses, while the men wore peasant ensembles with large mugs dangling from their hips. Passing by a group of vampires, Cash smiled. "Be careful," he warned. "The afternoon sun is of great danger to your kind."

A pretty, vamp girl smiled at him, showing off her sharp canines. "Blood helps us stay healthy," she replied, as she cast her eyes up and down his body. "Perhaps you would be a willing donor." She sauntered close enough for him to smell her perfume.

"My fair, young vampire," he said, stepping back. "I am afraid my body and blood are spoken for." He stepped away. "However, you may have my nuts."

The young woman faked a pout. "Well, I suppose I should settle for what I can get, then." She waved her hand. "Run along and do not return without your nuts."

Cash bowed and moved on through the crowd. Along the way, he ran into D. B., who was collecting trash.

"Good afternoon, Sir," he said.

Sitting on D. B.'s shoulder, wearing tiny black, bat wings, Spyder hissed and spat.

"And you too, my furry fiend," added Cash. He reached out and scratched the sleek, black cat under his chin.

Spyder leaned in and instantly purred loudly.

"So much for a protective familiar," quipped D. B.

"I thought you were working in the kitchen?" asked Cash.

D. B. shook his head. "I can't with Spyder. Something about food prep regulations." He shrugged dismissively, then reached up and rubbed the cat's head. "So, we're doing groundskeeping. I actually prefer it. I think Spyder does, too."

"Have you seen Zac?"

"Last I saw him, he was over at the stables," replied D. B.

"He's probably enjoying that."

D. B. chuckled. "He sure didn't look happy."

"Why not?"

"You'll see," replied D. B. He pointed. "He's at the small stables around the corner. Go check it out for yourself."

Cash nodded and gave Spyder one last good scratch, then spun around on his heels and made his way to the stables.

A line of giggling princesses stretched out from the corner, leading to a small pen. Cash passed, all the while remembering to bow and play the role of a peasant among nobility.

A gaudy sign in pink, turquoise, and lavender, heavily coated in glitter, hung over the makeshift wood frame of the entry gate. Inside the pen, Zac held the reins of a white pony, with a long, braided mane and a glittery unicorn horn placed between its ears. A young princess, dressed in a flowing, pink dress and sparkly crown, giggled while Zac clicked his tongue and coaxed the animal around in a circle. When the ride was done, he led the pony to a stall, then helped the princess from her saddle and escorted her to the gate where her parents awaited.

He locked eyes with Cash.

"Unicorns, eh?" asked Cash, with a wild grin.

"Beats selling my nuts," jeered Zac. He opened the gate to allow another child entry. "My young lady," he said, with a low bow. "Your pony awaits." The little girl, who couldn't be more than five, giggled and peered up at her mother.

"She would like to ride the black one," said the mom.

Zac peered over his shoulder. "Ah! The young lady has excellent taste, albeit a bit on the dark side." He walked over to a dark pony with a rainbow glitter horn, and scratched its head, then took the reins and escorted the animal to the gate.

The little girl jumped up and down, clapping her hands together with glee.

"Alright," said Zac, as he leaned down to talk to the girl. "Now, there're some rules when riding Smokey. First, no kicking or bouncing. He doesn't like that. So, when you get on his back, you must sit proper." He waited for the princess to nod her head in agreement. "Good. Second, no screaming or squealing. Smokey here doesn't know the difference between cries of joy and cries of fear. He might get scared, and that's not good." He waited again for a nod.

"And finally." He stood tall. "Smokey requires payment up front." He smiled at the little girl. "As the sign says." He pointed to a hand-painted sign. "One apple slice is required." He winked at the mom and pretended to scrutinize the little girl. "I don't see any apples. You do have apple slices for Smokey, don't you?"

The little girl nodded her head furiously as she struggled to contain her excitement.

"Okay, ma'am," said Zac. He reached out a strong hand and guided the princess to the pony. "Oh!" said Zac. "You like your fingers, don't you?"

The little girl peered up at him with a confused look on her face and nodded slowly.

"Good!" Zac held out his hand. "I want you to give Smokey the apple like this." He showed with a piece of carrot he pulled from the pouch on his waist.

The princess bobbed her head up and down.

"Alright, then," said Zac. "Go on, give Smokey his fee."

She held out an apple slice, letting the pony eat it from her open hand, afterward, she wiped the saliva onto the front of her sparkly dress.

Zac helped the little girl settle into the rhinestone-covered saddle, then with a nod of his head, he clicked his tongue and guided the pony around the ring several times. After returning the girl to the care of her mother, he walked back over to Cash. "Don't you have a job to do?"

"I do," replied Cash. "I'm just taking a break, watching you play with the unicorns." He looked Zac up and down. "Shouldn't you be wearing a pointy hat with tights or something?"

"Pshh," replied Zac. "They tried, but there ain't no way in hell." He waved his hands down his body. "Besides, I just told 'em I ain't responsible for what happens when all the ladies see this awesomeness in skintight clothes. I mean, they might not be able to control themselves. Things could go from rated G to triple X in a flash."

Cash laughed. "You're right, we wouldn't want that. I don't think my eyes could take it."

Across the way, a gaggle of people gathered around the dunking game. Knowing that Max was working there, Cash decided to wander over and see how it was going.

"Sir," said Max. "I'm afraid you are as disappointing as an unsalted pretzel."

The crowd cheered. A red-faced man stood at the table with a bowl full of baseballs in front of him, while several yards away, Max sat perched atop a contraption, hovering over a container filled with murky water. The man tossed a ball at the red and white target and missed.

"I see, it is impossible to underestimate you," taunted Max.

The man bellowed an unintelligible response.

"Keep practicing my man, you'll be able to talk like a human in no time."

The man lobbed three baseballs, each one missing the mark.

"I see your aim is on par with your IQ."

The crowd laughed.

The red-faced man emptied his bowl. With a dismissive wave of his hand, he stalked away.

"Don't go away," said Max. "The fun has only just begun!"

Another man stepped up to the bar and bought into the game.

"Let's hear it for another victim!" shouted Max.

The crowd cheered.

"Step up, let me get a good look at you," ordered Max. He squinted and flashed a wicked grin. "Ah! I love your hair. How do you get it to come out of your nose like that?"

The man spat on the ground and tossed a baseball. It missed.

"You seem nice. I bet you make everyone happy when you leave the room."

"Dunk him!" shouted a woman, standing nearby.

"Ah, my lady," teased Max. "If I had a face like yours, I would sue my parents."

The man tossed and missed again.

Max turned his focus back to the man. "It's amazing you've managed to live this long. You must be the reason shampoo has instructions."

"Yuck it up, smartass," said the man. "You're getting wet now." He tossed and missed.

The crowd moaned and turned their attention to Max.

"Aw, don't feel bad, a lot of people have no talent," he taunted.

The man grunted and walked away.

Max scanned the crowd. "Who's next?" He locked eyes with a teenage boy. "You, sir," he called out. "Step on up and take a turn. I'm sure your skinny, little arms are no indication of your true strength and ability."

Cash could have stayed and watched Max verbally assault people all day, it was truly an art form. But he was still in the middle of working hours, and he had a job to do. So, he left the laughing crowd and made his way to the storage area.

Chapter Eight

It had been two days since they left the cabin, Teague already missed it. A not so small part of him wanted to settle down. To set up a home that they could call their own. He didn't even care if it was in Louisiana or the mountains somewhere. He'd go wherever Finn wanted to go. He just yearned to stop the continuous movement for a while.

Of course, he didn't bring this up with Finn. He wasn't sure of the response. The last thing Teague wanted to do was to force him into an existence he wasn't ready for.

Overall, the time away was a success. It was good to be alone again, just the two of them, the way it used to be. For the most part, Finn was better. Many of the scars were still fresh and tender, but every day that passed brought more and more of the old Finn back to life.

It was nearly noon when they arrived at the Renfaire camping area. D. B. and Spyder met them at the roadside and helped to get them situated. After that, there was nothing left to do but go and find out what jobs they would be doing while there.

On their way to the main office, D. B. showed them around the festival grounds, stopping every third or so person so they could feed Spyder a treat. The little cat was a celebrity among the staff.

"Oh, my god!" shouted a familiar voice. River ran into Teague so hard they almost fell over. She wrapped her soft arms around him and hugged tightly.

There was something special about River. Her warm smiles, her way of making everything feel good, and her basic common sense were just a few of the things that earned her a special place in Teague's heart. He hugged her back warmly.

She stepped back, stared at him, then turned to Finn with her arms outstretched. "Get over here," she ordered, then she wrapped her arms around him. After a minute, she stepped back and studied him with her clear, green eyes. Her lips curled into a loving smile. "You look great!" she said. "I'm so glad you're back." A strange look swept across her face. She leaned close to Finn, and asked, "You didn't bring Walter, did you?"

He shook his head and laughed.

This made River's face light up all the more, if it was even possible.

Teague had to agree, the sound of Finn laughing was music to his ears too.

"Looks like they got you servin' beer," said Teague. "The clothing style fits you."

River flashed a coy smile and placed her hands on her hips. "I agree," she said. "I make an awesome, beer wench." She tapped the corset around her waist. "I could do without this thing, though. It gets sweaty in here."

"Ah," came another familiar voice. "I see the riffraff has arrived." Bells approached with a ready smile. She punched Teague in the arm and flashed a wicked grin, then wrapped her arms around Finn and pulled him in for a brief hug.

"How come he gets a hug" protested Teague, playfully.

Bells shrugged. "Fine," she said. "I'll make it even." She punched Finn in the arm.

"So, what are you supposed to be?" asked Teague, taking note of her pirate costume, complete with a realistic sword strapped to her leather belt.

"Today," replied Bells, taking a step back. "I am a pirate. My job is to go about, harass the patrons and keep things lively." She flashed a big smile.

"Nice!" exclaimed Finn.

"Ah!" came another familiar voice. "I see a couple of gentlemen with no nuts!"

Cash sauntered up carrying a pole with several bags of pecans dangling. He handed the pole to Bells and proceeded to greet both Teague and Finn with big hugs.

"I see they found something for you to do that puts your talent to good use," said Teague. He glanced around. "Where'd they put Zac?"

"He's working in the unicorn pen," replied Cash, grinning.

Teague tried to conjure up an image in his mind of what that looked like. He could hardly wait to see it for real.

"Who's hungry?" asked River. "Wait right here," she ordered. Not waiting for an answer, she spun around and disappeared inside the pub.

"You there, my fine sirs," shouted Cash, at a group of young men passing by. "Would you like to taste my nuts?"

The men laughed out loud; one shook his head.

"Now, now," said Cash, without skipping a beat. He pulled Finn forward. "You don't want to be like this man, do you?" He waved his hand at Finn with a flourish. "You see, he has no nuts." A wicked grin spread across Cash's face. "You don't want to be known as a nutless man, do you?" He leaned close. "You know, the ladies much prefer a man with nuts." He winked.

Laughter erupted all around them as another group of passersby overheard the conversation.

"I'll buy some!" shouted a short, round woman in a very tight-fitting pirate ensemble. She pulled a roll of bills from between her full breasts and handed it over to Cash.

As soon as he gave her the bag, Cash announced loudly, "This woman is holding my nuts!" He spun around. "Are there any other takers?"

Teague stood back and enjoyed the show. Cash was certainly in his element, performing and teasing the audience. Seeing his friends again, so happy and playful, made his heart sing. For the first time since leaving the cabin, he felt like he was home.

River materialized, carrying a tray above her head. She guided them over to a table and placed the food down in front of each one. Before she went back to work, she ordered them to make sure they ate their fill before moving on. Then, with a couple of quick pecks on their cheeks, she went back to work.

The food smelled delicious. Both Teague and Finn devoured every morsel, all the while watching Cash banter and play with the crowd.

Bellies full, they wandered over to the stables to say hello to Zac.

All around them, the festival was in full swing. A kaleidoscope of savory aromas wafted in the air, each one more tantalizing than the last. Revelers wandered along the dusty road, wearing every costume imaginable from pirates, to peasants, to nobility. There were several barbarians and even more Vikings.

It wasn't difficult to find the stables, all they had to do was follow the children. They strolled past a long line and made their way up to the corral, where they found Zac patiently escorting a white pony wearing a sparkly horn between its ears.

Upon seeing Teague, Zac's face lit up. He nodded, then finished the ride and helped the little princess from her bejeweled saddle. As soon as the child was back in the care of her mother, Zac announced he was taking a break.

He strolled up to Teague, wrapped his muscular arms around him. "It's great to see y'all again." He did the same for Finn, then, like River, he stepped back and studied them both. "Looks like the time away did both of you some good," he said. "Y'all got your color back."

Across the road, a large crowd had gathered. Between the shouts, cheers and raucous laughter, Teague couldn't make out what it was that had everyone's attention.

As if reading his mind, Zac said, "It's a daily occurrence. At least, whenever Max is on shift."

"Oh yeah?" asked Teague. "What do they got him doin'?"

"Come on, I'll show you."

They weaved their way through the crowd, coming to a stop along the wood fence that separated the dunk tank from the throng of people. Sitting upon a seat, hovering above a pool of water, was Max, spewing a steady stream of taunts and insults.

A thin man stood in front of the table with a bowl of baseballs. He threw one, but it missed the target by at least a yard.

"You know," teased Max. "There's this thing called a target." He pointed. "That's it, right there. The little red and white thing you keep missing."

The man growled and threw another ball, this time barely missing the target.

"It appears as though you couldn't hit water if you fell out of a boat!" jeered Max.

The crowd roared.

After emptying his bowl, the man gave a low bow of defeat, then stepped back to allow someone else a turn, but no one stepped up.

"Come now," said Max. "This water isn't going to come up and surround me on its own." He scanned the audience, then folded his arms and leaned back. "No worries," he said. "I'll just sit here and let the breeze keep me cool, because I sure ain't going into the water."

Teague shot a glance at Finn. The look on his face betrayed his thoughts.

Finn stepped up at the table.

Max sat up straight and smiled. "Well, well, well," he said. "Who do we have here? Is it perhaps a worthy opponent?"

The crowd grew silent as Finn pulled a crumpled wad of money from his pocket. In no hurry, he stretched each bill out and laid it flat on the counter.

From his perch above the tank, Max yawned, peered down at his fingernails, and swung his feet back and forth. He glanced at his wrist, pretending to look at a watch. "Come on, come on," he prodded. "We would like to do this today, if it's fine with you."

To his credit, Finn continued to move at a snail's pace. The subtle expression on his face told Teague he was very much enjoying himself. The fee finally paid, Finn held a ball in his hand and squinted at the target.

"Take your time," taunted Max. "I feel as though I'll still be up here an hour from now." He laughed. "Just remember, straighten your arm and then release the ball."

Laughter from the crowd.

Finn winked at Teague, then tossed the ball, missing the target by at least a yard.

"I've seen better pitching at a T-Ball game."

Finn smiled and lifted another ball. He set his focus on the target, the look of concentration on his face told Teague that this time he wasn't playing. The corners of his lips twitched; his jaw flexed.

From his perch in the dunk tank, Max seemed aware that the stakes had changed.

"Come on," said Max. "It's that little thing that looks like a target." His tone no longer quite so confident.

Finn reared back and flung the ball. Silence descended as all eyes were on the flying orb as it slammed dead center into the target. A buzzer rang out, followed by a loud splash as Max fell into the water.

The crowd cheered. A large man slapped a beefy hand on Finn's shoulder, congratulating him.

Inside the tank, Max wiped the water from his face and nodded at Finn, who smiled and waved back.

Chapter Nine

"I knew I was screwed when I saw you walk up," said Max.

Zac placed another log on their fire, sending a swirl of tiny sparks into the air.

"I wish I coulda been there," sighed Bells.

D. B. fed a piece of chicken to Spyder. "It was glorious," he laughed. "Just seeing the look on his face when he went into the water made everything worth it."

"Ha, ha," scoffed Max. He turned to Finn. "You ruined a perfect record."

Finn shrugged. "To be honest, I wasn't entirely sure I'd be able to hit the target."

"Bullshit!" scoffed Zac. "Nice try at humility though," he teased.

"Well, if anyone could take you down, it'd be Finn," said River proudly. After what seemed to be a lifetime, her boys were all back with her. She was so happy; her face was beginning to hurt due to the constant smile plastered on it. Her heart was full. Teague was positively glowing with energy and light; Finn was back to his healthy self again. His face wore a ready smile, but his eyes were different. If River had to find a word to describe the change, she would use maturity. There was a subtle maturity to the way he carried himself. After everything he'd been through over the past several months, she wasn't surprised. No person could possibly go through all of that and come out unchanged.

"Seriously, though," said Cash. "Our boy here has been tormenting people, unpunished this whole time."

Zac chuckled and shook his head. "The amount of people who walked away pissed off." He glanced over at Finn. "You'd be the man of the hour if they were around."

River leaned against Cash, reveling in the feeling of his chest rising and falling with each breath.

Their laughter was interrupted by the sound of several phones chiming at once. Someone was messaging the entire group through the server.

Bells was the first to open her phone. "Holy shit!" she exclaimed.

River quickly pulled her phone from her pack, opened the app, and stared down at the screen in awe.

Mara: He's here!

She posted a picture of a chubby, pink-skinned baby, with a tiny sprig of light-brown hair on top of his head. His eyes closed as he slept blissfully in Mara's arms. His momma was beaming with joy.

Mara: Everyone, say hello to our newest family member, Zephyr. Weighing in at nine pounds, eight ounces, he's a couple days early, but totally healthy. Isn't he the most precious thing you've ever seen?

Bella: Oh sweetheart! Congratulations! Give

Zephyr a hug from me. I can hardly wait to meet him in person.

Porter: Congratulations, Mom and Dad!

Max: Welcome to the world, little dude.

Spinner: He has got to be the cutest newborn I've ever seen.

Bells: Thank God he looks like his momma.

Gunner: Well, I'll be. He sure is a cutie. Congratulations, Mom and Dad.

Cash posted a meme picture of an actor holding a glass high for a toast.

Sam posted a meme of a woman clapping with glee.

Zac shared a happy dancing dog GIF.

Stoney: He sure is a cute little bugger.

Teague: You did good momma. Finn agrees. He'd say so himself, but he still doesn't keep his phone charged.

Mara: Posted a GIF of a dog laughing, holding his belly.

River: Oh, Mama, I am so proud of you. He looks precious. I agree with Spinner. He's the most adorable baby I've ever seen.

Tripp: Welcome little one. Hey, where's dad?

Mara: He's right here. The delivery was a little hard for him.

She shared a picture of Ben passed out on the floor during delivery.

Laughter exploded around the fire. River could only imagine that everyone on the chat was laughing as hard.

Tripp: Bruh

Zac: You're never gonna live this down.

Gunner: Shared a meme of a man standing with his hands on his hips, staring disappointedly.

Bella: Poor thing, all the excitement was too much for him.

Porter: Try not to feel too bad, my man. Take it from someone who lived through it. Childbirth is not for the weak.

Sam: Posted a laughing GIF.

D. B. did the same.

Cash shared a GIF of a man shaking his head.

Bells: Hahahahaha!!!!

Stoney: Son, you make us all look bad.

Ben: Laugh it up, smartasses. Until you walk a mile, I don't wanna hear it!

Max: But we're all living vicariously through you.

Spinner: I'm trying to feel empathy, but all I can do is laugh when I see that picture.

Mara shared another image, this one was Tanner holding the baby while a pale, sickly looking Ben cut the cord.

Tripp: Thank God for Tanner.

Ben: You have no idea how traumatic this all was.

Zac: How come Tanner looks fine?

Max: Right? It doesn't look like Tanner had a problem.

Ben: He's a combat vet! Of course, he's gonna have nerves of steel.

Nate: We had to pick Ben up off the floor and place him in a soft chair.

Ben: In my defense, I was operating on an empty stomach.

Tanner: Thank you all. He shared a laughing emoji.

Mara: I'm just thankful Nate and Tanner got here when they did.

Nate: Yeah, we literally walked in the door while she was in full labor.

Bella: How are you doing, Mama? Was it an easy labor?

Mara: It was painful and a little scary, but since I was in my home, with my sisters, Mom and Ben, it wasn't so bad. Tanner and Nate were a bonus.

River could hardly keep her eyes off the baby. He was tiny, but so pudgy. She never thought something so wrinkly and small would be so captivating. She was so busy staring at baby Zephyr, she missed most of the banter.

Mara: My mom says it's time for me to get some rest. I'll post more pictures tomorrow. Love y'all. Hugs to everyone!

A flurry of happy faces and congratulations appeared on the screen as everyone said goodbye.

River's phone chimed with a text message.

Mara: I can't wait for you to hold him.

River: Neither can I. I'm so happy for you. I can't get over how adorable he is. I never knew a baby could be so cute.

Mara: Wait 'till you have one of your own. She shared a smiling emoji along with a heart emoji. I'm gonna bet you and Cash will give us a run for our money on the cuteness scale.

River gasped quietly at the thought. Her? Have a baby? That was one image she couldn't conjure at all. In fact, just thinking about it made her break out in a cold sweat. She peered up only to find Cash smiling at her. She shoved her phone in her pocket and snuggled close to him.

"Looks like the family has grown by one more," said D. B.

"He sure is a cute, little guy," said Zac.

Max snickered, "I don't know about all y'all, but I am never letting Ben live this down."

A round of chuckles and agreement followed.

Cash kissed the top of River's head. "You okay?" he asked.

She nodded, though she wasn't quite sure what she was feeling. She went with the easiest answer. "I don't know, a part of me would've liked to have been there when Zephyr arrived. For Mara." She could feel him nod.

A comfortable silence descended on the group as everyone, lost in thought, stared into the fire.

It was Bells who broke the silence with a new subject. "So, what job did y'all get?" she asked Finn and Teague.

"We're gonna be manning the rope ladder challenge," replied Teague.

"Figures," nodded Cash. "You two are monkeys. It only makes sense."

Teague laughed. "I suppose if anyone wants to complain and say it can't be done, Finn here can show them it can." He wrapped his arm around Finn, who smiled sheepishly. "Starting tomorrow, we get to harass the patrons."

Max held his drink in the air. "All I can say is the next three weeks are gonna be lit."

A chorus of agreement made its way around the fire.

"Any thoughts as to what y'all are gonna do when we're done here?" asked Bells.

River shrugged. "I suppose that's up to Finn," she said.

A look of confusion swept across his face. "How so?"

"Well," replied River. "If you were gonna go find out about your bio dad, we'll be heading up to Gainesville."

A distant look took over Finn's face. When he snapped out of it, he glanced around at everyone. "I'm not sure," he said. "We don't know anything about him."

He had a point. According to Porter, the only solid bit of evidence was through Tricia. He found the official birth certificate, but the father listed was Daniel. But according to the man himself, he wasn't the father. The only piece of solid evidence they had to go on was that Tricia grew up in Gainesville, Texas and that she left shortly after Finn was born.

"The only thing we know for sure," said Finn. "Is where Tricia grew up." He stared into the fire. "What if that's a dead end?"

Teague nodded his head. "It could be," he said. "But then again, it might be a start." He shrugged. "Who knows, we could go there and find a trail."

"I agree," added Zac. "She could have people there who remember."

"What we know for sure," said Cash. "Is that she lied when you were born. Makes you wonder what else she lied about."

"Your bio dad has eyes like yours," added River. "There can't be a lot of people in that town who look like that. I'm gonna guess that he would have stuck out."

"Somebody for sure would remember him," said Teague.

"And if they don't?" asked Finn.

"Tricia has family," said Zac. "I bet they'd recall."

Finn shook his head. "I've never even heard her mention any family. She only ever said her parents died when she was young."

"According to Porter, her uncle raised her," said Cash. "She had a cousin about the same age."

Finn nodded in agreement. "But the cousin died long ago, and the uncle passed almost a year ago."

"We could still go and see if we can find something," said Teague. "Maybe someone else in town will remember her. It wasn't all that long ago."

River recalled a detail that Porter shared. She snapped her fingers and sat upright. "An aunt!" she shouted. "According to Porter, she had an aunt who still lived in town. She was related to the uncle's wife or something. I'll bet she knows something."

"And she might have come across your bio dad," said Teague. "We could go seek her out and ask."

Finn rubbed his chin. "What if she doesn't know anything or doesn't wanna say anything?"

"We won't know that unless we go find out," said River. She waited with bated breath for him to mull it over. While she understood his apprehension, deep down inside, River knew that finding Finn's father would be a good thing. If nothing else, it would give him closure. Of course, there was the possibility that he was dead or someone even more awful than Daniel, she pushed those thoughts away, preferring to focus on the positive side. Of all people, Finn deserved to have a happy ending regarding his family.

Finn turned to Teague. "What do you think?"

"I think we should go," he replied.

"Okay then," he said, nodding his head. "Looks like we're going."

River's heart filled with excitement. "Yay!" she shouted. She turned to Bells. "Looks like we're heading to Gainesville!"

Chapter Ten

The midnight breeze was cool against his skin. The presence of cloud cover overhead made it quite dark outside. This was a good thing, in situations like these, darkness was their friend. Shane sat in the passenger seat of the old pickup truck while Manny had the wheel.

"I'm not seeing anything," said Manny, peering through a set of night vision binoculars.

Shane was focused on keeping tabs on Odie's progress as he crept toward the run-down mobile home. He pointed. "Just beyond that cluster of trees over there," he said.

Manny nodded his head. "I see him now."

Parked on the edge of the road, behind a cluster of mesquite trees, Shane could just barely make out the giant silhouette of Pillar hiding among the trees, tracking Odie's progress through his high-powered rifle scope.

In moments of stillness, Shane's mind would always wander to his son. The world was a dark and dangerous place, many horrible things could happen, he ought to know, after all, Shane and his crew were personally responsible for many horrible things that had befallen a certain element of society. He convinced himself that they weren't the bad guys since their actions were only directed toward people who had committed some kind of crime.

Over the years, he'd seen some horrific things. There were some real monsters walking around disguised as human beings out there. They all shared one thing in common, they preyed on the young, the very old and the weak—they never seemed to have the balls to come after men like Shane. That's because the most wicked were also the most craven.

His thoughts drifted to Finn and his friends. How many monsters had they run into over the years? The thought of his son and his friends being in any of the situations Shane had witnessed broke his heart.

Shane despised the way his thoughts always led to disasters, hence he resorted to the only reliable distraction—immersing himself in his work. If he were a businessman, it would entail spending extended hours at the workplace, with his eyes glued to a computer screen. But Shane was anything but a normal businessman. His line of work was vastly different, it was also far more dangerous.

The truth was, he found the danger more appealing than anything else. It required his full focus, thus allowing him to avoid thinking of anything other than the immediate moment at hand.

Odie's silhouette slipped beneath a truck, sitting idle in the driveway.

Shane studied the windows of the trailer, watching for any movement that might be an issue. As far as he could tell, the occupants were too busy sitting around and getting high to notice the stranger lurking in the shadows outside.

It usually took Odie less than two minutes to lay explosives, so Shane launched a quiet countdown as he stood watch.

The cabin of the truck fell silent as Manny surveyed the perimeter of the property.

Shane barely got to one minute and thirty seconds when Odie slid out from under the truck and silently made his way back to Pillar.

So far, things were going exactly how they planned. He watched as Odie flashed him the ready signal.

"We're up," said Shane.

Manny pulled the ski mask down over his face. "I hate these things," he said. "They make me break out."

"What are you, fifteen?" taunted Shane.

"You don't have to be a teenager to have problems with acne," argued Manny, as he adjusted the mask. "It can affect anyone, at any age."

Shane shook his head and pulled his mask down. "You done worrying about your complexion?"

Manny nodded.

"Good, let's go!"

They exited the truck. With their weapons at the ready, they crept through the trees and took their place along the far side of the mobile home. Shane signaled Odie and Pillar—it was go time.

The countdown began. Ten, nine, eight, seven, six, five, four, three, two, one.

A sudden and intense burst of white light shattered the darkness. The ensuing explosion caused the truck to be hurled into the air before crashing down in a blazing inferno.

Shane and Manny stood ready.

The door of the trailer flung open, and four men emerged, their weapons at the ready.

Pillar dispatched them quickly with no problems.

Inside the trailer, another man barked commands.

With Manny stationed at the front door, Shane silently navigated his way to the back, closely monitoring the area with his gun in hand. As expected, the back door slowly creaked open. He stood still and watched as two men sneaked out and quietly descended the stairs. As soon as the first man hit the ground, Shane took out the one behind him, thus blocking the first man's escape back into the building. He fired two more shots, and the man toppled to the ground.

There was a commotion at the front of the trailer. Shane could hear a man shouting, followed by Manny barking commands.

Time to move. Stepping over the bodies of the two fallen men, Shane peered into the mobile home. He could see no sign of anyone. He entered the building and quickly cleared the rooms, then made his way to the front door.

The two men were standing at the bottom of the staircase. In front of them, they held two young boys, using them as human shields.

As Manny gave the order to release the children, the men pulled the boys closer to them, cowering behind their small frames.

Shane had little patience for people who harmed kids, he had even less for the ones who used them as shields. He raised his handgun, took aim at the back of the first man's skull, and squeezed the trigger. The creep fell to the ground.

Upon witnessing his friend's sudden death, the second man immediately shoved the child aside and raised his hands in surrender, hoping for mercy. He spun around to face Shane, his face covered in the splattered blood of his friend. "Please," begged the man. "I have a fam—"

Shane fired one shot, silencing the man forever.

Pillar and Odie erupted from the trees and made their way inside the mobile home.

The only noise he could hear besides the ringing in his ears was the sound of children crying. Shane approached the kids. One was a boy of roughly twelve, the other, also a boy, his best guess was that he was probably about ten.

The kids wept and clung to one another in fear.

Shane put his gun away and held his hands up. "It's okay," he said.

"Yo, Boss!" shouted Odie. "You're gonna want to see this."

Manny assumed the role of calming the kids so Shane could go inside and see what they found. He met up with Odie in the hall, gesturing toward a back bedroom.

He stepped into the room to find Pillar standing in front of the closet.

"Down there," he said, pointing to the floor.

Shane peered down into a small room, a bunker of sorts. The filthy face of a teenaged boy peered up at him. The poor thing was far too emaciated for Shane to even guess his true age. As he stared at the teen, two more crept out of the shadows.

"Get up here!" he barked.

Without hesitation, the boys did as they were told.

"Anyone else down there?"

The first boy shook his head.

"What's your name?"

"Alberto," he answered.

Shane stared at the next boy.

"Luis."

He moved his gaze to the third.

"Victor."

"Well, boys," said Shane. "Today is your lucky day."

The boys glanced nervously at one another.

Shane locked eyes with Alberto. "You and I are gonna go down there."

Alberto nodded and stepped in front of Shane.

The scent of dank earth mixed with teenage body odor assaulted his nostrils, making his eyes water. Dim light bulbs hung from a cord, strung along the ceiling. There were five mattresses, stained and moth-eaten, lined up against the walls. In the center of the room was a table, littered with white powder and plastic baggies, a small scale sitting at one end.

Shane wandered around the room. A collection of shelves stacked with blocks of white powder, coupled with containers brimming with small, pre-filled bags, all ready to be sold on the streets. Next to the shelving units, there were containers of infant formula, all stacked neatly. He turned to Alberto. "What's the drug?" he asked.

"Cocaine," replied the teen.

That was exactly what his sources said they would find, it certainly explained the cases of baby formula, but he had to be sure. The last thing Shane wanted to do was to touch fentanyl with his bare hands.

"Alright kid," he said. "Let's go join your friends."

Outside, Manny and Odie had the boys lined up on the ground. As Shane walked up with Alberto, Manny handed the kid a water bottle and told him to go sit with the others. Meanwhile, inside the trailer, Odie and Pillar scanned the building for any other hidden surprises. As soon as they gave the-all-clear, Shane typed a simple text on his burner phone.

```
Thank you for your interest, the home is move-in
ready.
```

Knowing there would be no response, he turned off the phone, shoved it into his pocket and waited. Having completed their scan of the trailer, Odie and Pillar took up positions in the trees, hidden from view, their weapons at the ready.

Shane stared at the group of scared boys sitting on the ground. He couldn't help but think about Finn. These kids were all somebody's sons. He walked over and took a knee in front of Alberto.

"You got a family?" he asked.

Alberto nodded and swallowed. Tears pooled in his eyes.

"Where are they?"

The boy didn't answer.

"I'm not gonna hurt them, nor are we gonna hurt you," said Shane.

"Ohio," answered Alberto. "They promised me that I could go to them once I worked off the money I owed." He swallowed nervously.

Shane understood. Alberto, and probably all the other boys, were migrants who were smuggled across the border and used as work-horses for the drug lords. These kids would never see their families. If they didn't die from disease or neglect, the men who forced them to work would kill them when they were of no more use. He turned to the other teens, and one by one, asked them where their people were.

Three black vehicles rolled into the driveway and came to a stop with their headlights still on, illuminating Shane, Manny and the kids.

The doors to the vehicles swung open, and five, burly men carrying firearms stepped out, followed by a slender man wearing an expensive suit.

"Put the guns down," he ordered. "We don't need them."

The men did as they were told.

"Shane," said the man. "Once again, you and your men did good."

"Cesar," replied Shane, as they shook hands.

"So, what do we have here?" asked Cesar, studying the teenagers. "I thought we agreed there would be no survivors."

"These kids weren't part of the deal," replied Shane.

Cesar clucked his tongue. "If they were in that building, they are part of the deal."

Shane stepped between Cesar and the boys. "This ain't a negotiation," he said. "Your father and I have a standing agreement. All kids that are found are our property."

Cesar studied Shane with a cold eye. "Well then," he said, with a light tone. "Far be it from me to interfere with an agreement made with my father." He stepped back. "I assume the merchandise is inside?"

Shane nodded. "Every ounce that was there when we came in," he replied. He never cared much for Cesar. Born into wealth and power, the kid had an itchy trigger finger and a short fuse.

"Good, good," replied Cesar. He gestured to one of his men who pulled a duffle bag from one of the vehicles. The man carried it over and tossed it to the ground, then opened it, exposing stacks of one-hundred-dollar bills. "You'll see that your full payment is in there."

Shane gestured for Manny to collect the bag.

"I'm sure it is," he replied. "After all, I know where to go if some is missing," warned Shane.

Manny had the boys climb inside the truck bed. Once they were situated, he tossed the bag inside the cab and gave a quick whistle, then climbed behind the steering wheel and fired up the engine.

"Be sure to give the old man my best," said Shane.

"I will, I will, my friend," replied Cesar. "You and your men have a good evening."

With that, Shane climbed into the truck.

At the property line down the road, they halted and retrieved Odie and Pillar. It was time to head back to the cabin and figure out what to do with these kids.

Shane's mind whirled with thoughts of Finn and his friends mingling with images of Alberto and all the other kids they've managed to come across over the years. By the time they pulled up next to the run-down cabin, his mind was in full catastrophic mode.

"Yo, you still with us?" asked Manny, snapping his fingers.

Shane shook his head and glanced around. Both Pillar and Odie were gone, so were the boys. The cabin lights were on, and he could see silhouettes moving around. He had no recollection of the drive at all. How did he miss everyone getting out of the truck?

"You're doing it again," said Manny. He lit a cigarette.

"Doing what?"

Manny exhaled a cloud of smoke and handed the cigarette to him. "That thing you do when you're spiraling."

Shane exhaled and passed the smoke back. He scoffed. "You sound like Catalina."

"Maybe that's because she's right," replied Manny. He took a drag and exhaled. "I can't believe I just said that out loud."

"So, what am I supposed to do? I can't control it."

Manny nodded. "I know, I've seen you like this before," he said. "You end up pushing everyone away." He took a long drag, then passed the cigarette. "The problem is this time you have Gabby to think about."

A sharp pain stabbed Shane's heart at the mention of his daughter. He thought of the last time he spoke more than two words with her, shocking himself at how long it had been. He shook his head and opened his mouth to speak.

"Stop," said Manny, his face serious. "You have to stop being such an asshole." He stared with his dark eyes. "I can't lie, none of us really know how you feel. But we've all stood by you before when you went into self-destruct mode." He took a drag from the smoke, exhaled, and tossed the filter out his window. "There's no more room for this shit. You have to get it together. You're messin' with more than your own life here." A sly grin spread across his face. "Don't make me have Pillar kick your ass."

Shane chuckled. "Pillar? Why not you?"

"Because I ain't stupid," replied Manny. He climbed out of the truck and peered back at him. "Now, pull your head out of your ass, and let's get these boys to their families. I'm ready to do something positive."

Chapter Eleven

The sound of the train whistle pierced the air, signaling their arrival at the rail yard.

Unlike the others, Finn could not sleep, his mind roiling with the many different ways this trip could go wrong. He spent the entire night gazing at the stars, envisioning all the possibilities. What happens if his bio dad turns out to be worse than Daniel? He figured he could deal with that fine. After all, he never knew the man, so it wouldn't matter if he forgot he existed and moved on with his life. In his opinion, the worst-case scenario would be that they find the man and he has a whole family where he's this great father. The type of father every kid would want to have—the type of father Finn never had. The mere thought of that being a possibility made him sad. He wasn't sure whether he could cope with the situation, if that was the case.

All around him, the others awakened, yawning, and stretching as they readied themselves.

"Did you sleep?" asked Teague.

Finn shrugged. "A little," he replied, instantly feeling bad for the lie. He sighed and shook his head. "Not a wink."

Teague smiled. "It'll be okay," he said. "Have a little faith."

"I wish I could. I'm scared of what we could find." Finn didn't bother to elaborate, fearing that if he put the words out into the ether, they might end up making his worst-case scenario happen. He cringed at how superstitious it all sounded in his head.

The train slowed.

Overhead, the sky was pale blue with sparse, fluffy, white clouds. He looked over the lip of the gondola. As the sun peeked over the horizon, its bright, yellow light illuminated the landscape.

They rolled through downtown Gainesville; the streetlights turning off as they passed. Not a single person in sight. He didn't expect to see anyone at this early hour.

"Alright," announced Cash. "We all ready?"

River cast a glance at Finn. "You ready, baby?"

He wondered whether or not he was, as he inhaled. He gave a curt nod of his head.

The train came to a halt with a sudden jerk beneath their feet.

"Let's go!" shouted Zac, then he disappeared over the lip of the car.

Cash went next, followed by River.

Teague clapped a hand on Finn's shoulder. "You go first," he said. He studied Finn for a moment, then smiled. "Try not to fret, even if this don't pan out to anything, you got your family right here." He tousled Finn's hair. "We ain't goin' nowhere without you."

Finn climbed the wall of the gondola and jumped over the lip, landing softly on the gravel. As soon as Teague landed next to him, they took off into the tree line, following the others.

"We should leave our gear here," said Zac, placing his pack down. He pointed. "Downtown's that way, a few blocks."

Finn's mouth was dry, his entire body twitched and trembled as every nerve was on end. He could scarcely recall a time when his body betrayed him in such a way.

The courthouse loomed up ahead. Tall buildings flanked the

streets, some of which had small shops at street level. River stopped and peeked through the glass windows of many as they passed.

"Hey now!" shouted Teague, then he sprinted across the street, standing in front of an outdoor mural, gesturing with his hands.

Finn read the sign, Teague Company. He couldn't help but smile.

"How weird is it that the town you were born in would have a business named Teague?" asked Cash.

"It means they were meant to be," replied River. She looked around. "Gainesville is kind of a cute town."

They walked on. Past a CBD shop, a barber, and what appeared to be a closed bakery. Skirting around the courthouse, a neighborhood came into view. Prestigious Victorians were shaded by the giant, old oak trees that lined the street. It was like the neighborhood was taken straight out of an old advertisement with its picturesque beauty.

Strolling past the beautiful homes, Finn imagined the rooms filled with happy families. Hard as he tried, he couldn't imagine Tricia in one of these places. As soon as her face came to mind, a sense of dread followed, casting an ugly glow on everything. He forced his mind to focus on the beauty of the neighborhood instead.

Zac stopped in front of a quaint, craftsman-style home. "This is it," he announced. "This is where Margaret Cox, Tricia's aunt lives."

Finn stood frozen on the sidewalk. He willed his legs to approach the cozy home, but they wouldn't budge.

"I'll go," offered River.

"No!" he shouted, much more forcefully than he intended. "It should be me." He glanced at Teague. "Just give me a minute." He breathed in slowly, then exhaled, as he attempted to calm his racing heart.

Taking one slow step after another, he climbed the stairs to the porch. He glanced behind him and noticed that everyone was staring at him with hopeful expressions on their faces. Before he lost his nerve, he turned around and pressed the doorbell.

From inside, a small dog barked, and a moment later, soft footsteps could be heard coming closer to the door. The lace curtain was drawn back, revealing the face of an elderly woman who gazed at Finn through the glass. Her jaw dropped. "Dear Lord!" she exclaimed, then quickly unlocked the door and let it swing open. The white-haired woman stared up at Finn as though she were looking at a ghost. Her eyes filled with tears. "I know who you are," she muttered, through trembling lips.

The world suddenly zoomed in and out, once again Finn felt weakness gradually settling in his legs. He didn't know what to expect, but he knew it wasn't anything like this. With his mind completely empty, he found himself unable to form any words. This turned out to be a blessing in disguise, as his mouth felt so dry that he doubted he could have managed anything beyond a weak, raspy utterance.

A sweet smile spread across the old woman's face. A tear ran down her cheek. "Do an old woman a favor," she said. "Take those sunglasses off, please." She stared at him.

Finn's hand trembled as he removed the sunglasses.

The old woman smiled. "I knew it!" she exclaimed, as she cupped her hands over her mouth. More tears sprung forth from her eyes. She smiled warmly at Finn. "I would know your face anywhere." She reached out and touched him tenderly. "And those eyes are all the proof I need," she whispered, her voice trembling with emotion. Without another word, the old woman lunged forward, her soft, woolen shawl brushing against his cheek as she wrapped her arms around him.

His nostrils filled with the soft, floral scent of cinnamon and lavender. He didn't know what to do, so he let the old woman hold him until she was done. When she pulled away, he glanced over his shoulder to find the others staring up at him with a mix of shock, humor, and love. He turned to the old woman.

"Where are my manners," she said. "Welcome home, Finnegan."

The world dropped out from under his feet; he felt lightheaded. How did she know his name? How come he didn't know her? What the hell was going on? Was he dreaming? For the first time since heading out here, he had the strongest sensation that he made a mistake. Maybe he should have stayed away. This was all too much. His heart pounded in his chest.

The old woman looked beyond Finn at the others on the sidewalk. "Those your friends?" she asked.

He could only nod.

She smiled and gestured with her hands. "Well, come on then," she said, loud enough for the others to hear. "Don't just stand there, come on up here and introduce yourselves."

Teague climbed the steps slowly, stopping alongside Finn, followed by Zac, then Cash and River.

"Who do we have here?" asked the old woman.

"I'm Teague," he replied.

"Zac."

"My name's River and this is Cash."

"Well, ain't you the prettiest thing?" cooed the old woman. "My name is Margaret." She gestured toward the porch. "Ya'll take a seat," she said enthusiastically. "I'll get us some tea and we can have a visit." She placed her hand on Finn's arm and smiled at him. "You go on over there and sit down. I'll be right back," she said, spinning around and vanishing into the house.

Teague placed his hand on Finn's shoulder. "Ça va?" he asked.

Finn swallowed against the lump in his throat. "Yeah," he croaked.

"Come on over and take a seat," said Teague. "Your face is white as a sheet." He guided Finn over to a chair.

"She said my name," said Finn. "She said, 'Welcome home, Finnegan.'" He licked his dry lips. "How did she know my name?"

Teague rubbed his chin, then shrugged. "We'll find out soon enough."

"She knew about my eyes."

"She's kin," replied Teague. "Of course, she's gonna know about them. That's a good sign."

Kin. The word rolled around in Finn's mind. It sounded so foreign, yet welcoming.

"But she recognized me before she saw my eyes," said Finn. "How is that?"

"I got nothing," replied Teague. He flashed a bright smile. "I guess it's a good thing we came here for answers."

Margaret stepped out onto the porch, balancing a tray that held glasses and a pitcher of tea. She set it on the small table and poured glasses for everyone. As soon as she finished passing out the drinks, she raised a finger, and said, "I'll be right back." Then she turned around and ran back inside the house.

"She's sweet," said River.

"So is the tea," said Zac. "I forgot how good real sweet tea can be." He took a large drink. "Makes my teeth ache." He grinned. "It's perfect."

Finn took a drink, hoping it would be enough to relieve his parched throat.

The door creaked open, and Margaret wandered out, carrying a photo album. She smiled and sat down in the chair beside Finn. "I figured you'd like to see some of these," she said. She flipped open the book and put her finger down on a black-and-white photo of three young women standing side by side. "That's my sister, Minnie." She slid her finger to another woman. "And that's Mary." She stared at Finn. "Your grandmother."

His grandmother. Gazing at the picture, he struggled to feel anything at all. After all, it was merely an image of a person he had never met.

Teague leaned forward and studied the photograph. He peered up at Finn, then nodded. "I can see a little resemblance," he said.

"May I ask you a question, Margaret?" asked River, using her most polite tone.

The old woman nodded.

"How did you know Finn's name?"

Margaret smiled. "Because I remember when he was born," she

replied. "I was working that night, so I wasn't there. I was a dispatcher for the local police back then." She winked. "My husband was the Sherriff." She sighed. "That was so long ago, it seems like another lifetime."

She turned and looked at Finn. "I was the one who took the emergency call. Sent my husband, James to the scene right away."

"The scene?" asked Finn, finally finding his voice.

Margaret nodded. "A horrible car accident," she replied. "I still don't understand what she was doing out there on that old road so late at night. As far as I can tell, there never was an explanation given as to why a woman in her condition was out there on that desolate road all alone. There was also never an explanation as to what caused the crash. Some speculated that she spun out trying to miss a deer or a dog or something."

"Who?" he asked.

"Melody," replied the old woman. She locked eyes with Finn. "Your mama."

Once again, the world zoomed in and out. Confusion washed over him. He shook his head. "Tricia—"

"Pshh," scoffed the old woman, waving her hand dismissively. "She may have raised you, but she wasn't your mama."

Dead silence descended on the porch. Finn looked around at the stunned faces of the others. He struggled to formulate a sentence, but words were hard to recall.

"Are you sayin' that Tricia wasn't Finn's mother?" asked Teague, slowly.

Margaret nodded. Tears welled up in her eyes. She placed a soft hand upon Finn's. "Melody didn't survive that night. She was too banged up by the accident. It was a miracle she made it through delivery." The old woman choked back tears. "She lasted just long enough to hold her baby."

Finn sensed dampness on his cheek, and instinctively reached up to wipe it away, only to realize that it was a tear. "But how?" he choked.

Margaret flipped through the book, landing on an image of a young Mary, wearing a wedding dress, standing beside a handsome young man. She pointed to the man. "That there is Ben Caldwell," she said. "His family was as well known around this town as our family. Their wedding was a big deal. Two, well-regarded blood lines uniting. They were the talk of the town." She smiled and gazed down at the image. "My little sister was such a lovely bride. And Ben, he had such a bright future ahead of him." She looked up at Finn. "He had recently graduated from law school in Austin."

"Mary was so elated. She told me they were gonna fill a house to the brim with babies." Margaret shook her head. "It didn't work out that way, though. After a few years of trying, the doctors told Mary the odds weren't likely she'd ever conceive."

"So, she got her degree and went to teach in the local grade school. It was the best thing she could think of to be around children."

"It was around that time when our youngest sister, Minnie got married." She leaned close to Finn. "Within a month, they announced they were expecting. Between you and me, I still think she was already with child at the wedding." Margaret winked. "She had packed some pounds on her." She sighed. "But folks weren't so ready to announce that sort of thing back then."

"Now, I don't know if it was the announcement or not, but whatever it was, Mary's ovaries kicked into high gear, and she found out not nearly a month later that she too was expecting."

"From that point on, Mary and Minnie were inseparable." Margaret waved her hands. "Always prattling on about how their babies would grow up to be the best of friends."

"The two girls were born within two months of one another. First, Minnie had Tricia and then Mary had Melody."

Finn's mind was reeling. He could barely keep up with all the information he was receiving. Each new revelation sent a whole new shock throughout his body. He wondered how much more he could take. He worried he might pass out.

"I will say," continued Margaret. "The two girls were very close. They were the cutest little things." She flipped the pages and pointed down to an image of two young girls.

For the first time, Finn saw a familiar face. A young Tricia stared up at him.

Margaret sighed. "Alas, our branch of the Cox family didn't have much luck. Minnie died of pneumonia when Tricia was five years old." She leaned back against the chair. "Since Mary had pretty much raised the girl, it only made sense that she and Ben take her." She shrugged. "Her daddy didn't try to keep her. Truth was, he was lost without Minnie. He let Mary and Ben take Tricia and left town. So, from that point on, the girl lived with them. I'm sorry to say, I don't know what became of him."

She took a sip of her tea and swallowed. "That was when Ben and Mary bought the old Victorian on the corner."

"The red one over there?" asked River, pointing.

Margaret shook her head. "No, my dear." A darkness swept over the old woman. "There used to be a grand home across the street. It burned down about a year ago. Took Ben with it." She rubbed her hands on her thighs. "Some folks think he did it intentionally."

"Why?" croaked Finn. "Why would he do that?"

"Because he was a haunted man, honey," replied Margaret. She flipped through the pages again, this time settling on a picture of a young woman. She pulled the photo from the book. "This is your mama," she said, beaming as she handed the image to Finn.

He took the photo with a trembling hand and stared down in confusion. She was beautiful, with large, soft eyes and long, flowing, dark hair. Her skin was as pale as his.

"You see the resemblance. Don't you?" asked Margaret. She smiled. "Of course, you do. That's how I knew who you were. You look just like her."

Teague and River peered over Finn's shoulder, both emitting audible gasps.

"She's so pretty," said River.

Margaret nodded in agreement. "She was the light of Ben's life." She sighed. "That is until she met your papa."

"Who is he?" blurted Finn, shocked at how suddenly his voice seemed to come back.

"Shane Ryan," replied Margaret.

He had a name. Finn finally had a name. Questions churned in his mind, along with a desire to know as much as possible about the man.

"I wasn't at the wedding," continued Margaret. "That one was a shotgun wedding at the courthouse. Now, I never got a full explanation from my sister, but she told me in the strictest of confidence that Melody was indeed pregnant with you at the time." She exhaled. "Old Ben was livid. He hated Shane. You could feel the hate pouring off him like poison whenever you got close, and Shane was around. When he got arrested, Ben was the only happy person."

"Arrested?" asked Finn. "For what?"

"Oh, darlin'," sighed Margaret. "There ain't no need to dig up old corpses."

"Please," he begged.

Margaret studied him for a moment, then sighed," Okay. But remember, nothing made it to trial, so no allegations were proven. In fact, all charges were dropped. Between you and me, by that point in time, Tricia was a well-known liar. And her envy for Melody was strong."

The old woman studied Finn for a moment. "Tricia accused Shane of assault." Margaret paused, waiting for the revelation to sink in.

"Did he hit her?" asked River.

"No sweetheart," replied Margaret. "She said he tried to rape her."

The words hit Finn like a sudden slap, leaving a painful sting that seemed to echo in his ears. He could almost feel the weight of them settling in his chest, like a heavy stone. The air around him felt thick and suffocating. It was a feeling unlike any other, a raw and visceral pain that left him reeling. His heart sank with the knowledge that his father was a rapist.

"I'll say it again," said Margaret. "Tricia was a known liar and schemer. After her mama died and her daddy deserted her, she turned dark. She envied Melody. I caught her more than once staring with pure hate at the girl. Everything that Melody was, Tricia was the exact opposite." The old woman shook her head. "Besides, my own sister told me the charges were made up." She stared at Finn.

"Made up?" he asked, wanting this to be true more than he cared to admit.

Margaret nodded. "My sister came to me one night, a couple of years after Melody passed. The poor girl was beside herself. She cried and told me that Shane was set up by Ben. He hated the boy. The mere idea of his daughter dating someone from a lower, social background infuriated him. So, with the help of Tricia, they devised a plan to get rid of him. He only changed his mind about putting Shane in prison when he found out his daughter was pregnant. An unwed pregnancy was far worse than a low-class son-in-law in his circles. During the arraignment, the judge gave him the choice of military service or jail. By the time Tricia withdrew the charges, the enlistment papers were all signed."

She stared at Finn. "I was just as shocked as you are right now," said Margaret. "But I had the benefit of knowing everyone involved, and let me tell you, I believe what Mary said. It all made sense." She leaned closer to him. "No father on this green earth would allow his daughter to marry a man who is truly suspected of rape. Especially Ben Caldwell."

"Why would he do something like that?" asked Finn.

"Shane wasn't from around here," replied Margaret. "He moved here when he was in high school. I don't know why, but word was that he had gotten into trouble back where he came from, so he was sent up here to live with his aunt. She had a house at the edge of town. They didn't have much money, and Shane was considered a troublemaker. A lot of the old folks thought he was the devil because of those eyes of his. I don't know much about his kin. I'm sorry I can't be of any help for you."

She took a long drink of her tea. "A week after she visited that day and laid all that truth on me, my sister Mary took her life." She wiped a tear from her eye. "I suppose she just couldn't live with the knowledge of it all any longer."

Finn's heart sank. Why was it that whenever things looked like they might be good, they always turned bad? Everything that had anything to do with his family was shit.

The old woman continued, "I saw Ben a week before the fire," said Margaret. "He'd been sick with cancer for a while. He was a mere shell of the man he used to be, broken and alone. He came to me and told me he ruined everything he ever loved. He felt bad about it all." She sighed. "I suppose he needed to purge his conscience. He told me everything. Some I already knew—some I had no idea about. He confessed to having a friend of his alter the birth certificate so he could hide the fact that the baby survived." She paused and locked eyes with Finn. "That would be you, son. He altered documents to make it look like you died when Melody died. We all thought that was what happened to you." The old woman's gaze didn't falter.

"So, wait," interrupted Teague. "He pretended Finn was dead?"

The old woman nodded.

"Why?" asked Finn, truly confused.

"To hide you from your father," replied Margaret.

Finn gasped. He could hardly believe what he was hearing. He locked eyes with Teague, unable to form any words to describe his thoughts or his feelings at the moment.

"Where was Shane?" asked Teague. "How could they hide his son from him?"

"My dear," replied Margaret. "Shane was in the Marines. He wasn't here when Finn was born." She took a drink. "I assume he heard about it from a phone call." She shook her head. "I can't imagine how he must have felt. In his mind, he lost his wife and son in one fell swoop."

She turned to Finn. "If you could have only seen how he looked at her, how he treated her like the most precious thing he'd ever had in his life. The news must have destroyed him."

"Did you ever see him again?" asked Teague.

Margaret shook her head. "He didn't come home for the funeral. And as far as I know, he never came back to town."

"He lied," muttered Finn. "The old man lied to everyone." He shook his head. "He ruined so many lives."

"He's dead now," said Margaret. "You rest assured, he's paying for all he's done. I'm sure there's a special place in hell where he's at."

Finn stared at the picture in his hand. His real mother. She was beautiful. His mind played out all the ways his life could have been different had it not been for the cruelty of an old man and the bitch Tricia. Why did she take him? Her coldheartedness toward him made sense. Hatred swelled in his heart.

Teague's voice interrupted his thoughts. "You said Shane had an aunt in town. Where?"

Margaret shook her head. "Darlin' that house is long gone. I'm not sure what happened to his aunt, she had to be close to my age. When you get old, everyone starts dying. If I had to guess, I would say she died. There's a strip mall where the house used to be."

Finn was spiraling in his thoughts. Another dead end. This whole trip was getting better by the minute.

"Tell you what," said Margaret. "You keep that picture. I don't need it any longer." She flashed a sweet smile. "I Know this visit probably didn't go the way you hoped it would. And I'm sorry for that. I, like everyone else, believed you were dead. I only found out the truth about it all a year ago when Ben came over and confessed." Tears pooled in her eyes. "Had I known the truth when I was young enough to do something about it, I would have taken you myself." She wiped her eyes.

"When I opened that door and saw you standing there, I knew who you were." She smiled. "The resemblance with your mama is strong. When I saw your eyes, I knew who I was lookin' at."

"She's buried at Fairview on the east end of town, just past the rail yard. You should stop by and pay your respects."

Margaret stood up and stretched her back. "I am too old to be sittin' so long," she said. "Would y'all like to stay for supper? I ain't the best cook, but I make do."

No one responded. Finn could feel their eyes on him. He peered up at Teague, unable to answer.

"Thank you very much, Ma'am," said Teague. "Unfortunately, we can't take you up on your hospitality. We appreciate it, though."

The old woman nodded. She smiled at him. "I can hear the Cajun in you, son."

"Yes, Ma'am," he replied proudly.

Finn climbed to his feet. "Thank you for everything," he said, trying to hide his deep disappointment. He was startled when the old woman pulled him in for a long hug.

"You come back anytime," she said. She stepped back and stared into his eyes. "You and your friends are always welcome." She flashed a warm smile. "After all, we're kin."

He watched as the old woman walked back inside her home and closed the door behind her. Standing on the front porch, Finn didn't know what to do next. There wasn't anything to do, it was all a dead end. He glanced over to find Teague busily typing away on his phone.

"What're you doin'?" he asked.

"Pullin' up a map to the cemetery," he replied. "She's right. You should stop by before we leave."

Finn gazed down at the photograph and nodded his head. He may as well, it would be the last time he ever stepped foot in this town.

He spent most of the walk to the cemetery deep in his own thoughts. There wasn't a whole lot to say.

It was River who finally broke the silence. "So, what are you thinkin'?" she asked.

Finn shrugged. "I'm not sure. I guess I'm thinkin' about everything." He shrugged again. "And nothing at the same time."

"It's a lot to take in," she said. "It's understandable that you need some time."

He nodded.

The conversation continued around him for the rest of the walk. Finn didn't mind, the sound of their voices made him relax. Teague's words from earlier came to mind, "You got your family right here."

They stopped in front of the cemetery. Finn never gave much mind to these places before, but this one was different. Beyond those gates, his real mother was buried. A mother who loved him, one he would never know. His heart ached in a whole new way. How could he feel this way about someone he never met? He wished he never learned the truth. Somehow, it was easier not knowing.

Teague placed a hand on his shoulder. "You ready?" he asked.

Finn nodded and stepped through the gates. The ground was carpeted with lush, green grass, and small avenues of tombstones were neatly lined up, each bearing a name. Teague guided him through the narrow paths, following the map he pulled up on his phone.

"Right over here," he said, pointing.

Finn stopped in front of a tombstone. Melody Anne Ryan was the name carved in the granite. The next line read, beloved daughter, wife and mother, followed by her date of birth and the day she died—Finn's birthday.

"You're gonna want to see this," said Teague.

Finn stared down at another tombstone. This one was tiny—child size. The name carved in the stone was Finnegan Shane Ryan, followed by his birth and death date, both the same as Melody's. This was his grave. He was standing in front of his own grave.

A whirlwind of emotions coursed through his body, like a storm of emotions raging within. He could hear the pounding of his heart in his chest and the rush of blood in his ears. He didn't know if he wanted to laugh or cry. Tricia had kept his first name and altered the middle. Why would she keep the first name?

"Whoa," exclaimed Zac.

Cash and River were dead silent.

"Why is it layin' down?" asked Teague. "It looks like someone knocked it over."

"Who would do that to an infant's grave?" asked River.

Something caught Finn's eye. A small, metal object sticking out of the ground at the base of the toppled headstone. He reached down and pulled it free from the soil. A dog tag. He flipped it over in his hand and read the name. Shane Ryan USMC.

"What's that?" asked Teague.

Finn's mouth went dry, his heart raced as he handed the tag to Teague.

"Well, shit!"

"What?" shouted River. "What is it?"

"It's one of Shane's dog tags!" exclaimed Teague. He looked up at Finn. "Do you know what this means?"

Finn shook his head.

"It means," explained Teague. "That we have a way to find him now."

Cash took the dog tag and studied it. "He's right," he said. Shane's social security number is on this. We can send this to Porter and he can do a search for him based on this number." He smiled at Finn. "We can find him now."

Finn didn't quite know what to say. He was still reeling from everything he learned. He wasn't sure he could take another dead end. He turned to Teague. "What do you think?"

"I think we should see what Porter can pull up," he replied.

"Okay," muttered Finn, not really sure if that was the right answer, but willing to follow Teague's lead on this.

Cash pulled out his phone and started typing furiously.

Finn knelt on the ground in front of his tombstone. His mind was numb—his emotions confused. How was one supposed to feel when looking at their own grave?

Teague's hand rested on his shoulder. He let out a deep sigh and slowly ran his fingers over his name, almost as if he hoped that tracing the letters would bring clarity to the situation.

Chapter Twelve

Beth awakened on the floor of some sort of vehicle. Her hands and legs were hog-tied behind her back, and a cloth stuffed in her mouth with a piece of duct tape holding it all in. Her head felt like lead, her eyes refused to focus. Where was she? How did she get here? She struggled to recall what happened.

She was on the beach with Kitty and Trace. She left them to go to the restroom before going to sleep. A creepy feeling washed over her. She stepped outside, and a hand wrapped around her face. A voice whispered in her ear—a familiar voice.

Terror ignited in her belly. Daniel. Daniel was alive, and he had drugged and kidnapped her. Now, she was tied up and heading to who knows where. She struggled to look at the driver, but her restraints made it impossible to turn around and see.

The cabin of the van was dark, with no modern comforts. Every time the vehicle hit a bump; Beth would be reminded that the floor was nothing but bare metal. There were no windows. She was trapped. Until the vehicle stopped, there was nothing she could do but lie there and wait.

The van slowed and finally came to a stop with the sound of squeaking brakes.

Beth listened as the door of the driver's side opened then slammed shut. Waiting in the dark, she ran through scenarios in her mind of ways she could fight back.

Several minutes had passed before the back doors to the van finally swung open. Beth immediately began screaming, or rather, she tried to scream. The gag tightly bound her mouth, reducing her sounds to unintelligible mumbles.

Daniel's face came into view, sporting a wicked grin. "You can do that all you want," he said. "But you'll see in a minute how much of a waste of time and energy it is." He reached for her.

Beth recoiled, trying to stay out of his grasp. It was useless. Her restraints were too tight.

He dragged her body across the corrugated metal floor and lifted her over his shoulder.

The fresh night air was cool against her skin. Beth glanced around. They were in the middle of the desert. Nothing but rocks and shrubs as far as she could see. There weren't even any distant lights from civilization. In fact, the only lights around were those of the van's headlights. A sense of defeat settled in her body. He was going to kill her in the desert, and no one would ever know. Her bones would probably be picked clean by coyotes. For the first time in months, her heart ached for her parents. They would never hear from her again and they would never know what happened to her. The thought of her mom, sitting alone, wondering whatever happened to the daughter she loved, brought tears to Beth's eyes.

Daniel dropped her to the ground, then wandered off, leaving her alone to wallow in her sorrow.

When he returned, he tossed a pack on the ground, then went to work building a fire.

Beth watched him with a wary eye. The entire time, wondering why he hadn't killed her by now. The best explanation she could come up with involved torture and a lot of pain.

He lit the fire and coaxed the flames to life. A warm glow illuminated their surroundings.

"I always loved the desert," he said. "The vast, empty space, filled with predators." He grinned. "It's my kind of place."

Beth studied his features. It was apparent that much of the damage Zac had done to him was permanent. His face was riddled with scars, including one that went from the side of his left eye down to his jaw. His once-dark hair had shocks of pure white mixed all throughout. He moved with a limp and his left arm seemed weaker than the right.

Daniel rose to his feet and moved closer to lean over her. "Now, just relax," he said. "I'm gonna cut those restraints."

Beth lay still while he cut the zip ties that held her arms and legs in place. As soon as they sprung free, she wasted no time in jumping to her feet. However, she underestimated the strength her legs would have after hours of being tied. She stumbled and nearly fell into the flames. The only thing that prevented her from being burned was Daniel.

He pulled her back over a sleeping bag he laid on the ground. "Beth," he said. "Now, you know me well enough to know, I've already taken steps to make sure there's no escape." He tapped the side of his head. "I always make sure I've planned for all contingencies." He glared at her with deadly eyes. "There's nowhere for you to go. Only I know where we are. If you take off running, you'd be dead by noon tomorrow."

Defeated and filled with a deep sense of hopelessness, Beth sobbed. Her emotions were a roller coaster of fear, anger, and sorrow.

Across the fire, Daniel prepared food over the open flames.

Despite her best efforts, Beth couldn't resist the alluring scent that wafted toward her nose, making her salivate uncontrollably. The savory aroma was so rich and tantalizing that she could practically taste it on her tongue. She could feel her stomach grumbling with hunger. Against her will, she found herself drawn toward the source of the mouthwatering scent.

He held a bowl out to her. "Go on," he prodded. "I'm gonna bet you're hungry."

Beth glared at him, unmoving.

Daniel laughed. "It ain't poison," he said, pushing the bowl closer. "I have no intention of hurting you." He paused and stared at her with amusement. "At least as long as you're useful to me." He gestured to the bowl. "Now, go on and eat. You should keep your strength up. We got a lot of traveling to do and people to meet." He shoved a spoonful into his mouth and chewed loudly.

Hunger overwhelmed her. With great reluctance, Beth lifted the bowl of stew and inhaled. With no more hesitation, she dug in, consuming every bite in a few minutes. When she was done, she placed the bowl on the ground in front of her and drank greedily from the cool bottle of water at her feet.

She wiped her mouth with her shirtsleeve and stared across the fire at Daniel. She knew what he was after, or rather who he was after. He had no idea the circumstances of her leaving the Nomads, and she intended to keep it that way. If he found out that she had severed all ties with the group and would never be welcome back, he would kill her on the spot for sure. After all, he said she had nothing to fear as long as she was useful to him. Her only hope of getting out of this alive was to play the part as long as she could until an opportunity to escape arose.

Daniel pulled a flask from his pocket and took a long swig. He stared at her with amusement. "I suppose you're wondering why I brought you here," he said. He waited for her to answer, when she didn't, he continued, "You, your friends and I have some unfinished business. I'd like to take care of that."

"Why didn't you just go away?" she blurted. "Why come back?"

The flickering flames illuminated his face, casting dancing shadows around him. However, he remained silent.

"Why not get on with your life?" she asked.

"There is no life for me," he bellowed. He took a deep breath, followed by another drink. "A mutual friend of ours made sure of that a long time ago."

"You could start over any time," said Beth. "You don't have to hang on to that hate."

He chuckled. "Spare me the psych 101 garbage." He glared at her with cold eyes. "This is over when I say it's over, not a moment before."

"Why do you hate him so much?"

Daniel drank heartily and stared into the fire. "He ruined my life."

"He was a kid," she replied.

"That's not an excuse!" he shouted. "From the moment I first laid eyes on him, all I wanted to do was to protect him. To be a good father and provider." He shook his head. "But that witch was determined to ruin me." He took another drink from the flask.

His demeanor shifted. "I almost had us out of there," he said, with a soft tone.

Whether it was the whiskey or his memories, something about Daniel had softened. Determined to keep that going, Beth prodded. "Out of where?"

"That house," he replied. "That whole situation." He shook his head. "That bitch drove me insane. She knew all the right buttons to push. He learned well from her."

"It didn't take me long to figure out she was a liar and a horrible human being, but I chose to turn a blind eye," he scoffed. "After all, I had my son to consider. My flesh and blood. I gave up everything that was good in my life for his sake. And it all turned out to be bullshit."

He glared at her with hateful eyes. "Can you imagine what it's like to find out that everything you thought you knew was a lie? That your son wasn't even yours?" He drank from the flask. "You wanna know how I found out?" He stared at Beth as though he was waiting for her to ask. When she didn't respond, he continued, "For years, we tried to have another kid, or so I thought we were. Turns out, she was never on board with that, so she never got off birth control."

Daniel lit a cigarette. "You would think that would be bad enough. Wouldn't you?" He shook his head. "Nah, it gets a lot worse." He took a long drag and exhaled a plume of smoke. "Turns out birth control can fail—which is exactly what happened. Twice." He stared at Beth. "She got pregnant twice." His voice was shaky as he held up two fingers for emphasis. "You know what she did? She had abortions. Both times." He took a large swig from the flask. "That witch murdered my children."

Beth was at a loss for words after hearing these revelations. She didn't say anything and simply waited for the rest of the story.

"You wanna know how I found out?" asked Daniel. "The clinic sent her a bill. I just happened to pick up the mail that day. She terminated a pregnancy the month prior." His face became stone. "I confronted her." He took a drag from the cigarette. "Faced with no possible way to lie her way out of it, she told me everything. Turns out, over the past few years, she had two abortions because the thought of having a child with me made her skin crawl."

He poked at a log in the fire. "You would think that would be bad enough." He shook his head. "But no, that witch had even more to share." He locked eyes with Beth. "That was when she told me Finn wasn't my son. That the kid I sacrificed for; the one I formed my plans around wasn't even my son. He belonged to some other man from her past." He shook his head. "She wasn't even his mother. That, too, was a lie. Her cousin was Finn's mother. I spent my life housing, feeding and raising a kid I wasn't even related to, with a witch who wasn't even his mother."

"Right then and there, I knew she had to die. There was no other option." He stared down at his hands. "I almost did it. I could see the light fading from her lizard-like eyes. She was almost gone." His lips curled into a viscous grin. "But he came in and saved her life. He chose her. She lied about everything, she abused him his whole life, and he chose her."

"When I came to, the police had already cuffed me. I was arrested for trying to murder the bitch who murdered my kids."

"It wasn't hard to convince her to bail me out," he continued. "After all, she didn't have access to any money and there's one thing that Tricia was above all, and that was greedy." He emptied the flask. "When I got home, just seeing his face enraged me. My kids died so I could raise some other asshole's brat. A kid who turned against me. He made his choice, so I made mine."

Daniel grew silent and stared at the fire for a long while.

The look on his face sent a shiver down Beth's spine. She was in the presence of a desperate man who was capable of anything. She didn't want to press her luck, so she asked no questions. Opting instead to sit in silence, staring into the fire.

Far off in the hills, a lone coyote called out.

It was several minutes before Daniel spoke again. "Why were you with those other hobos?" he asked, staring at her with eyes that pierced her soul. "Where's Finn and the others?"

Keeping his warning in her mind, Beth kept up the facade. "I went for a little trip with some other friends. I'm supposed to meet up with them soon." She studied his face intently, trying to discern whether or not he believed her.

"Your social media disappeared for a while," he said.

Beth nodded. Her mouth was so dry, she could hardly stand it. "I took it down for a bit." She shrugged, trying to appear indifferent.

"So, they went one way, and you went another," he said. "Sounds like y'all had a falling out."

"No, no, no," replied Beth, nervously. She cleared her throat and steadied her breathing. "I wanted to go hang with Trace and Kitty, and they wanted to go somewhere else."

"And where's that?"

"We went out west," she replied.

"Not you!" he shouted. "Where did Finn go?"

Her heart sank. She had no idea where they went. Opting for a lie, she prayed Daniel would buy it. "East," she replied. "They went east to Louisiana. It's too swampy out there for me, I hate bugs, so I opted to go where it was warm."

"It sounds like I'm wasting my time with you," he said, with a cold tone.

Panic welled up in her chest. Beth needed to make herself necessary, otherwise, she was sure she wouldn't live to see another sunrise. "I'm supposed to meet up with them," she blurted. Her mind quickly turning to create the next lie.

"Where?" he asked.

"If I tell you, what guarantee do I have that you'll let me go?"

He flashed a wicked smile, allowing her to see, for the first time, the gaps left behind from all the missing teeth in his mouth. "Now, why would I let you go?" he asked.

Beth struggled to remain calm. Fighting back tears, she replied, "If you kill me, you'll never find him."

Daniel nodded in agreement. "Good point." He glared at her.

She had to think of something quick. "I'm supposed to message them tomorrow!" she said quickly.

"Okay then," he said slowly. "Now, we're getting somewhere. Tell you what," he said as he climbed to his feet. He pulled a bottle from his pack and doused a rag with the liquid. "You're gonna take the rest of the night off." He stalked over to her. "And I'm gonna figure out what the next step is."

The cold, wet cloth pressed against her face, filling her nostrils with the pungent smell of chemicals. Beth struggled against his grip, but he was far too strong. Darkness closed in around the edges of her vision and the world went black.

Chapter Thirteen

Their visit to Gainesville certainly took some bizarre turns. River was having a difficult time processing everything they learned, she wondered how Finn was taking it all. After all, an info dump like that would be overwhelming for anyone, let alone someone who had recently had a breakdown.

As far as she could tell, he seemed to be doing fine. After they left the cemetery, he and Teague took a long walk alone, while River went with Zac and Cash to find something to eat. It was nearly two hours before they met up again and by then, Finn was back to his animated self again.

While it was good that Teague could be a sounding board for him, River wished he would open up a little more to the rest of them, it couldn't hurt to have more ears and shoulders to lean on. It seemed to be a heavy burden for Teague to always handle. Though he didn't seem to mind at all.

Thanks to the dog tag Finn found, it didn't take Porter very long to find Shane. Instead of waiting for a request, he also went ahead and included train info. A plan was made to catch on in Gainesville and switch out trains in Fort Worth. From there, they would ride until Odessa, and make one more switch to El Paso.

The hop from Gainesville to Fort Worth was easy. Both cities had good-sized train yards, and the routes were pretty straightforward.

Leaving Fort Worth was a different story. A storm had rolled in from the northwest, bringing with it heavy rain and strong winds.

This train hauled nothing but gondolas, with no cover, the ride was going to suck. They've done this before, so River knew exactly how to get on without slipping. However, she dreaded the inevitable puddle of water at the bottom of the car.

The howling wind carried hefty raindrops that relentlessly pelted against her face, each one stinging like a slap against her skin. The sky was a dark shade of gray, the clouds heavy with moisture, and the air was filled with the smell of wet earth. The sound of the rain and wind was deafening, drowning out all other noises.

Her rain poncho was doing a good job, protecting her clothes and her backpack, but it was going to be a real hindrance to getting on board.

She ran alongside the car, practically blinded by the pounding rain. There wasn't any time to make sure everyone else was doing what they needed to do, in situations like these, you had to believe everyone was capable of taking care of themselves.

The ladder came into reach; she grabbed hold and swung herself up, quickly climbing up and over the lip into the car. She made a gentle landing, causing a soft splash as she did so. After that, she pulled her hood back and waited anxiously for the rest of the group to appear. Zac was first over the lip, followed by Teague. He landed effortlessly and pulled his hood back. Anxiety swept over River as she noted the look on his face.

Teague dropped his pack then said something to Zac, who then adopted the same look of concern. Without knowing what was happening, River climbed up to peer over the ledge at the ground below.

Cash and Finn were nowhere in sight.

Panic washed over her; her heart raced in her chest. The driving rain made it impossible to see more than ten feet in any direction. She watched with bated breath, willing them to appear.

"Do you see them?" she asked Teague.

He remained silent and proceeded to climb over the ledge, giving the impression that he intended to leap off. Zac grabbed him from behind and pulled him down onto the floor of the car. As they struggled, River watched for any sign of the others. Nothing.

The train picked up speed. There was no chance for Cash and Finn to jump on, as the train was now moving far too fast.

Her phone buzzed in her pocket, she jumped down to the floor and pulled it out to read the message. It was from Cash.

```
Cash: Looks like we're catching the next ride.
Sorry.
```

Zac let up on Teague, they climbed to their feet and peered over River's shoulder to read the message. She glanced up, noting that the look of worry on Teague's face mirrored her own feelings. She typed a response.

```
River: What happened?
    Cash: I slipped on the gravel. Just about broke
my ankle.
    River: Are you okay?
    Cash: Yeah. My ankle and my ego are both
bruised, but we'll survive.
```

"Ask him where Finn is," said Teague. "He was right behind me."

· · ·

River: Finn with you?

Cash: Yeah. He saw me fall, so he turned around to help. Looks like we both missed our ride.

A sense of relief washed over her. This had happened a few times before. They would catch the next train and meet up with everyone at a designated place. She looked at Teague, hoping that he too was feeling a little better, the look on his face told her otherwise.

"He'll be fine," she said.

Teague didn't respond.

Cash: Tell Teague I'll keep an eye on his boy. I'll text Porter and we'll catch the next train.

River: Find some place dry to wait. And take care. We'll see y'all soon.

She closed her screen and put the phone away, then helped Zac construct a makeshift canopy out of her tent's rain cover. Finally, under protective cover, she removed her poncho and placed it on the floor of the gondola, to use as a barrier for her gear to rest on, then she sat down atop her pack.

The rainfall persisted. Ordinarily, River would relish the melody of the droplets drumming against the metal and the gentle sway of the train. Yet, this time, she was consumed by a sense of anxiety. It didn't help with Teague sitting beside her with that worried look on his face. This was gonna be a long trip.

Zac was already scrolling through the group chat, following the discussion with Porter, so River pulled her phone out and did the same. Beside her, Teague watched the conversation unfold, his phone in one hand, while he chewed nervously on the fingernails of the other.

Chapter Fourteen

"Well," said Cash. "According to Porter, trains are done for the night. Looks like we're sleeping here." He glanced up and realized that Finn was nowhere in sight. Chaotic shaking of the trees nearby caught his attention, then Finn burst into the clearing, zipping up his pants.

He smiled sheepishly and shrugged.

"Next time tell me," said Cash.

"Why?" asked Finn. "You gonna hold it for me?"

Cash didn't answer—he didn't have to. It was a silent agreement, they all had to monitor Finn. Almost like a PTSD response after having been separated for so long a few months ago. No one said it aloud, but deep inside, they all harbored an irrational fear that he could go missing once again. The thought sent a stabbing pain to his heart, Cash never wanted to see that look on Teague's face again. Mainly because it mirrored his own desperation during that whole time. Also, River would kick his ass.

"I found a place we can sleep," said Finn. "It's dry." He led the way to a concrete underpass.

While the space was indeed dry, it was far too exposed for Cash's liking. "I think we should find someplace more private," he said. "Anyone riding by would see us."

Finn scoffed. "That's why we're going up there." He pointed. Without another word, he scurried up the smooth, slanted surface, disappearing from sight. "You see me?" he called out from the shadows.

Cash didn't bother to answer, Finn had made his point. He followed the path, hoping along the way that the final spot would be flat. He loathed the idea of trying to sleep on an incline. When he reached the top, he was happy to see Finn sitting on a flat surface, wide enough to house them both comfortably. He placed his pack down and removed his rain poncho. "Excellent find," he said.

"I'm good at a few things," replied Finn. "Survival is one."

The rain continued to fall in sheets, cascading off the concrete where it splashed like a manmade waterfall onto the road below. The sound was almost soothing.

"I can't believe I slipped like that," said Cash. "Thanks for turning around."

"A man never leaves his brother behind," replied Finn. "To be honest," he continued. "I did that hoping we could get on the train." He pulled a granola bar from his pack, ripped it in half, and passed it over to Cash. "Had I known we'd end up spendin' some quality time alone together, I might not have turned around."

"Duly noted," replied Cash, with a nod and a chuckle. "I'll remember that for next time."

Finn laughed. "I'm just kidding. I'd have turned around, for no other reason than I ain't about to piss off River like that. That woman is pure fire." He shook his head. "She'd beat my ass for sure."

"No truer words have ever been said," replied Cash. "But don't fool yourself, Teague isn't anyone to mess with either."

"This is true," replied Finn, with a happy nod.

For the first time in a long while, Cash studied Finn, taking note of the subtle changes that had taken place over the past several months.

Finn had always been more of a feral cat if you had to compare him to an animal. It took a lot to get past his defenses. The wall he built up around him was tall and sprawling—it was more of a dome. The person who returned to them wasn't the same man he always knew. Gone was that familiar prickliness, in its place was a broken silhouette that was shocking to see. Cash never could have imagined he would have seen Finn so broken. To say it was earth-shattering would be the understatement of the century.

"How are you doing?" asked Cash.

"What do you mean?"

"I mean," said Cash. "How are you doing?" He tapped the side of his head.

"Ah," replied Finn. He shrugged. "I guess I'm doin' good. Though, I haven't really focused on much lately." He sighed. "A very wise man told me to take it one day at a time."

"I would say though," added Finn. "I could sure do with a lot less worrying about me." He locked eyes with Cash. "It gets tiring seeing the looks on everyone's faces most of the time. Y'all act like I'm fragile and it grates on my nerves."

"I suppose we do that," replied Cash. "I'm sorry. I'll work on it."

"It ain't like I don't understand why," said Finn quickly. "I get it. I really do. I just wish we could all get past a lot of that. Ya know?"

"I do," replied Cash. "Maybe it's time we all lightened up."

"How about you?" asked Finn. "River seems to have tamed the wild side of you."

Cash smiled. "I'm a happy man," he replied.

"I can see that."

"I can't tell you how great it is to see you and Teague together again," said Cash.

A serious look swept across Finn's face. "Hang on to what you and River have." He stared down at his feet. "I can't believe I fucked things up so bad the way I did." He clenched his jaw. "For a while there, I could hardly bring myself to look at him without wanting to scream, because every time I did, I saw what I did to him."

Cash listened in silence. He knew Finn long enough to know that if he was opening up like this, you just listen.

"Now and then, I still feel a stab," continued Finn. "That scar on the side of his face." He swallowed and tapped under his eye. "Knowing I did that—" He shook his head. "I can't believe I did that."

"Have you talked to him about any of this?"

Finn nodded, then shook his head. "Not entirely. He'd go out of his way to try to save me from my own feelings about it," said Finn. "I don't want him to do that." He stared at Cash. "I need to feel that pain. I need to be reminded—to be disgusted by my own actions, so I never slip and do something like that again."

"Can I ask you a serious question?" asked Cash.

"Sure."

"When you fought with him." Cash struggled to pull the right words together. He didn't want to say something that would possibly trigger Finn, but he needed to understand—for his own sake. "What went on in your mind? How did you not stop yourself?"

Finn shook his head. "You know," he replied. "I could lie right now and tell you I blacked out." He stared down at his feet. "Or that I was so caught up in the moment that I didn't see him, that I was just lashing out at the world." A tear slipped down his cheek. "I tried to convince myself that was what happened. But that's a lie." He peered up at Cash. "I knew what I was doin'. The whole time, I knew what I was doin'. I wasn't overcome with blind rage." He swallowed. "I was mad at him. I wanted to hurt him. I—I really wanted to kill him."

Cash stared in shock. Finn's confession shattered his own belief about what happened that night. His mind struggled with the reality of what he was being told, his heart refused to accept it as truth. Tears welled up in his eyes. He wanted to argue and make Finn admit that wasn't true.

Finn wiped his face. "For a long time, I blamed that all on that part of me that came from Daniel. I wanted it to not be something inside me—to not be my fault. But that ain't the truth. It was all me.

That animal who did all of that to Teague, to Beth and River, that was all me."

Finn shook his head. "I ain't got any excuses."

"But," interjected Cash. "That's actually a good thing."

"How's that exactly?"

"Because it means that you can control it," said Cash. "If it's your fault, you and you alone can take steps to control yourself, so it never happens again."

"You sound like a gentler version of Gunner now."

"Thank you for the compliment," said Cash. "But seriously, figuring out what force was behind it all is good. Accepting responsibility puts the power in your hands, so you can control it."

Finn sighed. "Doesn't feel like a good thing."

"But it is," said Cash. "You just have to get past the self-loathing part."

"Easier said than done," scoffed Finn.

"Just think about all the good things you have," said Cash. "For one thing, you got all of us. And Teague is right there with you. Daniel isn't even related to you, so that's a bonus."

"Yeah, but the man who is, was arrested for attempted rape," interjected Finn.

"And all the charges were dropped," replied Cash. "Besides, his accuser was Tricia. And we all know what a stellar person she is."

Finn nodded in agreement.

"Margaret was very clear about the way he treated your mother." Cash thought about Shane. Without a picture of him, it was impossible to conjure an image of the man in his mind. Hearing that he was an outsider from a working-class family garnered him some sympathy. After all, Cash could relate to that scenario quite well. "He was a kid who got screwed over by a bunch of self-serving, elitist assholes."

"That was a lifetime ago," said Finn. "He's probably a lot different by now."

"Well, thanks to the dog tag you found and Porter's expertise, we know he owns a ranch just north of El Paso. Which is why we're heading down there."

Finn scoffed. "Watch him end up being some outlaw or something. It'd be just my luck that he's all wrapped up in some illegal shit."

"Nah," replied Cash. "My guess is he's probably a rancher, just living his life out there."

"I like your scenario better," said Finn.

"Then hang on to it. Either way this goes," said Cash. "We're going down there to find out about him."

Finn's face became serious. "I don't wanna talk to him." He stared at Cash. "I just wanna see him with my own eyes. To know he's real. He thinks I'm dead, it's probably best to leave him be."

"I hear ya," replied Cash. "But, how 'bout we take it one step at a time."

Finn's lips curled up into a wry smile. He nodded, then pulled his phone from his pocket.

Seeing him hold the device was startling. Cash could count on his two hands the number of times he had seen Finn pull out his phone without being prodded to.

The cold light illuminated Finn's face. "Time for check-in," he said, then started typing away.

Cash didn't have to ask who he was texting, he knew. He pulled out his own phone and fired off a text to River. After all, it was time to check-in.

Chapter Fifteen

The morning sun sliced through the darkness like splinters of yellow glass. Beth blinked her eyes, her head ached worse than any hangover she had ever felt. Her hands and legs were tied again. Unable to move, she lay there, staring at the tiny dust particles floating in the sunbeams, wishing she could wipe the drool from the side of her mouth.

It was a long time before the door to the van swung open. Daniel loomed above her, his large frame blocking out most of the fresh morning air.

"Up and at 'em," he said, as though he weren't talking to a young woman he kidnapped and had tied up in his van. "I whipped up a pot of coffee, and I'm about to make us some breakfast."

He reached behind her and cut the zip ties, this time, she didn't even flinch at his touch. She knew as long as he thought she was of use to him; she had nothing to fear.

Daniel moved away from the doorway and gestured with his hands. "Come on," he said. "I got some water for you to clean yourself up." Without another word, he turned his back to her and strolled over to the fire.

As Beth watched him, she imagined herself jumping out of the van and cold cocking the maniac, then stealing his keys and running away. The pounding in her head told her that was a bad idea, that she wouldn't even get close enough to him to shove him. The scenario would more than likely end up with her unconscious and hog-tied in the van again.

She wiped her face and scrubbed her fingers through her hair, then followed him over to the fire.

"Come on," he prodded. "Take a seat."

His joyful demeanor was off-putting. Beth found happy Daniel far more creepy than angry Daniel.

She took a seat, doing her best to remain as far away from the man as possible.

He poured a cup of coffee and passed it over to her.

Beth inhaled, letting the aroma awaken her senses. She peered over the mug at Daniel, imagining that she splashed the hot liquid on his face. As he screamed in pain, she could grab a log from the fire and beat him senseless with it. Then she could take his keys and drive away, never to see the man again.

She glanced around at her surroundings, realizing that she had no clue where she was. She didn't even know what state they were in. If she were to drive off, how was she to guarantee that she wouldn't end up driving farther into the desert, eventually running out of gas, and finally dying from exposure?

"What's goin' on in that head of yours?" asked Daniel. "Planning some grand escape?"

Startled by his accuracy, Beth quickly took a sip from her coffee and shook her head. "I'm just trying to wake up," she offered, hoping he would believe her. She decided it was best to play the role of a confused, stupid, teenage girl as long as possible. "My head hurts."

Daniel nodded. "That'll wear off soon enough."

To Beth's surprise, he was a pretty good cook. She could see where Finn learned all his skills. Finn. She hadn't thought about him in a long time. A large part of her wanted to forget all about him.

Wherever he was, she hoped he was suffering. The anger of her own emotions startled her. She stared at Daniel, thinking about his swagger, and his attitude. The way he purposely went out of his way to be intimidating. She could clearly see him through the eyes of a young child, and it made her blood boil. Her heart filled with hate for the man—with empathy for Finn.

"Alright, let's clean up," said Daniel. He stacked some of the dishes together. "We got a long drive ahead of us."

Beth didn't answer, instead, she scanned the area for some sign of civilization. Of course, there was nothing.

Daniel rinsed the dishes off. "It'll be an hour before we get to the nearest town," he said.

The nearest town. Beth's heart raced. She could call out for help or get free somehow and run away to safety. Surely there was a sheriff in the nearest town. Once there, she could jump out of the van and run for help. That's exactly what she would do.

He finished kicking dirt over the last glowing embers of their fire, then reached a hand out for Beth.

She stared at it as though it were a poison vine. She had no intention of touching this man voluntarily.

"Get up," he said, with that evil tone of his.

Beth climbed to her feet and brushed the sand from her clothes, then held her hands out in front of her, ready to be tied up again. To her surprise, Daniel strolled over to the van and pulled open the passenger side door.

He gestured toward the seat. "Well, come on," he said. "Get in. We don't have all day."

She climbed inside the van and settled into the leather seat.

Daniel grabbed her hand roughly and cuffed her to the door handle. He flashed a wicked smile. "Can't be too cautious now. Can we?"

He slammed the door closed and left her sitting there, pondering her fate—conjuring a new scenario where she could get away after she somehow managed to get out of her new restraints.

By the time Daniel settled into the driver's seat, the morning sun was high in the sky. He turned on the ignition and threw the engine into gear. A perplexed look spread across his face. He looked at Beth. "Now, which way do we go?"

Fear welled up inside her. For the first time, she wondered, what if he didn't know how to get out of here? What if they were lost?

He laughed maliciously. "Just kiddin'," he said. He stared at her with cruel eyes. "Now, let's head to town." He pulled a phone from his pocket and wiggled it in the air. "You got a phone call to make."

Her phone! Beth hadn't even considered the device since first awakening in the van. She gazed intently at the phone, hoping it would magically land in her empty hand.

Daniel stuffed it back in his pocket; her heart sank. Was he actually going to have her call the Nomads? What if they hung up on her? Daniel would know she was no use to him and he would kill her. Panic swelled in her chest. How was she going to work her way out of this one? If she told him she didn't have their numbers, he would know something was wrong.

Their numbers. She suddenly realized she deleted them all long ago—all of them but Zac's.

Chapter Sixteen

During the night, the storm never let up. The steady, constant cascade of rain, driven down in sheets by the wind, made for a very uncomfortable ride, soaking Teague to the bone. Overhead, the morning sky was painted a dismal, dark gray as the heavy cloud cover loomed low. The skyline of Odessa was barely discernible in the distance.

River was the smart one, having pulled on her rain poncho before the storm hit, consequently, she was dry under the plastic cover and both he and Zac were dripping wet. It made no sense at all to put his poncho on now, water had already saturated every inch of his body.

There was no respite from the rain, and to compound matters, there was no shelter under which to take cover. The trees were all too short, and there was no overpass. As far as he could recall, having ridden this track before, the nearest shelter was an old, abandoned gas station roughly three miles away. Who knew if it was still standing, the entire state of Texas was being overrun with house farms and suburban sprawl. Up north, there were some areas around the cities that reminded him of California. Odessa and west Texas were not immune to this. In a few years, the whole state would be unrecognizable.

Teague ran his hand down his face, in a futile effort to clear away some of the water, only to have it replaced immediately. He blinked his eyes, feeling the cool rain drops pelt his eyeballs.

On the ground, crouching under her poncho, River was doing something with her phone, as was evidenced by the cold glow emanating from the green camo plastic sheet over her.

She stood up and shouted over the rain, "Porter says another train is coming through in a minute."

"Heading where?" hollered Zac.

"El Paso."

Teague shook his head. "We weren't supposed to leave until Finn and Cash arrived," he argued.

"We can't stay here," said River. "The storm is stalled; it'll be hours before it rains itself out or moves on."

"I ain't leaving."

"It's not raining in El Paso," argued River. "We can stay there and wait for Cash and Finn."

Teague shook his head.

"Dammit!" shouted River. "Teague! Now is not the time to be stubborn."

Zac, who had been silent this whole time, stepped into the conversation. "She's right," he said. "Whether we wait for them here or a couple of hours south of here makes no difference."

"We agreed to wait for them here," argued Teague.

"I know," agreed Zac. "But the weather has a mind of its own."

As if on cue, a sudden gust of wind ripped through the air, almost knocking Teague off his feet. "They're expecting to meet up with us here."

"They'll understand," said Zac.

"Look, baby," said River. "I wanna see Cash as much as you wanna see Finn. But I also understand, they're two of the most capable men either of us know." She paused and waited for him to acknowledge that he heard what she said. "It's just one more night. We can survive texting with them for one more night."

"Finn's phone is dead," said Teague. "He can't message anymore."

"Then he and Cash will share," she replied.

"Look man," said Zac. "I don't wanna stay out here in the rain, I'd rather be dry. But if you insist on staying out here, I'll stay with you."

"Me too," added River.

Zac locked eyes with him. "It's up to you, do we go a little farther south of here where it's dry? Or do we stay here in the rain?"

Teague studied their faces. As much as he wanted to remain in Odessa and wait for Finn to arrive, he couldn't make Zac and River suffer. Besides, his own body was already protesting over being wrapped in a layer of soaking-wet clothes. He bowed his head. "Okay," he said. "We'll head south and wait for them there."

River jumped up and wrapped her arms around him. "They'll be fine," she said. Then, once again, she hunkered down under her poncho, presumably to let Cash know about the change of plans.

Just like Porter said, the next train rolled in. His heart heavy, Teague readied himself for the hop. The train whistle blew, one long, one short and another long, signaling its entry to town. It was time to go.

Keeping pace with the iron beast, Teague grabbed the ladder and pulled himself onto a grainer. Finally, out of the rain, he settled in under cover on the metal porch, shaking his head furiously, sending droplets of water everywhere.

River pulled her hood back. "Cash said they're fine. They don't want to ride into the downpour, so they're staying put for a few hours. Porter has a new ride all slated for them as soon as the storm clears."

A small modicum of relief washed over Teague. His phone chimed in his pocket. He had forgotten all about it. He pulled it out and peered down at the screen; it was a message from Finn on Cash's phone.

. . .

Finn: We're good. Don't worry so much.

Teague: Y'all stay dry.

Finn shared a thumbs-up emoji.

Finn: We'll see y'all in a few hours.

Teague shared a thumbs-up emoji, followed by a heart.

Finn responded with a heart of his own.

Teague stuffed the device back into his pocket. He needed to stop worrying so much. River was right, both Finn and Cash were some of the most capable men they knew. If anyone could take care of themselves, it was those two.

Zac handed him part of a sandwich he saved from earlier, then he handed another piece to River.

As he nibbled on the sandwich, the curtain of rain gradually diminished. The clear, desert sky emerged, sprinkled here and there with light, puffy clouds. The air smelled of fresh rain; the breeze was cool against his wet skin. He shivered. A change of clothes would have to be the first thing he took care of when they finally arrived at their destination.

Chapter Seventeen

The dingy motel room was filled with the pungent stench of stale cigarettes, mixed with a sickly-sweet undertone of vomit and the unmistakable smell of body odor. The buzzing of the flickering fluorescent light overhead seemed to amplify the musty smell, making it even more oppressive. The walls were stained with mysterious blotches. Everything in the room had a yellow tint to it, Beth recalled a similar room not long ago. As she peered up at a painting on the wall, a faint smile spread across her lips.

She had spent the past several months pretending that she didn't care about the Nomads—that she was better off without them. But here, in the seedy, little motel room, there was nothing to divert her thoughts, nothing to change her feelings. Truth was, she missed them all—even Finn.

The night she left was filled with a storm of emotions. Anger, fear and indignity roiled inside, triggering a response she came to regret, but refused to acknowledge later. Since leaving, she spent lots of time around other riders, many of whom were wonderful people, but there really was no replacement for the Nomads.

She wondered how they were doing. Were they happy? Did any of them miss her? Did River ever think of her? Did Finn ever make it back? Was he dead? It saddened her that she didn't know the answer to any of these questions.

Across the room, Daniel was busy staring at a computer screen. From where she sat, handcuffed to the bedpost, Beth was unable to see what had his attention. It occurred to her that the more time she spent with the man, the more she understood Finn.

Daniel was a complex individual, though kind and understanding were never traits that could be attributed to him. Most of the time, he stared forward, with an evil glint in his eyes, lost in whatever demonic world he lived in. Even when he smiled, it came off as dark and foreboding rather than pleasant in any way.

She thought about her own father. How full of love and happiness he was. Even when he was angry, he never came close to the level of malevolence that Daniel emanated on a regular basis.

An image of her parents floated to the fore of her mind. Christmas tree lights sparkling in the background, while her mom and dad danced slowly, their love so strong that Beth could feel it all the way across the room.

Her heart ached. Tears welled up in her eyes, overflowing down her cheeks. She missed her mom and dad. How were they doing? Did her leaving cause them to fight? She knew they missed her, that was never a question in her mind. How absolutely selfish of her to run away. Blinded by her own desires, she hurt the people who loved her the most in this world. Beth felt a stab of guilt in her belly, followed by a deep ache in her heart. She had a loving family, and she threw it all away to do what? Ride trains? Party? Hang out with a bunch of sketchy people? It all seemed so stupid now. Here she was, held prisoner by a man who would kill her in an instant. She was a selfish and cruel jerk to those who loved her. There was no one to blame for her situation but herself.

"Okay, Beth," said Daniel. He swiveled around in the chair to face her. "Ready to reach out and touch someone?" He dangled her phone in the air.

Her mouth went dry, fear wrapped its icy fingers around her heart. She willed herself to remain calm. Do not let on. Do not give him any reason to doubt you're useful.

He strolled across the room and sat down on the bed beside her, holding the phone out. When she reached for it, he pulled it back and glared at her with a cruel eye. "Don't even think of doing something stupid," he warned.

Beth nodded. Her whole body trembled.

"I won't give you another warning," he said. "Don't test me. You won't like the outcome."

She took the phone in her hand and stared down at the device. So cold and lifeless. It was hard to believe this was once the center of her universe.

Stupid Beth.

She swiped the screen, opening her contacts. Only one remained of the Nomads, so she quickly scrolled down to the letter Z. Zac's face beamed up at her with that loveable face of his. A pang of sorrow stabbed her chest, hot tears collected in her eyes.

Beth knew she could call him, but she also knew a personal conversation would involve a lot of explanation that she didn't want Daniel to hear. She had to maintain the facade that she was still very much a part of the inner circle of the Nomads. That she was merely traveling with others for a little while. Her best course of action was to text. At least that way, there was a higher likelihood that she could direct the conversation.

"What do you want me to say?" she asked.

Daniel glared at her. "What do you think I wanna know?"

With a trembling hand, she clicked Zac's icon and sent a text.

Chapter Eighteen

Zac's phone vibrated in his pocket. Worried that it might be Cole, he pulled out the device and peered down at the screen.

"Beth?" he said aloud, not meaning to.

River peeked over his shoulder. "Is she okay?"

Zac raised an eyebrow. "I thought you'd given up on her."

"No," replied River. "I admit I was angry when she left. We were going through an awful time and all she could think about was herself." She shrugged. "But I never stopped caring about her. I want her to be okay." She gestured to the phone. "Has she messaged you before?"

He shook his head, feeling more than a little guilty over the fact that he let his connection to Beth slip away. All his talk about family and he dropped the ball on this one as soon as she was out of sight.

"I feel bad sometimes that I just let her go on those terms," said River. "She didn't deserve that. My mind was singly focused on Finn and Teague." She sighed. "And me and Cash."

"Yeah," replied Zac. "I guess we all sorta let her slip away. Didn't we?"

"What's she sayin'?"
Zac opened the message.

```
Beth: Hey Zac, just checking in. How's it going?
  Zac: Good. Where you at?
  Beth: Tucson. How about you?
  Zac: On our way to El Paso. So much has
happened, too much to type.
  Beth: I hear ya. Wanna meet up in El Paso?
```

He stared at the screen then glanced up to River. "What do you think?"

"Absolutely!" was her immediate response. She paused and turned to Teague.

"Why you lookin' at me like that?" he asked.

"Is it okay with you?" she asked.

Teague scoffed. "We all did her dirty," he said. "I suppose a little meetup is the best way to mend that fence." He looked at Zac. "Wouldn't you think?"

"What do you think Finn would say?" asked Zac, recalling that night when Beth pushed him over the edge.

"He and I have talked about that," said Teague. "He doesn't hold any hostility toward her. But I can see how she would to him." He shrugged. "I'm pretty sure he wouldn't mind." He nudged River. "All the same, we should make sure."

River pulled out her phone and typed a message to Cash.

```
River: We just got a message from Beth, asking if
we could meet up in El Paso. What do y'all think?
  Cash: Beth? Wow! It's been a hot minute. Hold
up, I'll check with Finn.
```
                    . . .

Time ticked by slowly. "I hate to admit it," said Zac. "In all these months, I haven't thought much about her. Seems we had so much going on, her leaving was good for all of us. I hope it was good for her, too."

River nodded.

"I'm almost ashamed," said Zac. "I mean, I don't know anything about what she's been up to."

"Max showed me her social media a while back," said River. "She was riding with other people. It seemed as though she was enjoying herself."

The phone chimed with a new message.

```
Cash: Finn says he's in. He'd like to apologize
to her.
```

Zac cocked an eyebrow. "Did he misspell a word there?" he asked.

Teague chuckled. "I told you, my boy's done a lot of growing," he said.

"Yeah but," replied Zac. "That's a total personality change."

"Are you complaining?" asked River.

Zac shook his head. "No, no, no," he replied. "I ain't at all. I'm just stunned and impressed by the way our boy has grown." He flashed an impish smile. "He's almost a real boy."

"We're workin' on it," replied Teague.

"Well," said River. "Go on and tell her."

```
Zac: Sure. How long before you get to the city?
  Beth: I can be there in a few hours.
  Zac: Sounds good. Text when you get here and
we'll come and meet you.
  Beth: Sounds like a plan. See y'all in a few
```

hours.

Zac responded with a thumbs-up emoji.

He put his phone away, an odd feeling washed over him. That whole exchange was strange. Of course, he didn't have much experience with families making amends, so he didn't have any solid reason to feel that way. Still, it was kinda odd that after so many months, she would message as though she had just seen him. That didn't sound like Beth—at least not the Beth he knew. His Beth would've held a grudge for a long time, after that, her pride alone would have held her back. Maybe Finn wasn't the only one who's grown up.

So many things had happened over the past few months—things he never would have imagined possible. But all of them turned out to be good things. Could it be that the universe was finally making things right? Finn was back and doing a whole lot better than Zac ever imagined possible. If he could change, anyone could. River and Cash were happy. He himself chatted daily with Cole, and now Beth. Maybe it was just time for a positive change. For his family to come together again.

He leaned back against the wall and stared up at the sky, smiling.

By the time they rolled into the El Paso rail yard, it was well past noon. According to Porter, Shane's ranch was north of the city, just east of the Franklin Mountains. The plan was to meet up there and camp for a few days while Finn did some poking around. Zac wasn't sure what the plan was regarding Shane, he figured it was best to let Finn make all the decisions on that, after all, it was his family.

Their first order of business was to stop and pick up some supplies. Not wanting to haul things longer than necessary, they opted to hit a store when they got closer to their destination.

Moving through the city was easy. It took them no time at all to make their way north, stopping along the way at a supermarket where they picked up most of the supplies they needed. A quick check-in with Cash told them they were a few hours out.

The last item on their list of supplies was wood for their campfire. Crossing through the convenience store parking lot, Zac noted the motorcycle parked outside.

"Hey Zac," teased Teague. "Think that belongs to your dream girl?" He gestured toward the bike.

He responded with a scoff then dumped his pack on the ground. "I'll go in," he said.

The cold, artificial air hitting his damp clothes sent a shiver down his spine. He wandered the aisles, searching for matches. It never ceased to amaze him that the things you needed most were always the most difficult to find in these stores. He rounded the corner of an aisle, accidentally knocking over several bags of chips to the floor.

He quickly scooped them up, then stood up and found himself face to face with a beautiful woman.

Her long, dark hair was pulled back into tight, neat braids. She smiled at him with dark, brown eyes that stared into his soul.

A flash of heat rushed through his body, his pulse quickened.

"Find what you're looking for?" she asked, with a smooth voice.

He flashed a smile. "I believe I have," he replied. His whole body was on fire.

The beautiful woman held out her hand. "I'm Marisol," she said. "You can call me Mari."

He took her hand, realizing that his was quite sweaty. "Zac."

She made no move to pull away, rather she stepped closer. As they stood together, their bodies were barely an inch apart. The air around them was thick with the floral scent of her perfume, over-whelming his senses. Time was frozen, a perfect stillness that he never wanted to end.

"Nice to meet you, Zac," she said, flashing a warm smile.

His mouth went dry. He struggled to find something to say, but he was too lost in her dark eyes to come up with anything.

"Are you always this chatty?" she asked.

"Cat's got his tongue," said Teague.

Startled to hear the voice, Zac turned to find Teague standing next to him with a sly grin plastered across his face.

"I was wonderin' what was takin' so long," said Teague. He winked at Zac, then turned to Mari. "But now I see it was something good." He held out his hand. "I'm Teague," he said.

"Pleased to meet you," replied Mari, still standing painfully close to Zac. She raised her arm to lean against the shelf, bringing her body even closer to his.

Zac shifted his body, inadvertently knocking several items off the shelf beside him.

Teague chuckled. "You'll have to excuse my friend," he said. "He only gets this way around beautiful women."

"Women?" asked Mari. She stared into Zac's eyes. "You meet a lot of beautiful women?"

Zac swallowed. His mouth was so dry. "No ma'am," he croaked, then shook his head. "At least, none as beautiful as you."

Mari leaned back and let loose the most beautiful laugh he had ever heard.

She smiled at him. "You have me intrigued," she said.

Unable to recall what words were, Zac turned to Teague with a pathetic look.

"Do you live around here?" asked Teague.

Mari nodded and glanced around. "Y'all passing through?"

"We are," replied Teague. "We're waitin' on a couple of friends to join us." He pointed. "We're camping in the mountains for a few days."

"Sounds like fun," she replied.

"You're welcome," blurted Zac, his voice cracking like a pre-pubescent boy. He cleared his throat and spoke again. "You're welcome to join us." He glanced over. The look on Teague's face told him he was never going to live this down.

"Hmm," replied Mari. "Unfortunately, I gotta go to work." She snapped her fingers. "I know," she said. "I work at a bar up the road a little ways. Y'all can come and hang out 'till I get off work." She flashed a smile. "Are you hungry?"

"Always," replied Teague.

Zac could only nod.

Mari's eyes shifted from him to someone over his shoulder. She nodded her head and said, "My name's Mari."

"River," came the voice right behind him. "Please tell me these two weren't giving you a hard time," she said, smirking.

"No," replied Mari. She locked eyes with Zac. "At least not yet, anyway."

A sudden flush of heat spread throughout his body; he was sure his face was deep red.

Behind him, Teague snickered.

River chuckled.

Mari turned her attention to River. She stepped away from Zac and moved closer to her. "They said you were waiting for friends. How many?"

"Two more," replied River. "Did I hear you offer food?"

"I did." Mari glanced around at everyone. "If you're up for it, y'all can come and hang out at the bar where I work." She placed a soft hand on Zac's chest. "I can make it worth your while." She flashed a coy smile. "I promise, you've never tasted anything so good."

Zac's pulse was racing so fast, it was difficult to keep himself from panting and drooling like a dog. Every time he looked at River or Teague, he could hear their silent laughter. He was so enthralled with Mari, he almost didn't care.

"Well," said River. "I can't speak for these two, but I'm hungry."

"Me too," added Teague.

Mari gazed into Zac's eyes. "How about you?"

He moved his dry lips, but no sound came out.

"He'll do just about anything you want," laughed Teague.

"Great!" said Mari, never taking her eyes off of Zac. She slid her hand into his and tugged. "Follow me." She guided him toward the door, outside and over to the motorcycle.

This was too much. His knees had become weak.

Mari gestured to the bike. "Unfortunately, this is all I can offer by way of transportation." She grinned. "I can give you a ride, but you're gonna have to ride bitch."

"I'll be your bitch," muttered Zac.

Behind him, Teague laughed out loud.

River cleared her throat and placed a firm hand on Zac's shoulder. "Tell you what Mari," she said. "How about we meet you there when our friends arrive?"

The look on River's face told Zac there was no room for debate. He turned back to Mari. "Mom says no bike ride."

"What are your friends' names?" asked Mari.

"Finn and Cash," replied River.

"Hmm," said Mari. "When are they arriving?"

"Last word was they were two hours out," replied Teague.

"I got a better idea then," she said. "How about I go get my dad's truck, then come by and pick y'all up? We can wait for your friends to get here. I know a spot by the rail yard where we can park and wait."

"I thought you said you have work," said Teague.

"How did you know we came in by train?" asked River.

"Oh!" replied Mari. "I just assumed." She smiled innocently. "I've seen lots of riders come through here." She turned to Teague. "As for my boss, he'll understand."

"If you say so," said River.

"So, it's settled then?" asked Mari. "I'll come back with a ride."

Zac was in, he knew Teague was good, but he was a little nervous about River. Something in her tone was off. This worried him. He really wanted to spend time with Mari. He stared at River, silently pleading with his eyes for her to go along.

"Sounds good to me," replied River. "We'll wait here." She wrapped her arms with Teague and the two strolled over to their gear, leaving Zac alone with Mari.

She swapped numbers with him before hopping onto the bike, then slipped on a pair of black leather gloves. She paused momentarily and smiled up at him, then grabbed him by the collar, pulling him in for a kiss.

As soon as their lips met, a blazing heat erupted inside him.

She pulled away and peered into his soul. "Now, you stay right here until I return," she said.

Unable to catch his breath, he licked his lips and nodded.

With a final smile, Mari started her motorcycle and drove away.

As he stood in place, watching her taillight fade into the distance, Zac could hear the sounds of laughter behind him. He let out a deep sigh and pivoted, bracing himself for the inevitable wave of teasing that was about to hit him.

Chapter Nineteen

Shane stared at the computer screen. His eyes twitched and spasmed as he tried to make sense of the spreadsheet in front of him. Why on earth did Cat insist he look over this crap? She was perfectly capable of doing all of this.

He rubbed his eyes before opening the drawer in the center of his desk. Inside, he gazed at the brand-new eyeglasses he had purchased just a week ago. He only went to the eye doctor on Catalina's prodding, he didn't want, nor did he feel he needed help to see.

A picture of Finn sat next to the eyeglass case. After his talking to by Manny, Shane put more effort into the here and now. It made no sense to throw away his family for a ghost. So, he put more effort into Catalina and Gabby and a lot less worry and hyper-fixating on Finn. It wasn't easy at first, but each day it got easier. His relationship with his family flourished. This, in turn, eased some of the heartache. He took down all the photos from the wall, keeping this one in his desk and the rest in a box in his office back home. Seeing the boy's face every day hurt too much.

The door to the office swung open. "How late are you planning on staying tonight?" asked Catalina, as she took a seat at her desk.

Shane was about to answer when there was a timid rap on the door.

"Enter!" he shouted.

The afternoon bartender, Kyle, stepped timidly inside the office. "Hey, Boss," he said quietly.

"Son," said Shane. "How many times do I gotta tell you? When you're speaking to me, use your outside voice." He tapped the side of his head. "I got a hard enough time hearing on most days; I don't need you whispering."

"Sorry Boss," said Kyle.

"What do you need?" asked Cat.

The kid glanced around nervously. "My shift is over," he said.

Shane waited for the rest of the sentence when nothing else was said, he leaned forward. "And?" he asked, with a cocked eyebrow.

Kyle cleared his throat. "Well, Mari's not here yet." He shifted his weight from one leg to the other.

"What do you mean, she's not here?" barked Shane.

Catalina switched the cameras to scan the parking lot. "Her bike's not here," she said, shaking her head.

"Well, where the hell is she?" demanded Shane.

Catalina shrugged.

Shane sighed. That girl was gonna be the death of him. "Can you stick around 'till she gets here?"

Kyle nodded.

"Good," stated Shane. "Get on out there. I'll pay you double for your time."

The kid's face lit up. He smiled and closed the door.

Cat sauntered across the room and climbed onto his lap. "I guess this means my plans for tonight are canceled," she said, then kissed his neck.

He smiled and kissed her on the lips. "Care to fill me in on these plans of yours?"

His gorgeous wife smiled down at him. "Well, Gabby is with my mom, and Mari has the closing shift." She smiled. "I was hoping we could get some time alone."

"I'm listening," he replied, with a grin.

There was a loud knock on the door. A second later, Manny stepped into the tiny room.

"Gah!" he shouted, making a big show of covering his eyes. "You two ever hear of getting a room?"

Catalina climbed off of Shane's lap and strolled over to Manny. "Ain't nothin' happening here that you haven't done yourself," she scoffed, then punched him in the arm.

Manny rubbed his arm and moved away from his sister, creating an opening for Shane to peer down the hallway just in time to see Mari heading toward the office.

"It's about time!" he barked. "Get on out there and relieve Kyle. The poor kid's been here since lunch."

"Actually," said Mari, as she slid into the room. "I'm not here to work, I'm here to get the keys to your truck."

Catalina scoffed and shook her head.

"Are you fucking kidding me?" bellowed Shane. "If you weren't blowing off your shift, I still wouldn't let you drive my truck." He shook his head. "Now, get out there and get to work."

"Fine!" shouted Mari. She threw her arms into the air and spun around. "If you don't want me to pick up Finn and his friends from the rail yard, then so be it!"

"Wait!" shouted Catalina, grabbing the girl by the arm.

Shane was still reeling from the sound of Finn's name. He heard what she said, but for some reason, his mind was acting as though it couldn't process those words. He jumped to his feet. "Did you just say Finn?" he asked, in a half-whisper.

Mari stepped closer. "I ran into Zac in town. You remember, the handsome ginger?"

Shane nodded, every muscle in his body was vibrating.

"Are you sure it's him?" asked Catalina.

"Oh, I'm sure," replied Mari. "He was with the girl, River and the blond one."

"Teague?" asked Cat.

Mari nodded. "They just rolled into town."

"Where's Finn?" blurted Shane.

"He and the one named Cash aren't here yet," replied Mari. "They should get here in a couple of hours."

"Did you talk to them?" asked Catalina.

Mari smirked. "No, Mom," she replied sarcastically. "I read their minds, that's how I know all of this."

Cat's eyes lit up with anger.

Shane stepped in front of her, placing his body between the two women. Now, was not the time for an argument. "What do you need the truck for?"

"I invited them to come and hang out here," replied Mari. "I sorta promised them food." She glanced over his shoulder at Cat. "I told them I'd be right back with the truck so I could give them a ride." She held out her hand and stared at Shane. "Well?"

Cat dropped the keys into the girl's hand. "Go!" she shouted. "Go bring our boy and his friends back here!"

"It's gonna be a couple of hours," said Mari. "We're gonna go wait by the rail yard for Finn and Cash to arrive."

"I'm coming," said Shane.

Mari placed a hand against his chest. "No!" she shouted. "I got this. Besides, it'll freak them out if an old man shows up." She spun around on her heels and strolled down the hallway. "Be back in a couple of hours," she called, over her shoulder as she jingled the keys in the air. "And keep the kitchen open!"

Shane was in shock. Finn was two hours away. How was this possible? What were the odds that they would stumble into his random neck of the woods? Was this really happening? His heart raced in his chest. His thoughts swirled out of control.

"Earth to Shane," said Manny, snapping his fingers in front of his face. "You still in there?"

Shane blinked and shook his head. He glanced around, taking note that Pillar and Odie were now standing nearby, but Catalina was nowhere to be seen. "Where's Cat?"

"She went to make sure the kitchen was ready," answered Manny. His face became serious. "You should probably take a seat. You look a little green."

"I'm fine!" replied Shane dismissively. He turned to Manny. "Is this happening?"

"It sure as hell is my brother." Manny slapped a firm hand on his shoulder. "Our boy is about to walk through that door."

Shane didn't want to get his hopes up. There have been too many moments lately where he allowed himself to feel hope, only to have it smashed. He had no intention of falling down that hole again. He shook his head. "Let's not get ahead of ourselves," he said, more for himself. "He ain't here yet."

"Okay, Brother," said Manny. "You go ahead and pretend like this ain't happenin'. I'm gonna be over here waiting anxiously for my nephew to arrive." He smiled and walked to the bar. "Yo! Kyle!" he shouted. "A round of drinks for the house! We got some celebrating to do!"

Shane went back into the office and closed the door behind him. Finn. The boy was here. Well, he was on his way. His friends were here. Teague was here, that certainly meant that Finn would follow soon. At least he hoped that would be the case.

He had dreamed of this moment ever since he found out his son was alive. What would he say to the kid? How does one even approach something like this? For all he knew, Finn thought Daniel was his father, was he even going to believe the truth? What's the best way to drop such a revelation on someone? How the hell did he end up coming here? Of all places, why here? And why now?

Chapter Twenty

"What do you think of her?" asked River. Peering over her shoulder, she attempted to make out what was happening inside the truck where Mari and Zac were seated.

Teague smiled. "I think Zac is completely enthralled," he replied.

"I know that," she said. "Does she seem a little weird?"

"Like, how?"

River shrugged. "I don't know." She snapped her fingers. "Like how she knew we rode trains."

"Lots of people figure that out," replied Teague. "Especially if they're in a place where riders come through. We got a specific look. You're gonna have to do better than that."

"Yeah, I suppose you're right," she replied, tapping her chin. She stared at the truck. "I'm being silly, ain't I?"

Teague shook his head. "Don't be so hard on yourself," he said. "You're only acting on how you feel." He tapped his chest. "You care about your family. That's a good thing." He stared down the tracks. "After everything we put you through over the past year, I'm surprised you still care."

She scoffed and shoved him playfully. "Y'all are the only family I got," she said. "Lord knows, y'all ain't perfect, but a girl's gotta work with what she's got. Besides, I love you."

"Ain't perfect?" Teague placed a hand against his chest in protest. "That's special comin' from a woman who snores like a buzz saw."

"Again with the snoring," argued River. She placed her hands on her hips. "You got no proof."

He shook his head. "You're right, I don't. Am I gonna have to record you one of these nights?"

"If you do, I'll have to kill you," she warned.

"Duly noted," he replied.

River paused and studied Teague. It felt like old times. She never thought they would all get back to the way it used to be. She recalled the way Teague was right after Finn left. He was shattered, barely even present most of the time, always lost somewhere in the abyss of his broken heart. The weeks following were awful. It was like being around someone made of cracked glass. Every word she said to him was carefully calibrated so as not to push him. Rather than walking on eggshells, it was more like walking on thin, cracked ice. At any moment, you could take the one fateful step that would plunge you into the icy waters where you would surely drown.

When Finn and Teague went off on their own, she was more than a little worried. After all, they had no guarantees that Finn wouldn't lose it again. Who knew what damage he could do if he snapped and no one else was around to stop him from hurting Teague. It was Cash who told her to trust that things would be okay.

If she hadn't witnessed the change take place with her own eyes, one video call after another, she would hardly believe it. Gone was the tension and sorrow, in their place was a sublime sort of contentedness.

"What?" asked Teague, eyeing her warily.

"I'm just thinking about how different you are," she replied.

"Different? How?"

"You're calm." She smiled. "And there's an air of contentedness all around you."

"Now, you're soundin' like Bella," he chuckled.

"It's true though. Both you and Finn are different."

"Is that good?"

She nodded. "I think so. You're both older." She shrugged. "More mature."

Teague laughed. "Mature, huh? You wouldn't say that if you saw him with Walter." He looked back at her. "You've changed too," he said. "I mean, you always were the mama bear but, it's so much more prevalent now." He smiled. "You've also managed to bring that out in Cash."

At the mention of his name, River's lips curled into a tiny smile.

"That right there," said Teague, pointing a finger at her. "That smile. That's a sign of true love." An impish grin appeared on his face. "Nothin', but true love could possibly get past all that snorin' you do."

"Shut up," she said, and shoved him playfully. "I do not snore."

He put his hands up in surrender. "Okay, okay, whatever you say."

River glanced back at the truck, listening to the playful giggles that erupted from the cab. Zac was certainly smitten with Mari. She smiled, recalling the way he could hardly string together a whole sentence when he first met the woman.

Zac laughed loudly, his voice bouncing off the surrounding trees. It was good to see him so happy. It made her heart sing to see the people she loved most in the world come back to their old selves. Come to think of it, they were better than their old selves.

She thought about the past few weeks. Zac had regular contact with Cole. Seeing him take part from time to time in the group chat was fun. And now Beth was gonna come visit.

Over the past several months, River tried hard not to think much about Beth, it was too painful. She hated the way it all went down—the way the poor girl left. She must have felt as though everyone had abandoned her.

Wherever it was she went to, River pretended Beth was happier. She never looked into it, because she was afraid she might find out otherwise. And that would have broken her heart.

Truth was, she missed Beth. Her laughter and the way she used to tease River; it differed from the guys. Beth was her little sister, and she broke her heart.

Maybe now, once Beth arrived, she could talk it over with her and they could start anew. Even Finn seemed to want to repair that bond.

The train whistle rang out, one long, one short and one long. A bright headlight appeared on the horizon, a tiny speck of light at first, but growing as the giant, metal beast rolled closer.

Chapter Twenty-One

The city lights glowed bright up ahead, they were rolling into El Paso. Finn scanned the landscape along the side of the tracks, hoping to catch a glimpse of the others, but all he could see was the occasional shrub or tree and a whole lot of nothing.

The train slowed as the engineer applied the brakes, causing the car to jerk under his feet, it was almost time to jump. He donned his pack and readied himself.

The tracks split into two, then three and four, they were in the rail yard. The sound of the brakes pierced his eardrums, their speed dissipated, they were now moving at a slow crawl.

Finn gave a quick nod to Cash, then jumped. A moment later, Cash landed softly beside him. The others were somewhere close by, but they had no way of knowing where exactly. He scanned the tree line in search of a signal.

A tiny glimmer of light pulsed to their left. He smiled and slapped Cash on the arm, then pointed. "This way," he said.

Teague burst out with a broad smile across his face when they got within twenty feet of the trees.

"Finally," he said, as he wrapped his arms around Finn. "Was your ride smoother than ours?"

Finn pulled away. "It certainly was a lot drier," he said, pretending to be disgusted by the soggy nature of Teague's clothes.

"Mais oui," laughed Teague. "That storm kicked our asses."

River ruptured from the trees and fell into Cash's arms. After a long kiss, he looked around. "Where's Zac?"

"With his new girlfriend," she replied, with a wide grin.

"Girlfriend?" asked Finn. "We were only gone for a few days." He turned to Teague. "Our boy works fast." He grinned. "Who is she?"

"She," replied Teague, guiding him into the trees. "Is our host tonight. She's bringing us to the bar she works at to hang out. Oh, and she offered us dinner."

"She borrowed her father's truck," added River. "She seems okay. At least when I've been able to talk with her." She chuckled. "Zac's been all up into her, so that's not often."

They stepped out of the trees onto a side road, where an old pickup truck sat. Teague gave out a sharp whistle, and the doors flung open, dumping Zac onto the gravel. He quickly made his way over. A pretty, young woman with long, dark hair approached slowly behind him, keeping her distance as Zac said hello to both Finn and Cash.

She stepped forward and held out her hand. "You must be Finn. I've heard a lot about you," she said, with a smile. "I'm Mari."

Finn took her hand only to be surprised when she wrapped her arms around him for a hug. This startled him, he wasn't used to getting hugged by women he didn't know. He didn't know where to put his hands or what to do with his arms, so he stood there awkwardly, waiting for it all to end.

Mari stepped back and stared into his eyes. "You're almost exactly how I imagined you to be." She smiled.

Cash cleared his throat and introduced himself.

Mari nodded at him and smiled, but never took her eyes off of Finn. "Happy to meet you too," she said.

Finn couldn't help but notice that she didn't even bother to hug Cash. So why did she do it to him?

"Who's hungry?" she asked, as she stepped back and smiled at everyone. She locked eyes with Finn. "You look like you could use a big steak."

"I know I could," interjected Cash.

Finn glanced at Teague, who was standing at a distance and observing the situation. His eyes shifted to Zac, who was beaming with joy as he observed Mari interacting with everyone.

"Okay!" announced Mari. "Let's all load up. I gotta get to work, and your dinner awaits." She flashed a bright, happy smile and spun around on her heels.

Finn stood in place, waiting for Teague to come up alongside him. As soon as he did, he pulled him close and whispered, "This is weird."

Teague chuckled softly. "I agree," he replied. "Can you ever recall seeing Zac this way before?"

"I ain't talking about him." Finn shook his head. "I'm talkin' about her. What's her deal?"

"She seems normal." Teague shrugged. "Or, as normal as one could be living way out here." He gestured with his arms. "She seems authentic. At least I haven't caught her lying yet. She said she would be back with a truck to give us a ride, and she came back with a truck."

"What was she driving when you met her?"

Teague smiled. "A big, black motorcycle."

"Seriously?"

"Oui."

Finn shook his head and laughed. "Well, that explains Zac goin' all puppy dog-like." He mulled over his feelings. "There's somethin' off."

"With her?" asked Teague. "Like what?"

He shrugged. "I don't know. Why'd she hug me?"

Teague laughed. "She was sayin' hello."

"She didn't hug Cash."

"Maybe you're just more of the huggable kind," he teased.

"It felt weird."

"Well, she's a girl," chuckled Teague. "And she touched you, so you probably got the cooties now."

The truck horn blew twice. Mari hung out the window. "Come on," she said. "Dinner's waitin'."

Teague gave him a playful shove. "Come on," he said. "You can worry about everything when we're done filling our bellies."

Finn stood back for a moment, trying to reconcile his emotions with his thoughts and his eyes. Teague was right, there didn't seem to be anything about the girl that he could put his finger on. Still, it was creepy how she acted as though she already knew him—but that could be explained by the time she had already spent with Zac. No one else seemed to be concerned, so why was he?

The truck rolled backward, coming up alongside him. Teague pulled a door open. "Come on," he said.

With a shake of his head, Finn brushed aside his apprehensions, chalking them up to his deep distrust of new situations. He climbed in beside Teague and pulled the door close. A moment later, they were rolling down the road toward some bar he had never heard of before, for a free dinner. As they rolled along the dark, desert road, he quietly made note of the landmarks he could see.

Chapter Twenty-Two

Tap, tap, tap.

Manny sat across the desk, nervously tapping his finger on the side of his beer bottle as he stared into space. Pillar sat next to him, shifting his body trying to find a comfortable position to no avail. Leaning against the bookcase in the corner was Odie, lost in deep thought, all the while pulling at his beard hair, while Cat sat at her desk, biting off the tips of her nails.

Tap, tap, tap.

The sound punctuated Shane's emotions. It was almost as annoying as a leaky faucet. Each clang was like a drumbeat against his eardrums. He considered asking Manny to give it a rest, but he realized that would only result in an awkward silence among them all. He glanced down at his watch. How long had it been since Mari left? He knew he should have gone with her. What if they had an accident? What if they changed their minds and left? From what he had learned so far, Finn was cagey, he didn't come to trust people easily. What if something triggered his flight response, and the whole group left?

"Could you please stop that?" asked Catalina, glaring at Manny.

In true brotherly fashion, Manny locked eyes with her and continued to tap on the side of his bottle, only now, the sound was much louder.

"I mean it," warned Cat. "If you don't stop that right now, I'm gonna climb over this desk and bust that bottle over the top of your hard head."

Manny smirked and continued tapping.

Shane weighed his options. Should he intervene? It was never a good idea to get between those two when they were arguing, things would start flying and they weren't always words. On the other hand, it was a nice distraction from his own thoughts. He leaned back and watched.

Cat pushed her chair back, ready to get up and slap her brother. She stopped in her tracks when Odie stood up straight and pointed at the monitor.

Shane looked up at the screen and caught a glimpse of the truck pulling into the parking lot.

Time stopped; all eyes were glued to the screen.

The air in the room was like thick liquid, or at least that's how it felt to Shane until he realized he was holding his breath. His heart raced in his chest as he watched the black-and-white screen for any movement. How long did it take them to get out of the truck? What the hell were they doing in there? Irritation mixed with anxiety as he waited for what seemed an hour.

The doors swung open, and a gaggle of young people climbed out. Shane scanned the faces, his heart skipping a full beat when he laid eyes on his son.

"There he is!" shouted Manny, pointing at the monitor.

Chatter continued around him in the tiny office, but Shane was too fixated on Finn. He watched the boy stand beside the truck, studying the area. His eyes scanned the building until they found the security camera. He gazed directly at it, as if he could see Shane and the others watching him on the monitor, and then he quickly donned a set of sunglasses. Teague stood nearby, the two leaned close, obviously discussing something, then, with a shrug and a gentle shove, they followed Mari into the bar.

Catalina switched the camera on the large monitor to the one inside the bar. This one had a much better resolution, so it was easier to see small details.

The big redhead, named Zac, followed Mari close, clearly infatuated with the girl. Shane smiled; the boy had it bad. The girl, River, came next, holding hands with the sly one named Cash. Finn and Teague hovered close to the door, taking in the bar before stepping all the way inside. While Teague seemed open and cheerful, Finn's face was unreadable.

Shane leaned over and adjusted the controls, zooming in on Finn's face. He was desperate to see any indication that Finn felt at ease in the bar.

The door to the office creaked open and Mari squeezed in. She tossed Shane's keys onto his desk, then glanced around the room and smirked. "It's kinda tight in here," she said. Her eyes followed their gaze to the monitor. "Yeah," she scoffed. "That's not creepy."

No one made a move, nor did they respond to her, their eyes fixated on the screen.

She shook her head. "So, are y'all gonna sit in here and stare at him through the monitor or are you gonna come on out and meet him?"

"What's he like?" asked Cat, nervously.

"Quiet," replied Mari. "He hasn't said a whole lot." She shrugged. "He mostly sits and observes." She chuckled softly. "I hugged him. I think it freaked him out." She waited for a response, when none came, she turned to the door. "Since I brought Finn home, can I get the night off?"

Silence.

Mari grinned. "Since y'all ain't answering, I'm gonna take that as a yes."

"Kyle's been here all day," blurted Catalina. "He should go home." She gestured toward Mari. "You can flirt with your ginger while you're working. From what I've seen already, he isn't going anywhere."

"I can help out," added Odie. He shrugged. "Wouldn't want to get in the way of young love."

Mari squealed and planted a kiss on his cheek. "Thank you!" Without another word, she flung the door open and left the room.

Shane sat transfixed; his eyes locked on Finn on the monitor.

"So, what are we gonna do, Boss?" asked Pillar.

"What do you mean?" scoffed Manny. "We're gonna go out there and meet my nephew."

All eyes were on Shane.

"What do we say to him?" asked Cat.

"I don't know," replied Shane. "I mean, you see how apprehensive he is. We can't just go up to him and shout out, I'm your father!" He stared at the monitor. "He'll bolt for sure. Besides, he thinks Daniel is his father. Remember?"

"So, what are we supposed to do?" demanded Cat. "Sit in here and watch him on that monitor all night like a bunch of peeping toms?"

"Well, we can't just run up to him," replied Shane. "You see what I see. He'll leave, thinking we're a bunch of nuts."

"Would he be far off?" quipped Manny. When everyone scoffed and glared at him, he put his hands in the air in mock surrender. "I'm just sayin' we can't sit in here all night and just watch the kid."

"He's got a good point," offered Odie.

Pillar grunted in agreement.

Shane looked around, they were all waiting for him to make a decision. He cleared his throat. "No matter what, we can't tell him who we are until we can guarantee we can do it without sending him running," he said firmly.

"So, just pretend like he's just another patron at the bar?" asked Cat. She shook her head and sighed. "I don't think I can do that. The mom in me wants to hug him tight and bring him home." She studied the monitor. "He looks so skinny."

Manny chuckled. "You sound like Mom."

She rolled her eyes and waved him off dismissively.

"Can we be serious for a minute?" asked Shane. "We have to do this right. I don't want to mess up the first time I ever get to meet him. If we screw this up, it could be the last time we ever see him."

"We'll do whatever you want, Boss," replied Odie.

Manny pushed his chair back noisily and climbed to his feet. "I don't know about all y'all, but I'm gonna go meet my nephew." He moved for the door. "And don't worry, I ain't gonna say shit." He nodded to Shane. "When you think the time is right, you can let him know. I'm just gonna go and play a few rounds of pool with the kid." He pulled open the office door and stepped outside, followed by Odie and finally Pillar.

The door closed, leaving Catalina and Shane alone with the monitors.

She strolled over and rubbed his shoulders. "This is what we've wanted since we found out he was alive," she said softly. "He looks good. Doesn't he?"

Shane spun around and peered up at her. "Is this really happening?" He pinched his eyes against the tears that were welling up. "I can't believe this is real."

Cat smiled. "It's real, Babe." She gestured to the door. "Our son is out there, just a few feet away from us."

"I'm scared," blurted Shane. "What if he hates me?"

"That's impossible," she replied. She stepped back. "Now, come on, let's go see our boy."

After one more peek at the monitors, Shane allowed Cat to guide him through the door and into the bar.

Chapter Twenty-Three

Beth gazed upward at the massive, metal statue of a roadrunner. In the distance, the lights of Las Cruces glimmered and glowed. The feeling of loneliness that she experienced at that moment was unlike anything she had ever felt before. It was fitting that the first public place she was allowed to venture out into would be a hilltop rest stop in the wee hours of the night. Not a person in sight and nowhere to run for help.

Examining the intricate sculpture, she took note of the various bits and pieces that were used to construct the bird. A set of headlights reminded her of her uncle, he would know exactly what make of vehicle they came from. Old golf clubs made her think of her dad. A random trophy brought forth memories of her brother Tomas during his soccer days. She used to hate going to his games when she was little. There were never enough seats, and she never got to eat any of the snacks. What she wouldn't do to be back at one of those games again. It was amazing how a collection of other people's trash could make her feel so nostalgic.

Hot tears pooled in her eyes. She refocused on the bird and eventually noticed a small set of shoes encased in metal. Her mind immediately snapped to her own baby shoes that her mother had encased in bronze when she outgrew them. A flood of tears streamed down her cheeks.

Standing beside her, Daniel lit a cigarette. He exhaled a cloud of smoke. "Aw, don't be so sad, we're almost there, princess," he said. He stared out at the city below. "Sure is pretty this time of night. Ain't it? You could almost forget all about the scumbags, asshats and harpies that live down there." He took a long drag and exhaled a cloud of smoke, then stared long and hard at Beth. "You should be happy," he said. "You're going to see your friends." A malevolent grin spread across his face. "And I'm gonna have a little visit with family."

"You could let me go!" she blurted. "I won't tell anyone. You can let me go right here. I'll stay right in this spot 'till morning then get a ride west." She shook her head. "You'll never hear from me again."

"Now, you know me better than that," he said. "Or, shall I say, I know you better than that." He exhaled another cloud of smoke. "No, sweetheart, you're coming with me for the whole ride."

"Please," she begged, with tears streaming down her cheeks. "I promise, I won't tell anyone." She swallowed as she struggled to control the tears that streamed from her bloodshot eyes. Images of her parents played in her mind in such a vivid display, she could feel their sorrow. How could she have been so cruel to them? She was a horrible person, maybe she deserved to end this way.

Daniel sneered. "Turn off the waterworks. You women always go for the tears, expecting us to cave. Well, I ain't falling for it."

Beth wasn't ready to give up. Clinging to the tiniest spark of hope, she continued, "You could turn around right now. Head west and start a whole new life," she said. "Everyone thinks you're dead. It could be a whole fresh start—"

"And why do you suppose everyone thinks I'm dead?" he shouted. His eyes were full of hate. "There's no such thing as a new start for me." He stared out at the city. "At least not until I finish what needs to be done. If I do nothing else with my life, I'll at least have the satisfaction of seeing the life drained from that freak's eyes."

The tiny flame of hope she had left in her heart went cold and flickered out. She wasn't getting out of this. There was no convincing him to turn back.

Daniel pulled her cell phone from his pocket and held it up.

"No," she said, shaking her head defiantly. All fear had left her body. She accepted her fate. If she was to die, then let it be here and now. She was done living in fear of this monster. "I'm not helping you anymore."

He laughed diabolically. "You're a funny one," he jeered. "But I don't need you for this part." He slid his finger across the screen and input the passcode then he opened her messages.

She watched in horror as he typed a message in her name.

```
Beth: I'm just outside of Las Cruces. I'll be in
El Paso soon. Where y'all at?"
    Zac: We stopped here for the night. Think you
can make it?
    He sent a screenshot of his map, showing their
location.
    Beth: Yes. Absolutely.
```

The phone chimed with a new message. There was something about this particular one that sparked a look of pure joy on Daniel's face. He laughed out loud and held the phone so she could see.

```
Message: Beth, this is Finn. If it's OK with you,
I'd like to meet up and talk before the whole
group is around. Just you and me.
```

. . .

Her heart sank. Finn was reaching out to her as a friend, and she was bringing death. A torrent of tears burst forth from her eyes, drenching her already damp cheeks. "Please," she muttered to Daniel.

"Looks like you haven't been entirely truthful to me, princess," he sneered. "What is it you two have to talk about? Seems as though there was a falling out. Wasn't there?"

Beth refused to answer.

Daniel scoffed. "Oh, well, it doesn't matter. Whatever went down between you two is good for me." He grinned. "Now, I don't have to come up with a way to get him away from the group."

The evil man, full of malice, stared at her with disgust. He then shifted his focus back to the small screen.

```
Beth: Yes. I'd love that. I'll text when I get
close.
```

Daniel shoved the phone in his pocket and grabbed Beth's arm, his eyes glinting with malice. "Let's go, princess," he said. "Finn's waiting."

He shoved her roughly into the van, then reapplied the hand-cuffs. As they rolled back onto the highway, Beth's mind reeled with all the different scenarios that were possible. None of which involved an escape.

Chapter Twenty-Four

The bar was like a million other bars, nothing special, nothing notable. A building with outside seating, patio lights and from what he could hear, loud rock music playing inside. He scanned the parking lot. It wasn't very crowded, a few work trucks, an SUV, and what he could only assume was Mari's motorcycle.

Security cameras hung high up on poles, staring down at the parking lot. Finn stared up at one, noting the red light that showed the device was recording—that someone was watching.

"Come on," shouted Mari, waving her hands as she held the door open.

Slowly, he followed the others inside. Large, flat-screen TVs were suspended low around the bar, each broadcasting a different sports event. Finn gazed intently at one of the screens displaying a hockey game, attempting to identify which teams were playing. A tiny pang of remorse stung deep as he recalled Craig.

He scanned the room. Small and medium-sized tables lined the walls, while a series of pool tables sat in the far corner, away from the loudest music. Cameras sat on high perches overhead, seemingly covering every inch of the building.

Mari disappeared down a narrow passage, only to reappear a moment later. With a bright smile on her face, she approached Finn. "Come on," she prodded. "Why don't y'all take a seat at the bar. I gotta get to work." She strolled over to the bartender, whispered something, then began wiping glasses while the young man gathered his things and left.

Finn stood back and watched as the others made their way over to the pool tables. He wished he could be as relaxed as they were, but he had never been able to run into a new environment blind. A very dark part of him always needed to know where all the exits were.

Teague, noticing he hadn't moved, wandered up alongside him. "Whatcha waitin' for? Come on," he said, as he shoved Finn over to join the others.

He didn't want to bring anyone down, especially since he had no real reason to be so apprehensive. He didn't even have a gut feeling that anything was wrong, his reaction to this place was all him and his lifelong wariness of new things.

The pool tables were mostly unused, with a few, gnarly regulars gathered around one. Cash grabbed a cue from the rack and twirled it around in his hand. With a joyful grin, he made his way toward the closest table and began to set up the balls.

A burst of men's laughter erupted from the corridor; Finn glanced over just in time to see three men wander out into the main room. The leader was a tall and thin Latino, his unruly, black hair was peppered with streaks of white. As he sauntered over to the bar, he smiled and nodded at Finn. After a brief conversation with Mari, he walked over to the pool table, whiskey bottle in hand, accompanied by the other two men.

"Hola, my friends," said the man. "My niece, tells me you're visiting."

He walked up to Zac, holding out his hand. "My name's Manny," he said. "And you must be Zac."

"Yes, sir," replied Zac, taking the man's hand.

"Nice grip," said Manny. "I like it." He turned and stopped in front of River. "And who is this beautiful lady?" he asked.

"River," she replied.

"I'm pleased to meet you," he said.

"This is Cash," she added quickly.

Manny said hello. "You any good?" he asked, gesturing toward the pool cue.

"I don't like to brag," replied Cash, with a grin. "But I can hold my own."

Manny gave a nod of approval. "My man Odie here is a pretty good player too." He waved his hand over to the shorter of his two friends. "Don't let his height or lack of vocabulary fool you. He's slick. He took a hundred dollars from me last week," continued Manny. "It'd sure be nice if someone could put him in his place. I don't even care if you get the money, just so long as he doesn't have it by the night's end."

Odie snickered and shook his head. "That's right," he said. "Ask the kid to do it for you, because Lord knows, you ain't gonna be able to."

"You see what I'm up against here?" said Manny, with a shake of his head. "He's insufferable when he wins."

Cash chuckled. "Well, step on up," he said to Odie. "I'm always up for a challenge."

The older man pulled down a stick and moved closer to the table. That was when Finn noticed the burn scars all over his hands. Whatever the man did for a living, it must involve fire.

Manny's face became serious. His eyes moved over to Teague and then Finn, where he paused for an uncomfortably long period of time.

Finn was quick to acknowledge that he wasn't particularly skilled at comprehending other people's motives. However, he was able to sense when someone was summing him up. He stood firm as Manny approached with an open hand.

"And who are you two?" he asked.

"Teague."

"Happy to meet you," said Manny. His dark, piercing eyes glided over to Finn.

"And what's your name, my young, sunglass-wearing friend?"

Finn stared.

Teague nudged him. When Finn didn't respond, he said, "This is Finn."

Manny seemed to get the hint. He gave a quick nod, then backed off. Lifting the bottle of whiskey in the air, he announced, "What are we waiting for?" He turned to the bar. "Mari, bring us some shot glasses. We're gonna watch this kid beat Odie's ass."

"What's with the long face?" asked Teague.

"Do they seem a little weird to you?"

Teague shook his head. "They're friendly, but I'm not reading any sort of threat from them." He shrugged. "They probably don't get many non-regulars here." He studied Finn. "What's got you so worried?"

"I don't know," he replied. "Something feels weird."

"Can you describe what it is?"

Finn shook his head.

"We've met folks like this before," said Teague. "They're strange, but not in a threatening way." He smiled. "Come on. Try to relax and enjoy the night." He nodded toward Zac, who was hovering near Mari. "Besides, our boy deserves to spend some time with his dream woman."

Finn sighed, of course, Teague was right. He watched Mari approach with several shot glasses, taking the time to flirt with Zac before going back to work.

An older woman wandered out of the corridor, she was beautiful —an older version of Mari. Behind her, a tall man with a thick, well-trimmed beard followed close. They strolled up to the bar where the man took a seat. With a friendly smile on her face, the woman sauntered up to the pool table, stopping right in front of Manny.

"Are you going to introduce me?" she asked him.

He shook his head and sighed. "Because my sister doesn't seem capable of doing it herself," he teased. "Everyone, this is Catalina." He gestured around the table. "This is Zac, Cash, River, Teague and Finn."

She nodded hello to everyone, then turned to Teague and pulled him in for two quick pecks on his cheek. "Call me Cat," she said.

Before Finn could step back, the woman drew him in and embraced him warmly, pressing a kiss on each of his cheeks. With her hands still on his arms, she leaned back and looked at him. "You boys make yourselves at home," she said. "Mari says she promised you dinner. Are you hungry?"

"Always," replied Teague.

Finn stood silently.

"Relax Mijo," she said to Finn. "You're among friends here." She stepped away and called over her shoulder, "I'll go have the kitchen whip something up for you."

Without another word, she disappeared behind a set of double swinging doors, leaving Finn to ponder why the hell everyone was so touchy-feely around here. His skin tingled where she touched him. These people had to be some of the friendliest people he had ever run into, and it was making his skin crawl. From what he could tell, there wasn't anything wrong with them. Even so, something was off. It was almost as though they knew something he didn't. His mind wandered over his recent memories of the people he met, pausing briefly on Violet and Tayo, two of the kindest folks he ever met. He mulled it over, realizing that these people were more like Tigre— friendly, but deep down dangerous if need be.

Manny whistled. "Yo! Boss!" he shouted. "Why don't you come on over here and meet our new friends."

The man from the bar looked stunned at first, but his expression quickly changed to one that could only be described as fearful. He downed what was left of his drink and let Mari pour him another, then he made his way over.

"They tell me you're the man I need to beat," said Cash, as he chalked his cue.

"I see you're putting Odie through the paces," said the man. "It's always a good day when he loses."

Cash grinned. "Spoken like a man who's lost many times." He gestured to the table. "You feeling lucky? There's always room in my wallet for more," he teased.

"That's some serious bravado."

"I like to think of it as confidence from years of winning. What do ya say, Boss," prodded Cash. "You ready to empty your wallet?"

Laughter erupted all around as the older man pulled down a cue. "Alright, son," he said. "Get ready." He stretched his arms. "You're about to learn something."

Finn watched his friends' banter back and forth with the men as they played pool, carefully studying their gestures and facial reactions. A bizarre sense of déjà vu washed over him. He scraped his memory, trying to figure out why it was that he felt like he knew these people. The contagious laughter and camaraderie lured him in and before long, he was fully engaged in the conversation.

"I tried to warn you," quipped Cash, scooping up a pile of dollar bills from the table.

The boss man turned to Finn. "Is he always this way?" he asked.

"Nah," replied Finn. "He's usually much worse."

The man laughed heartily and poured some shots. He handed them out, then held his high. "Salud!" he said aloud. He nodded toward Finn, then downed his shot, twitching his nose as he swallowed.

Finn downed his, slamming his glass on the table at the same time as the boss man. He glanced up to find Teague staring with an odd expression on his face.

"Have we met before?" Teague asked, the older man. He squinted his eyes. "I swear we've met. Something about you is familiar."

The man twitched his nose. He opened his mouth to speak, but stopped short when Mari, followed by Cat, strolled out of the kitchen carrying large trays laden with food.

"Who's ready to eat?" asked Cat.

Finn was more than ready. The savory aroma of grilled meat filled the air, pouring into his nostrils, making his mouth water. He promptly sat down at the table, snatched a fork, and impaled the steak. Raising the entire piece toward his mouth, he chomped down, taking a sizable bite.

Chewing sloppily, he glanced up to see that everyone was staring at him, their faces a mixture of humor, shock and horror.

"Ah, Mijo," said Cat, as she handed him a napkin then placed a soft hand on his shoulder. She leaned close to him. "I see you're hungry. Eat up," she said. "We can make more if need be." She turned to Mari and said, "Come on, Mija, let's leave them to eat in peace." With a final wink at Finn, she wandered back over to the bar.

Zac's phone buzzed with a message. "It's Beth," he announced. Then tapped a response. After a brief back and forth, it was established that she would come and meet up with them at the bar.

"Let me have it," said Finn, holding his hand out. He still harbored a lot of guilt over the way he treated her. He saw her reaching out as a perfect opportunity for him to make things right. After all, most of what happened was his fault. She was just a naive kid who found herself in a nasty situation, he had no business taking his rage out on her. Just like he had no right to take it out on Teague.

He handed the phone back to Zac.

"What was that?" asked Teague.

"An opportunity to fix somethin' I broke," replied Finn.

Teague flashed a warm smile and gave a nod of approval.

The hearty dinner sat heavy in his stomach, a welcome change from the past few days of light eating. Finn rose to his feet and stretched his arms, basking in the overall feeling of well-being that had washed over him. Another round of pool had begun, this time it was Manny who was challenging Cash. Finn turned his focus on the rest of the bar, noticing the random photographs that hung on the walls. He wandered around, inspecting each one.

A black-and-white one caught his eye, a happy family peered up at him. He studied their faces, noting that he was staring at very young versions of Cat and Manny. Farther down the wall, he came to an image of a group of young men in desert camouflage, gathered around a red flag with the Marine Corps logo on it. He studied their faces, all wearing sunglasses, their uniforms covered in sand. The desert sun, cast a pale glow on all of them. Manny stood out, wearing his familiar grin, his tanned skin darkened by the bright sun.

Finn studied the other men, he could make out one who resembled Odie and the giant beast of a man who stood in the back was definitely the one named Pillar. Standing on the side, tall, muscular and proud, was the one they called Boss.

"We were probably about your age when that picture was taken," said a deep, familiar voice.

Finn startled and looked over to find the boss man standing beside him. He looked back at the photograph and pointed. "That you?" he asked.

The man smiled. "It is," he replied, then tapped his belly. "A lifetime ago when the food wasn't nearly as good." He scrubbed his fingers through his beard. "And I wasn't quite as gray."

"Y'all have been friends for a while," said Finn. "Haven't you?"

"When you find family," replied the man. "It's best to keep it." He glanced over at the photo. "Those boys helped me through some tough times." He sighed. "I wouldn't be here right now, if it weren't for them."

Finn recalled the past few months. He could relate to the man's words.

The older man gestured toward the pool tables. "Looks like you got yourself a tight-knit crew of your own."

"I wouldn't be here right now without them," he replied.

"Then I would say you are truly blessed." He placed his firm hand on Finn's shoulder. "Can I buy you a drink?"

Finn gave a nod and followed the man as he led the way toward the bar.

"Mari, would you pour us a couple of shots?" he asked.

She winked and smiled. "You got it, Boss," she said.

"So," said the man. "Mind if I ask what brings you all the way out here?"

"Some family business," replied Finn.

"Really?" asked the man.

Finn chuckled. "If I told you half of it, you'd never believe me."

"You'd be surprised," said the older man. "Believe me when I say I've seen some shit."

Teague sauntered up and took a seat beside Finn.

"Just in time," said the man. "We're about to share another drink. Care to join?"

Mari poured three glasses. When she finished, she stared at Finn. "What's with the sunglasses?" she asked.

"He likes to hide his eyes," replied Teague.

Finn nodded sheepishly.

"Really?" she asked. "And why is that?" Without waiting for an answer, she placed one hand on her hip and held out the other. "Come on," she prodded, wiggling her fingers. "Let's see."

Teague nodded and nudged him gently. Finn pulled the glasses off and peered up at Mari. To his surprise, she didn't gasp or even react. He turned to look at the man, he too was unfazed, but there was something weird about his facial expression.

"You shouldn't hide those," said Mari. "I think they're cool. How about you, Boss? Wouldn't you agree eyes like that are too cool to hide?"

The man didn't reply to her. He held his glass up. "Cheers," he said, then clinked glasses with both Finn and Teague.

Mari grinned. "You know, when I was fifteen, I bought a couple of pairs of those colored contact lenses. You know the ones." She waited for Finn to nod in understanding. "I split up the sets and wore one brown in this eye and one blue in this one."

"What made you think of doing that?" asked Teague.

"I guess I saw it somewhere," she replied with a shrug. "But seriously though," she continued. "Eyes like that are genetic. Aren't they?"

Finn nodded. "That's what I've been told." Knowing that his father had the same eyes, it suddenly occurred to him that maybe one of these two had seen him around. After struggling with his apprehension, he finally blurted, "Have y'all ever seen a man with eyes like mine?" Immediate regret settled in. What if they knew Shane? He meant what he said when he was talking to Cash, he didn't want to meet the man, he just wanted to see him. He glanced up at the shocked faces staring back at him. Even Teague seemed to be stunned.

Over by the pool table, Zac's phone chimed. "It's Beth," he announced. "She's almost here."

Thankful for the distraction, Finn stood up. "Looks like I'm on," he said, ready to put some space between himself and his impulses. "Hold my place, please. I got something I gotta do," he said. As he stepped away from the bar, he called out to Zac, "Tell her to meet me by the road."

Chapter Twenty-Five

"Ça va?" asked Teague, stopping at the door.

Finn nodded. "Do you think it was a mistake asking them about Shane?"

Teague shrugged. "I don't know."

That response did nothing for Finn's anxiety.

"I'm proud of you," said Teague. "I never thought we'd ever see the day you felt like apologizing to someone who did you wrong."

Finn shook his head. "She didn't know she was doing anything wrong." He sighed. "I shouldn't have reacted the way I did. She's just a kid."

"Want me to come with you?"

Nah," replied Finn. "It's gotta be just her and me for this."

Teague nodded. "Ya know, I have some shit to apologize for as well."

"Save that for when I'm done," replied Finn. "When we come in, she's all yours."

Stepping outside, Finn allowed the door to close behind him, shutting out the music and laughter emanating from inside the bar.

He found himself standing alone in the hushed parking lot. There was no sign of Beth, maybe she was still on her way up the road.

Finn walked past the trucks, listening to the crunch of gravel under his boots, basking in the warm feelings of friendship and good times, doing his best to avoid thinking about his outburst. Maybe the folks inside knew Shane—maybe they didn't. Tomorrow he would go by his father's ranch and check it out. He wondered what the man was like. Aside from their eyes, did he share a resemblance with Finn? What about his life? Was he happily married with a family? Finn had so many questions and he was terrified of many of the answers.

Those worries were for tomorrow. Tonight, it was all about having fun. The group in the bar was a pleasant surprise. He enjoyed their company. Once again, he wondered if Shane knew these people, and if so, did he get along with them? A not-so-tiny part of him wanted the man to be like the people inside the bar.

Finn scanned the area, still no sign of Beth. He wondered what she had been up to all these months. Did she ever find the adventure she was looking for? He felt more than a little guilt over how things went down. She was a young kid who was looking for excitement and adventure. She never signed on to deal with his messed up past. No one did. Hell, even he didn't sign up for that shit.

He passed by a big, white van as he made his way toward the edge of the parking lot. A chill ran down his spine—something was off. It was too quiet. A heavy sense of dread descended on him.

"Hello, shithead," said a gruff, familiar voice.

At first, his brain refused to process what he just heard. It couldn't be. He was dead and dead men don't talk. Panic gripped his heart. What if Daniel wasn't dead after all? What if somehow the monster survived? Finn spun around and found himself face to face with his worst nightmare, then something hard hit the side of his head.

The world around him went black.

Chapter Twenty-Six

Teague watched the door close behind Finn. Life was so strange. Just a few months ago, he was sure his entire world had come to a crashing end; he wasn't even sure from one day to the next if he wanted to keep going. And now, here he was, surrounded by the people he loved most in the world. Even Finn was working his way to become a better man. His heart was full.

He returned to the bar and took his seat. Things were going well, it was even looking as though Beth would be back with them. He sincerely hoped that whatever happened over the next few days wouldn't derail all they had achieved. Finn had overcome so much, and even though he seemed strong at times, Teague knew all too well that Finn's grip on things was still fragile.

"You look pretty worried," said the boss man.

Teague sighed. "It's been a long year," he replied, with a slight shake of his head.

"I hear ya," said the man. He poured another glass and held it up. "To good times ahead," he said.

"Now, that," replied Teague. "Is something I can drink to." He took a sip and watched as the man did the same.

The older man put down his glass and twitched his nose.

Déjà vu washed over Teague with a strange intensity. Once again, it occurred to him that something about this man was very familiar. He watched him closely, trying to figure out what it was. Had he met them before? Was it even possible that somewhere over the years they had crossed paths?

Teague glanced around the bar at the other men, Manny, Pillar and Odie. Nope. He would remember if he ever met them before. He turned his focus to the one everyone called Boss. There was something familiar about him. His mannerisms reminded Teague of someone, he just couldn't put his finger on it.

A chorus of phone alerts went off, even Teague's vibrated in his pocket. Zac, Cash and River all glanced at one another confused.

Teague pulled the device out and peered at the screen. It was a group text from Max, telling them to check out the server.

He opened the app and scrolled down, reading all the messages. They had been quite busy, there was a lot to read.

Max: Hey, y'all check this out.

There was a screenshot of a post from someone Teague didn't know. The person went by the name Kitty. She shared an image of a backpack sitting on the beach. The wording read, "We need your help. Our friend has gone missing. She disappeared a few nights ago and the police can't even be bothered. They think she just left, but we know she wouldn't leave without her gear. This is her backpack."

Teague's heart sank. Across the room, River gasped, holding her hand to her mouth in shock.

He didn't want to read on, but he had to. The second post was another screenshot. This one was an image of Beth, smiling brightly. The words written below the post read, "This is our friend Beth.

Please, we're begging everyone to share this. If you've seen her, please tell us. Let her know we're looking for her and we have her gear."

Nausea hit Teague like a huge wave crashing onto the shore. His mind sputtered, refusing to connect the dots. The messages on the chat continued as the group processed what Max had shared.

```
Bella: Has anyone heard from her?
  Max: I'm ashamed to admit, I haven't done much
to stay in touch.
  Bella: What about River and the others?
  Mara: OMG! I hope she's okay.
  Tripp: It could be a mistake.
  Max: Not likely.
```

The chat went on, but Teague could read no more. His heart raced in his chest as he jumped to his feet and bolted for the door. He burst into the parking lot, Zac, Cash, River and all the bar patrons close behind.

"Finn!" he shouted, as he scanned the parking lot.

There was no sign of him anywhere. Panic sucked every bit of oxygen from his lungs. "Finn!" he shouted again, his voice sounding foreign to his own ears.

Dead silence.

Zac took off in one direction while Cash went in the other, each of them hollering Finn's name. The fear evident in their voices reflected the way Teague himself was feeling.

"Where is he?" asked Boss. His face a mask of desperation. "Go look around back!" he bellowed to his men, who promptly took off. He turned to Teague. "What's going on?"

Cash came jogging back, followed by Zac, both shaking their heads.

Panic took hold. Teague ran to the edge of the road and called, "Finn!" The darkness answered with pure nothingness.

Chapter Twenty-Seven

eth craned her neck as far as possible, yet she couldn't catch a decent glimpse of Finn. The only thing visible to her was a motionless, shadowy mass resting on the floor of the van.

The whole time Daniel was stalking outside, waiting for Finn, she struggled against her restraints, but all she could accomplish was serious bruising around her wrist and a small trickle of blood that ran down her arm from her raw skin. The handcuffs were simply too tight.

Finn let out a moan, and his body thrashed about in a seizure.

Beth's heart broke. She had only ever seen him suffer those under the careful eye of Teague. Was he aware that he was alone? Was he scared? Was there a danger of serious injury for him if left to struggle through it by himself?

"He needs help," she said.

"So?" asked Daniel, focusing on the road while reading a map on his phone. He glared over at her. "He'll be fine." An evil grin spread across his face. "At least until we get to where we're going."

Beth gazed out of her window, seeing nothing but a vast expanse of emptiness stretching as far as her eyes could see. There were no other lights in sight except for the van's headlights and the stars shining above. She needed to do something—anything was better than sitting there patiently along for the ride, as this madman murders both her and Finn. It was now or never—she had to do something.

As Daniel was driving, a coyote suddenly darted out onto the road, prompting him to swerve the van to avoid colliding with the animal.

This was her chance.

Beth used her free hand to grab the steering wheel and abruptly turned it to the right, causing the van to veer off the road. They crashed through a barbed wire fence and flew into the air, coming to an abrupt stop upside down.

She was the first to regain her composure, as she was the only one who had been wearing a seat belt. Unfortunately, she was upside down. Behind her, Finn moaned—at least he was alive.

Daniel groaned as he found himself crushed against the van's roof at an awkward angle. He raised a hand to his head, but quickly pulled it back, as it was covered in blood.

Good! Now was her chance.

She struggled against her seatbelt, but it wouldn't release. Feeling desperate, she reached for the keys that were still in the ignition.

A strong hand grabbed hold of her. "Stupid bitch!" growled Daniel. "You're gonna regret doing that."

Daniel squeezed her hand so tight she could feel the tiny bones snapping in her little finger. She cried out in pain. He hovered menacingly above her, blood oozing from the wound on his head and splattering onto her face. Still hanging upside down, she could feel the blood rush to her head. She was sure she would pass out soon. Unwilling to give up so easily she tried to shrink into the seat, but there was nowhere to go. If this was it, so be it. No matter what, she managed to disrupt his plans by throwing a monkey wrench into them.

Beth gathered her courage and locked eyes with him, refusing to show any trace of fear.

With a wicked grin on his face, Daniel lifted his fist and slammed it hard just beneath Beth's jaw.

Tiny lights erupted in the corner of her eyes. Pain shot through her skull followed by a wave of nausea. She begged for the release of unconsciousness.

Daniel repeatedly raised his fist and brought it crashing down on her.

The pain subsided; Beth let go. Her mind focused on Finn in the back, hoping that she had bought him enough time to save his own life.

Chapter Twenty-Eight

Teague leaned forward, his hands gripping his knees tightly. His heart pounded against his ribs, each beat thundering in his ears. He could feel his pulse racing in his temples and his breaths came in short gasps. The air felt thick and heavy, making it difficult for him to breathe. Confusion and fear churned in his gut, twisting his insides into knots.

Through blurry vision, he watched as River sprinted off with Zac and Cash. Teague wanted to go with them, to help in any way he could, but his body wouldn't cooperate. The chaos of the situation was overwhelming, a deep sense of helplessness washed over him.

"The security camera!" shouted Cat.

The boss swiftly dodged under Teague's arm and helped him back into the bar. They made their way through the narrow hallway and entered a small office, where he carefully seated Teague in a comfortable leather chair positioned behind a desk.

"Pull it up!" the older man barked.

Cat was busy typing on a keyboard, while both Teague and the older man were fixedly gazing up at the security monitors.

The image on the screen played backward. Finn appeared in the corner. "Stop!" he shouted.

Cat hit play, and the video began in real time.

Finn walked out of the front door of the bar, then disappeared from the camera's view.

Teague slammed his hand on the desk out of frustration.

"Hold on," said the boss man calmly. "Check the other camera." He nodded to Cat who was already typing.

The screen changed, this time picking up where the last camera left off. Finn wandered toward the edge of the parking lot. As he passed a white van, a man stepped out of the shadows and hit him on the side of his head with some sort of blunt object. Finn slumped to the ground.

Teague let out a guttural moan, his chest heaving as he struggled to draw in a breath. With a sense of dread, he watched as the man carried Finn's limp body toward the back of the van. Unable to look away, he stared at the monitor, his mind reeling with horror at the sight playing out before him. The man turned and glanced back at the bar, his eyes cold and calculating. A shock of pure dread ran through Teague's body.

"Stop it there!" shouted the boss.

Staring at the screen, Teague struggled to make sense of what his eyes were showing him. The image on the screen was burned into his memory, haunting him with every blink. The face staring back at him was the source of his purest nightmares, and the panic that exploded in his chest was suffocating. His mind reeled with questions. How was this possible? He shook his head in disbelief. "No, no, no, no," he muttered, as if saying those words would undo everything he had just witnessed. "He's dead! He's supposed to be dead!"

"Son of a bitch!" shouted the older man, as he swept everything on top of the desk onto the floor.

"Shane!" shouted Cat. "That's not going to help!" She turned to Teague. "Son, open the drawer and give me a pen so I can write down the license plate number."

Teague watched her lips move, even heard the words, but for

some reason, his brain refused to translate. She might as well have been speaking a foreign language.

The older man leaned across the desk and slid the drawer open, then grabbed something and tossed it over to Cat.

Teague's mind was still catching up. Did she just call him Shane? His eyes moved down to the desk drawer, taking note of the pens, paperclips, rubber bands, and a photo of Finn.

His mind snapped with sudden and intense clarity, like a bolt of lightning striking his brain. The sound of his own voice muttering, "What the fuck?" echoed in the silent room, bouncing off the walls and back into his ears. With a trembling hand, he reached out and lifted the photograph, feeling the weight of it in his palm. Slowly, he shifted his gaze to Shane, studying his face with a mix of confusion and suspicion.

"Hold on, Son," said the older man, his hands held up in front of him.

Teague's eyes blazed with fury as he launched himself across the desk. The sound of Cat screaming echoed through the room as his body collided with Shane's, sending them both crashing into the hallway. He swung his fist with all his might; the impact jarring his arm as he connected with the older man's jaw.

"Hold up!" shouted Shane, still standing there pathetically with his hands up.

Every ounce of rage poured from Teague's body into his fist. He punched the man's face again and again, the sound of flesh hitting flesh bounced off the walls. His knuckles throbbed with each impact. He swung once more, but this time Shane was prepared, catching Teague's arm in mid swing, and spun him around. Before he knew what was happening, the older man had Teague wrapped tightly in a choke hold. As hard as he tried, he could not break free.

"I don't wanna hurt you, Son," whispered Shane. "Please, calm down."

Teague bucked and struggled, to no avail. Every effort made Shane's grip tighten. It was getting hard to breathe, his body was getting weak. Cat was shouting, but he couldn't make out anything she said.

Something heavy crashed into Shane, the impact sending shock-waves through his body and causing his arms to flail uncontrollably.

Teague crumpled to the floor, gasping for air. Through the haze of pain and confusion, he managed to look up just in time to see Zac hurling Shane out of the hallway and into the main bar area. The sound of shattering glass and splintering wood was deafening.

Cat tried to help Teague up, but he shoved her away, sending her crashing into the wall.

Teague stumbled out of the hall, his body still adjusting to the influx of oxygen. Zac was relentlessly pummeling Shane, who stood there, seemingly frozen in place, making no effort to strike back. In the doorway, Odie, Manny, and Pillar stood watching the whole thing with amused looks on their faces.

Cash attempted to intervene, but Zac brushed him off. However, it was Mari who finally succeeded in reaching out to him.

"Please, stop!" she begged, placing a calm hand on his shoulder.

Zac stepped back from Shane, his breath coming out in heavy gasps, creating enough space for Cat to rush over to the older man.

"What the hell is going on?" demanded River.

"He attacked Teague," said Zac.

Shane stood up, catching everyone's attention. He wiped the blood from the corner of his mouth and ran his fingers through his hair. "He came at me," he explained. "I was just trying to prevent him from doing something he'd regret."

With questioning eyes, the entire room turned to stare at Teague. "He has a picture of Finn in his desk. He knows who we are. He's known this whole time."

River let out a gasp and stepped closer to Teague, standing beside him.

"Explain!" boomed Cash.

Zac readied himself for another fight.

"Please," said Mari, softly. "Hear him out."

Chapter Twenty-Nine

Shane made his way toward the bar and scooped up a handful of ice from the bin, dropping it onto a towel. He then slumped down onto a chair and applied the ice to his lip. "I have an explanation," he said. "But before we begin, I suggest you all take a seat." He gave a stern look toward Teague. "And don't come at me again. If you do, I'll have to knock your ass out and deal with it later." He then turned his gaze toward Zac. "And you! Don't make me do something I'll regret."

"I'm not sitting down to have a nice chat!" shouted Teague. He turned to Cash. "He's got him! He ain't dead!" Tears pooled up in his eyes.

"Who?" asked Cash. "What are you talking about?"

"Daniel," stated Shane. "Daniel's got Finn."

The silence in the room was deafening.

"That's impossible!" shouted Zac. "He's dead!"

Teague shook his head. "He ain't."

"So, why are y'all fighting?" asked River. She turned to Shane. "And how the hell do you know who Daniel is?" She glanced around the room. "Who the hell are you people, anyway?"

"I'm Finn's goddamn father!" Shane's voice boomed around the room, reverberating off the walls. He reached up to his eyes and plucked out the brown contact lenses, revealing one blue eye and one amber brown. He locked eyes with Teague.

Once more, the room lapsed into silence as Teague stumbled forward, his gaze unwavering.

Shane turned to Manny. "In the office," he said. The van is on the monitor, get the plate number and get a search going."

"On it," replied Manny.

"One more thing," bellowed Shane. "You let everyone know that they're to leave that son of a bitch for me." He stared. "He's mine."

With a quick nod of understanding, Manny disappeared into the office.

Shane shifted his attention toward the kids surrounding him. He pushed out a chair with his foot and signaled for Teague to sit down. "Take a seat," he said. However, the boy remained motionless. "I'm not asking, Son," he warned.

River came up behind Teague and placed her hand on his shoulder, then gently guided him to take a seat.

Shane waited for everyone to get situated, then he spoke, "You know, I thought he was dead for so many years." He fumbled with his lighter, trying to light a cigarette. The sound of the lighter's sparks echoed in the room. Finally, he got it lit and took a long drag, exhaling a cloud of smoke that swirled around his head. "I found out less than a year ago that it was all a lie." He paused and took a deep breath. "A lie created by a sick woman and an evil old man."

Shane's voice trembled as he spoke, "When he and his mother died, a big part of me died with them." He looked up at Teague, eyes filled with tears. "You have no idea what sort of pain it is to bury the person you love alongside your own child."

"But you didn't bury him," argued Teague.

"I understand that now," Shane responded, while taking another puff from his cigarette. "But I had no idea back then."

River pulled a chair up to sit alongside Teague, while Cash and Zac, along with Mari, sat nearby.

"The day Melody told me she was pregnant was the most terrifying and amazing day of my life," explained Shane. "We were kids. I had no idea what to do but she—" He swallowed and struggled to hold back the tears that threatened to spring forward. "She had it all planned." His lips curled into a mournful smile. "All the way down to the names of the small army of kids we were gonna have."

"She used to sing to her belly. She was so in love with him. I was home on leave for a few days when it finally hit home." He took a drag from the cigarette and exhaled. "She had me touch her belly. He wriggled and moved around. I swear, he reached out and touched my hand." Shane stared at his hand. "I can still feel it to this day. It's like a physical memory burned into my flesh."

"Why didn't you say something?" asked Teague.

"How? Say what?" asked Shane. "How do you suppose that would have gone down?"

"Besides," he continued. "I ain't ashamed to admit, I was more than a little nervous and scared. I didn't know that he knew about me. I was operating under the impression that he believed that asshole was his father."

Teague nodded.

"By the time I figured out he knew about me, all y'all's phones went off."

Manny walked out of the office with Pillar and Odie in tow. "Sherriff pulled up the traffic cams. The van was spotted on the old highway, heading west, out of town." He stopped long enough to take a drag from Shane's cigarette. "We're heading that way now."

"We're coming with you!" shouted River.

"We all are," added Shane. He stood up and approached Teague with an extended hand. "I'm sorry it had to happen like this, Son," he said. "I hope you can forgive me and we can move forward from here."

Teague looked down at Shane's hand and then shot him a hateful glare.

Shane opted to view it in a positive light; at the very least, the kid didn't try to attack him again.

"Um, excuse me, Sir?" Zac stepped closer and cleared his throat. Shuffling his feet like a guilty child, he uttered, "I want to apologize for beating you up, Sir."

"Let's get one thing straight, kid," replied Shane. "You did not beat me up, I wasn't fighting back." He stared directly into Zac's eyes. "And if you ever raise a fist to me again, I will not show the same restraint. Are we clear?"

Zac nodded sheepishly.

Shane stalked over to the door. On his way past Manny, he leaned close and asked, "Why the hell didn't you intervene?"

"You had it under control, Boss." He flashed a toothy grin. "Besides, it's been a hot minute since I've seen you get your ass beat. Seeing it happen at the hands of a kid." He kissed his fingertips. "It was just too good."

Pillar cleared his throat and extended his hand. With a deep sigh, Manny retrieved a twenty-dollar bill from his pocket then handed it over.

"What's this?" asked Shane.

"We made a wager about how long it would take before you snapped and defended yourself."

"I won," said Pillar, with a wink. "I had faith in you. I knew you would hold back."

"I gotta say, brother," said Manny. "I am truly impressed with your ability to control that temper of yours. I've known you for decades and I've never seen you hold back like that." He shook his head. "I was sure you were gonna blow." He clapped a firm hand on Shane's shoulder and walked out into the parking lot.

Chapter Thirty

For a moment, Finn felt weightless as his body floated in the air. Suddenly, he was slammed hard against a cold, unforgiving metal surface. The impact caused his head to ache, and waves of nausea overtook him, in perfect tune with the throbbing pain in his brain. He could smell blood as he reached up to wipe it away from his brow, feeling the sticky warmth on his fingers. Slowly, he pulled himself up onto his hands and knees, his body feeling weak and disoriented. As he looked around, he couldn't make sense of his surroundings. The surface beneath him was unfamiliar, and he had no idea where he was.

He blinked his eyes, adjusting his vision. Scanning his surroundings, Finn noticed something that appeared to be a rear tire well. He lowered his gaze and ran his hands over the rough surface, realizing, with a jolt that, he was touching the roof of the vehicle. The air inside the van was stuffy and stale, and the overwhelming scent of gasoline lingered in his nostrils. He couldn't see outside because there were no windows, so there was no way to tell where he was. With a sinking feeling, he understood that he was trapped inside an overturned van, and his heart raced with fear.

In a desperate attempt to shake off the cobwebs from his brain, he shook his head, but the excruciating pain that instantly followed made him regret it. The sharp pain felt like a million needles piercing through his skull; he winced, unable to bear it. A wave of nausea washed over him, causing his insides to churn. Unable to control it any longer, he leaned forward and emptied every bit of food from his belly, feeling the hot, burning acid in his throat.

Something was happening in the front of the van. He strained his eyes in the darkness, trying to make out the shapes and movements. A loud thud bounced off the metal walls, followed by the sickening sound of flesh meeting flesh. As his eyes adjusted to the dim light, he saw a massive figure looming over the passenger seat. The figure shifted, and a sliver of moonlight pierced through the shattered windshield, illuminating the face of Daniel!

Finn's blood turned to ice in his veins as the memory flooded back. The dimly lit parking lot, the chilling voice, and the excruciating pain in his head all came rushing back in a torrent. Another wave of nausea hit him like a ton of bricks. The taste of bile rose in his mouth, this time, he didn't try to fight it. He doubled over and retched, his stomach heaving as he purged whatever remained in his gut.

The soft whimper that reached his ears served as a reminder of why he was in the parking lot.

Beth!

Straining with every last drop of strength within him, Finn dragged himself upright. The sound of his labored breathing and the pounding of his heart filled his ears. The stench of gasoline and burned rubber lingered in his nostrils, a reminder of the crash that brought him here. A sharp, throbbing ache shot through his left leg, a familiar pain that hinted at a possible fracture. Wincing in agony, he flexed his fingers, grateful that his hands were uninjured, he was gonna need them.

The cargo tie-down anchors in work vans were always exposed. In the dark, he searched above his head until he located them. Grabbing hold of the loops with his fingers, Finn lifted his lower body and swung forward. His feet collided with Daniel, who was caught off guard and propelled him through the shattered windshield, onto the ground outside.

Finn hobbled over to Beth and checked for a pulse. She let out a soft moan as her eyes slowly opened. "C'mon," he encouraged. "Wake up." As she stared up at him, he supported her body with one hand and released her seatbelt with the other. Once she was free, she regained her composure quickly, glancing around in terror.

Finn raised a finger to his lips. He leaned close so she could hear. "Run," he said. "Get out of here now!"

Outside, Daniel was climbing to his feet.

Finn took a deep breath, feeling his heart race as he steeled himself for what was to come, then he launched out of the van.

Fortunately, the accident had also harmed Daniel, giving Finn a level playing field. The older man was moving slower than usual and nursing his left arm. Finn took notice of this and aimed for the injured area. He swung at Daniel's head, anticipating a dodge, which happened as expected. Finn then seized the wounded arm and pulled with all his might. The tendons snapped under the pressure, and Daniel screamed out in agony.

There was little time to celebrate. His victory was soon cut short.

With his good hand, Daniel reached out and grabbed a handful of hair, then slammed his forehead into the center of Finn's face.

Stars erupted in his vision, Finn staggered back, forgetting for a brief moment about his injured leg, only to be reminded by stabbing pain. He shifted his weight, feeling the rough ground beneath his feet. He could hear the sound of his own breaths, heavy and ragged.

Daniel crashed into him, knocking them both to the ground.

Finn's lungs gasped for air as his body hit the ground with a loud thud. The impact reverberated through his bones and made his head spin. A fist connected with his jaw. The metallic taste of blood rushed into his mouth. Daniel wrapped his large hand around his throat, squeezing with an iron grip. Finn's eyes bulged as he tried to breathe, but the pressure was suffocating him. He clawed at the dirt beneath him, searching for a weapon to defend himself. Blackness danced at the edge of his vision as he felt consciousness slipping away. Suddenly, a surge of adrenaline rushed through his body. He reached up, his fingers clawing at Daniel's face. He felt the squish of his thumb sinking into a wet eye socket. The older man howled in agony. The sound echoed in Finn's ears, and he felt a wave of satisfaction wash over him. He watched as Daniel stumbled backward, his eyeball bouncing freakishly against his blood-stained cheek.

Finn needed a weapon. Searching the ground around him, the only things he could find were small stones that were of no use. He needed something more substantial. The tire iron. He hobbled around the van, smiling with relief when he saw one of the rear doors was open, hoping that meant that Beth got away. He glanced behind him, but there was no sign of Daniel. Fear gripped his stomach, and he quickened his pace, determined to end this once and for all.

He turned the corner and immediately felt a sharp impact in his stomach. The force of the blow knocked the wind out of him, his hand clutched his gut. Gasping for air, Finn looked up at Daniel's face, his one eye staring back at him with a cold, calculating gaze.

Finn's mind reeled, struggling to make sense of what was happening as he stared at the horrifying mask of blood and gore in front of him.

His eyes were drawn down to Daniel's hand wrapped around the hilt of a hunting knife, which was buried deep in his abdomen. The pain was excruciating, a searing heat that spread throughout his entire body, making him gasp for air. He could hear the sound of his own breathing, ragged and uneven, as he struggled to stay conscious. The world around him seemed to blur as he fought to stay alive. With a desperate burst of energy, Finn reached out and grabbed Daniel's arm, his grip tightening as he struggled to hold on to the fraying threads of life.

"There was a time," whispered Daniel, his voice shaking, "when I could never imagine doing something like this to you." A tear slid down his cheek. "But you chose her," Daniel hissed through gritted teeth. He turned the blade of the knife. His face went cold as he stared into Finn's eyes and slid the blade. The metallic tang of blood filled Finn's nostrils as the knife sliced through his skin. "You chose this."

Blood oozed down Finn's legs, warm and sticky, as he clutched his abdomen with a desperate grip. He could hear his heart pounding in his ears. His knees buckled; weakness washed over him.

The sound of metal striking metal reverberated loudly. Daniel jerked to the side and fell over, pulling the blade of the knife with him.

Finn was completely bewildered, his mind racing as he collapsed to the ground. His only thoughts were to hold his body together.

Chapter Thirty-One

Beth fought to come to her senses, feeling disoriented as she tried to open her heavy eyelids. When she finally managed to open them, she found herself face to face with Finn hovering over her.

"Run!" he commanded. "Get out of here now!" Then he unclipped her seatbelt while holding her up so that she didn't fall on top of her head. A moment later he was gone.

She tried to speak, but as she moved her mouth, she felt a sharp, stab of pain in her jaw. She reached up to her face and winced at the touch, feeling the throbbing pain shooting through her cheekbone. Her right arm, still cuffed to the handhold, had gone numb. The death-like chill in her fingers was suddenly apparent, sending a deep shiver throughout her body.

Outside, in the glow of the bright headlights, Finn was fighting for his life.

She had to get free! In a fit of panic, Beth pulled and tugged at the cold, unyielding metal handcuffs that bound her wrist, each attempt sending searing pain through her arm. The keys! Her eyes darted over to the ignition; a glimmer of hope flickered to life within her when she saw the keys dangling tantalizingly close.

Beth stretched her arm as far as possible, but it fell short. No matter how she tried, the most she could do was barely brush her fingertips across the keys.

She quickly glanced out of the window and saw the terrifying sight of Daniel on top of Finn pummeling him with his fists. If she didn't do something, he was going to kill Finn. Her feet! Beth quickly untied one of her boots and then, using her bare toes, she pulled the keys from the ignition, only to drop them to the floor.

A fit of despair threatened to overwhelm her. Cursing under her breath, she ordered herself to stop it and keep it together. For once in your life, don't be Beth, she commanded.

Daniel howled. She turned to look just in time to catch him spring back, his eye dangling uselessly from its socket, bouncing against his cheek. Dark, red blood gushed forth from the black hole where his eye used to be. He raised a trembling hand to his face in a futile attempt to hold the eyeball.

Beth couldn't look away. The gory spectacle was unlike anything she had witnessed before outside of horror movies.

Movement in the corner of her eye caught her attention. She glanced down and saw Finn scurry backward on the ground.

Beth shook her head and redirected her attention to the keys. She took three deep breaths and exhaled before using her toes to grasp the keys and bring them within reach of her hand. Once she had them, she let out a sigh of relief and sifted through them to locate the one she needed. In the dim light, she held the small key and allowed herself a momentary smile before promptly unlocking the handcuffs. Her arm felt lifeless and cold, as though it belonged to a corpse. Gradually, blood flowed back into it, causing unbearable agony as her limb regained sensation.

There was no time to waste! Beth quickly made her way to the back of the van and pulled down the spare tire compartment, causing the metal jack and crowbar to come crashing down onto her head before clanging loudly onto the metal floor. Rubbing her head, she cursed herself for not considering this earlier, all the while groping around in the dark to find the crowbar. Once she had a firm grip on it, she pushed open the rear door and jumped out of the van, ready to use the weapon. She ran around to the front of the van, jumping out into the glow of the headlights. Neither Finn nor Daniel was there. She scanned the area carefully, listening closely to the sound of shuffling on the rocky ground.

Tiptoeing around the van, her heart raced as she strained her eyes in the darkness, trying to make out the two shadows. Beth could hear her own breaths coming in short, sharp gasps, and the sound of her blood rushing through her skull was almost deafening. Crouching low, she crept closer as she waited with a tense and watchful eye, knowing that sooner or later one of the shadows would move in a way that would tell her who was who.

The shadows collided. In the darkness, she could see the glint of a steel blade, followed by a strange sound she was unable to identify.

Daniel's voice spoke softly.

Beth crept forward cautiously, her heart pounding in her chest like a drum. She placed one foot in front of the other, taking care to be as silent as possible.

Close enough to hear his breathing, Beth tightened her grip on the crowbar as she prepared to strike. The metal bar swung through the air and connected with the side of Daniel's head with a sickening thud. The impact was so forceful; the crowbar continued to swing, hitting the side of the van with a sharp clang. Beth felt a rush of adrenaline as she watched Daniel crumple to the ground, his body twitching uncontrollably.

There was no way this bastard was getting a second chance. She lifted the iron rod and struck his skull repeatedly, each blow giving her more energy to hit harder. Blood splattered everywhere, covering her face, arms, and the side of the van. The warm, sticky wetness coated her hands and made it difficult to keep a firm grip on the rod.

Daniel lay motionless on the ground, but Beth didn't care. This time, he wouldn't survive. The nightmare was ending now. Tears streamed down her face, mixing with drops of blood as she relentlessly pounded away. She struck so many times that her hands and forearms went numb.

"Beth!" shouted Finn.

The sudden sound of his voice caught her off guard; she had completely forgotten about him. She halted mid swing and spun around to find him on his knees. He flashed a smile at her and remarked, "I don't think he's getting up." He chuckled softly and then crumpled to the ground.

Beth stared down at the lifeless body lying at her feet, noticing that where the head should be, there was only brain tissue and gore. A crazed giggle erupted from her chest, surprising even herself. She lifted her hand to wipe the blood spatter from her face, but instead, she smeared more of the sticky liquid from her hands all over her cheek.

On the ground, Finn stared down at the growing pool of blood.

The crowbar thudded to the ground as she fell to her knees beside him. In an attempt to see how bad his injury was, she tried to push his hand aside, only to have him take hold of her hand and shake his head.

"Don't," he said.

The pool of deep, crimson blood grew beneath his prone body. They needed to call for help. Beth raised her hand to her ear, making the sign of a phone, hoping he had one they could use to call someone.

Finn chuckled softly. "You know me better than that," he said. "When was the last time you knew me to have a working phone on me?"

Beth sighed in exasperation and gave a disapproving shake of her head, then remembered her phone. The last time she saw the device, it was in Daniel's possession. She dug her hand deep into the pocket of the corpse and pulled it free. There was no way she could make the call, so she unlocked the screen, found Zac's contact, hit speakerphone, and held the device close to Finn's face. Less than a full ring later, Zac's worried voice boomed through the speaker.

"Beth!" shouted Zac. "Where are you?"

Finn inhaled. His breathing was slow and shallow. "It's me," he croaked.

"Tell us where you are," said Zac.

"Fuck if I know," Finn replied weakly, followed by a pathetic chuckle. A thin rivulet of blood trickled from the corner of his mouth. He licked his lips, then continued, "Beth can't speak. I think her jaw's broken. Imma have her send you a screenshot."

Beth opened the map app, then zoomed in on their location and took a screenshot. She took a second, a little farther out, then quickly sent them via text chat.

Zac's voice came over the speaker. "Got it!" he said. "We're on our way. Hang in there."

"You might wanna hurry," said Finn.

Teague's panicked voice came through the speaker, "Finn, how bad is it?"

He licked his lips, coating them with fresh blood instead of saliva. "It's bad."

Beth got up and ran into the van, grabbing a bottle of water, then returned and lifted Finn's head on her lap so he could take a sip.

"Talk to me," said Teague, over the phone, his voice mirroring the panic that Beth was feeling.

A man in the background bellowed, "Five minutes! Just hang in there!"

"Stay on the line," said Teague.

Finn swallowed. "I am," he replied weakly.

The phone went black. The battery was drained. Their contact with the others was severed.

"Looks like I rubbed off on you," said Finn, attempting humor.

Beth shook her head in mock disgust.

Finn's breaths became weaker with each passing moment. His eyelids slowly drooped as his head lay heavily on her lap. The pool of liquid beneath him continued to expand, now encompassing a larger area than his entire body. Beth knew he couldn't hold on for much longer.

Saying a silent prayer, she wiped the bloody hair from his face and held his free hand as she waited for help to arrive.

Chapter Thirty-Two

Try as he might, Teague wasn't able to shake his apprehension toward Shane. There were far too many unanswered questions for his liking. Finn had already gone through too much with family, he didn't need any more deceit.

Still, there was something genuine about the man and the people he surrounded himself with. They seemed to care deeply for Finn.

When he first heard Finn's voice over the phone, he allowed himself to feel hopeful. But the longer he stayed on the line, he could hear Finn growing weaker. His breathing was labored. When the phone went dead, Teague wanted to scream and throw the device. Why do people have these damn things if they never seem to have them properly charged?

The tension inside the cramped cab of the truck was suffocating. The wind whipped through the open windows, filling the space with the smell of dust and sweat. Teague gazed out at the endless expanse of sand and rock. The roar of the wind, combined with the rattling of the engine made it hard to think straight.

In the front seat, Manny navigated, his voice calm and unwavering. This was a sharp contrast to Shane who seemed determined to hit every pothole on the road. Teague couldn't help but wonder if it was a good idea to let the man drive.

"Right here," shouted Manny, pointing.

Before the truck came to a full stop, Teague leaped out of the vehicle with such desperation that he stumbled upon hitting the rocky ground and skittered a few feet before regaining his balance. The smell of gasoline permeated the air. He ran past the front of the van, with its broken-out windshield, crunching on the scattered glass shards all over the ground. He circled around to the back of the vehicle where he found them, a sense of relief washed over him, then quickly dissipated.

Beth was seated, her back against the vehicle, with Finn lying motionless on her lap.

Teague skidded to his knees. "Finn!" he shouted.

A flurry of activity erupted around him as the others arrived.

"How are you doing, Darling?" Shane asked Beth.

She wept uncontrollably while shaking her head.

"Jesus!" exclaimed Manny, staring down at the mangled corpse on the ground. He made the sign of the cross. "One of you took old boy out," he said.

Finn's eyes fluttered open, and he scanned his surroundings until he spotted Teague.

"Let me see, Son," said Shane, trying to lift Finn's hand. Blood gushed from the wound. Even in the darkness, it was obvious this was a mortal wound.

Shane locked eyes with Teague. "We gotta get him to Doc's," he said.

"The hospital," argued Teague. "We need to get him to a hospital."

Shane shook his head. "Son, I need you to listen to me. The nearest hospital is fifty minutes from here. Our friend Doc, on the other hand, has a clinic that's about thirty minutes that way." He pointed. "You can do the math."

The older man didn't wait for an answer or approval. "Pillar!" he barked. "Get over here and help me lift him."

Teague stepped back and watched.

"Alright," said Shane. "On the count of three." He began counting. At three they lifted Finn who immediately let out a deafening scream of pain, causing a spray of crimson spittle to fly out of his mouth. A waterfall of thick blood cascaded off of him, splattering all over the ground.

"Teague!" bellowed Shane. "Get in the truck and buckle up. We're gonna hand him to you."

As instructed, he sprinted forward and climbed inside the vehicle. Shortly after, Finn was placed inside with his head laying on Teague's lap. Shane then secured him with the seatbelt.

The older man leaned into the door, his face dead serious. "Listen to me, Son," he said. You keep pressure on that wound. Do not let up." He stared at Teague. "Think you can do that?"

Teague nodded.

"Good boy," he said. He slammed the door closed, then climbed inside behind the steering wheel. "This is gonna be a bumpy ride," he said, over his shoulder, then he too buckled up.

Amid the hum of voices outside, Finn's labored breaths filled the small space inside the truck. The metallic scent of blood hung heavily in the air. As he applied pressure to the wound, he could feel the warm stickiness of blood seeping through his fingers. Looking around, he noticed that the backseat was already covered, a gruesome sight that made his stomach churn. Despite everything, Finn was still hanging on, as was evidenced by his ragged breathing and his death-like grip on his belly.

Cash settled into the passenger's seat and glanced over his shoulder as he fastened his seatbelt. "How's he doing?" he asked.

"I don't know," replied Teague, fighting against the tears he could feel clawing their way to the surface.

Cash nodded. "He's ornery," he said. "If he's breathing, he's doing okay."

"Alright," said Shane. "Everyone hang on." He glanced over his shoulder at Teague. "I meant it when I said this is gonna be a rocky ride," he warned. "Keep that pressure on." He gave a final nod, then threw the truck into gear. A moment later, they were barreling down the dark highway.

Shane wasn't lying; the ride was anything but smooth. The vehicle jolted at every turn; combined with the uneven terrain, Teague felt as though he was riding a rollercoaster. Each time they hit a pothole, the rattling of the truck was deafening, and it felt like they were going to be tossed out of their seats. Thankfully, the seatbelts held them in place, providing some measure of security.

As warm liquid coated the side of his leg, Teague couldn't help but wonder how much blood a man could lose and still survive.

Finn's body tensed, his head pressed hard against Teague's thigh. Why was life so cruel? He kept the pressure on the wound while gently talking to Finn. "Shh, shh," he whispered. "It's okay."

Teague was getting impatient as the drive seemed to be taking an eternity. He looked out of the window, hoping to catch a glimpse of the clinic, but all he could see was the barren desert landscape. The thought of being lost crossed his mind. What if they didn't make it in time? Teague couldn't even fathom the idea of losing Finn.

Tears flowed down his face while he sat in the darkness, overwhelmed with a sense of powerlessness.

As the truck screeched to a halt, the bright glow of the clinic lights flooded the inside of the truck. At that moment, Teague could see the full extent of the damage. Sticky blood covered everything, including himself.

The door swung open, and a familiar face appeared. Doc. The same man who stitched his face and saved Cash's life stared back at him.

He flashed a gentle smile. "We got him," he said to Teague, with a nod.

Shane and Doc carefully lifted Finn and transferred him onto a gurney. Surprisingly, Finn didn't scream this time. Instead, he looked frighteningly pale in the bright glow of the lights.

Teague followed close as they entered the clinic.

"I don't have enough blood for this," said Doc. "That's gonna be a problem with his wounds."

"You got plenty," replied Shane. He held out his arms. "You can take every drop of mine."

"We have to do tests," argued Doc. "To see if you're a match."

"He's my son!" shouted Shane. "We're the same blood type." He pinched his eyes. "Just save his life," he said with a trembling voice. "You can drain me dry if you need to."

"Okay," replied Doc. "One of us will be back to get you in a moment. Right now, we have to get him stabilized." Without another word, the short man turned on his heels and disappeared behind a set of metal, swinging doors.

Teague stood in the hallway, the buzzing sound of electricity emanating from the ceiling lights, filling his ears with white noise. He leaned his back against the cool wall. As he slid down to the hard floor, he could feel the coldness seeping through his clothes, sending shivers down his spine. With his arms resting heavily on his knees, he tried to calm his racing heart, but the memory of Finn's blood all over him was too much to bear. He ran his fingers through his hair, feeling the sticky residue on his fingertips. Unable to hold back any longer, he broke down into uncontrollable sobs, the weight of the situation finally crashing down on him.

With a blast of dry desert air, the doors to the clinic whooshed open as River rushed in with Mari. Zac followed closely behind, carrying Beth.

As soon as she saw him, River ran over and wrapped her arms around him. "How is he?" she asked.

Teague shook his head, he didn't have the ability to answer.

"They just took him back," explained Cash. "We ain't gonna know for a while."

A woman wearing scrubs materialized and assessed Beth's condition. Following a short conversation, she provided an ice pack to the girl and instructed her to take a seat. She then administered a pain-relieving injection to ease Beth's discomfort.

Roughly ten minutes later, a different nurse emerged, fully attired in surgical clothing. She lowered her mask and gestured for Shane to accompany her.

Chapter Thirty-Three

Rolling up on the wreckage, Shane's heart sank deep into his belly. The fact that there was no sign of any survivors made things far worse. He threw the truck into park and ran around the vehicle.

As soon as he noticed the kids lying on the ground, he felt a brief moment of relief. However, it was quickly replaced by an intense feeling of apprehension. Finn appeared lifeless, not making any movements. He was lying there, looking pale and death-like, with a pool of blood surrounding him that was almost the same size as his own body.

Shane fell to his knees, the sound of his own heartbeat pounding in his ears. He lifted Finn's hand to get a look at the wound. What he saw sent a shiver down his spine. The wound was gaping, a deep slash in Finn's belly—the boy was literally holding himself together. Shane had seen injuries this severe before, and he knew that time was everything.

Teague didn't seem to fully comprehend the severity of the situation, in a way that was good, because if Shane was going to save Finn's life, he needed all the help he could get. Luckily, his guys knew the protocol. Manny immediately called Doc, while Pillar and Odie assessed the situation with Daniel, or the other body they believed was Daniel, there was no real way to identify him. The head was completely crushed and mangled. Shane wondered which of the kids had done such damage? Whoever it was, he admired their thoroughness.

A slight feeling of resentment crept into his being—Shane wanted to be the one who stared into the bastard's eyes as he took his last breath. He stared down at Finn, barely able to believe he was able to fight back in his condition. The boy had more balls than most men Shane had known.

The drive to the clinic was pure hell. The father in him wanted to collapse into a miserable heap and wail. He wanted to hold his son and comfort him and cry. But there was no time for that. His boy was in the back seat on the brink of death. He needed to be strong and keep his wits about him. Now was not the time to collapse in despair.

As he barreled down the highway, he willed himself to keep it together, all the while ticking off the miles with each marker.

Shane held himself together all the way until the moment Finn disappeared behind the doors. At that moment, the weight of the situation crashed down on him like a tsunami, crushing his heart and soul. He looked down at his hands; they were covered in blood.

Teague fell to the floor in a near catatonic state, leaving a trail of red on the white wall of the clinic as he slid down.

Breathing was difficult. Shane's heart hurt with a deep pain he knew all too well. He walked outside for some cool, night air. At least, that was what he told himself. The doors to his truck were still wide open. As he peered inside the cab, he saw the horrifying sight in the backseat and his heart shattered into pieces. Collapsing to his knees, he cried out in a mix of rage and agony.

A soft hand touched his shoulder. Catalina whispered, "It's okay, Babe."

The dam burst, releasing a flood of tears from his very soul. Years of guilt, remorse, and heartache surged forward, overwhelming him. He crumpled against her soft body, weeping uncontrollably.

Upon his return to the clinic, he found everyone present. A nurse was attending to the young girl, Beth, while River sat beside her, offering her assistance in any way possible. Shane had some questions that only Beth could answer, but it seemed that she wouldn't be able to speak anytime soon.

Manny had sent a message to inform him that they were almost done with the cleanup. Their plan was to take the body out to the desert, dismember it, and scatter the pieces along the coyote trails in the region. The aim was to ensure that by morning, there would be barely anything left of the bastard.

The atmosphere in the clinic was grave. Teague remained silent on the floor, staring into space, lost in heartache and worry. Shane could relate. He struggled against doing the same thing.

Cash sat calmly next to Teague, with Zac and Mari sitting close by.

A nurse came out and signaled for Shane to follow her. It was about time. He was ready to do his part. She escorted him to the back where they had him take a seat, then hooked up the needles. The nurse tried to smile and relieve some of the tension, but her efforts fell on deaf ears. The only thing that could possibly alleviate some of the tension in the room would be to see Finn sitting up and smiling in his bed. Shane meant it when he told Doc they could take every drop of blood from his body, if his son didn't make it through this, he wouldn't have much use for it any longer. He didn't have it in himself to live through losing the kid again.

He wasn't sure how much blood was taken from him, but by the time they were done, he was weak. So weak, in fact, he could only stand up with help. The nurse handed Shane a glass of orange juice. "You need to rest," she admonished. "You also need to eat something hearty. We might need more blood in a little while." She made sure he understood her orders, then she guided him to a bed where he promptly fell into a deep, nightmare-fueled sleep.

Chapter Thirty-Four

River moved a sweaty lock of hair from Beth's face. Her heart broke seeing the poor girl in this condition. No part of this was supposed to turn out this way; it was supposed to be a happy reunion. She took note of Beth's injuries—all the bruises and the broken jaw. The poor girl had suffered greatly, she was so fragile looking.

"Girl," said River, jokingly. "I see you're still the drama queen you always were."

Beth let out a chuckle, but quickly followed it with a painful moan.

"I'm sorry, baby girl," said River. She locked eyes with Beth. "Can I get you anything?"

Beth shook her head. From the look in her eyes, the pain meds were kicking in.

River wrapped her arms around the younger girl, coaxing her to lean against her for support. Stroking Beth's hair, she whispered, "I'm so sorry all this happened to you, baby girl." Fighting back tears, she inhaled. "If I could take it all back I would."

The sound of Beth's sobs were enough to trigger River's own

breakdown. She kissed the top of Beth's head and cried until she had no more tears left. Across the hall, Teague sat in a catatonic state staring at nothing, lost in his head. She had seen him like this before. In fact, it wasn't all that long ago when he sat in this very clinic in the same state of mind.

Next to him, Cash appeared lost in his own thoughts. He glanced up at River with a halfhearted smile but then resumed staring at the ground.

Zac hovered nearby, Mari staying close, offering comfort when needed. At least he had someone to hold on to.

To be honest, River was a bit hesitant when she initially met Mari. Learning about her association with Shane and Finn didn't ease her worries either. She was unsure if she should like or dislike the girl. Nonetheless, discovering that Mari was related to Finn helped River understand her actions. Mari treated Finn like a younger brother, and it all made sense.

In just a few hours, so much had occurred that it was difficult for River to wrap her brain around. The only certainty she had was that some of her family members had been hurt, and one of them might not survive. She could deal with everything else later.

Finn. She wondered how he was doing. It had to be good that she hadn't seen hide nor hair of the doctor or his staff since the lady came to get Shane. She told herself it was good. After all, if Finn hadn't made it, they would have known by now. Exactly how long has it been now? It felt like hours.

Beth sat up and brushed her hair aside. She looked almost unrecognizable with her face swollen and purple, poor thing.

"Do you need anything?" asked River.

Beth shook her head and pointed.

As River shifted her gaze, she caught sight of the doctor strolling toward the double swinging doors. The rest of the group also took notice of him and climbed to their feet, but Teague remained seated.

Doc pressed the button, causing the doors to swing open. His scrubs were stained with a dark shade of red. He let out a deep sigh and made his way toward Teague.

River didn't have to coax Beth into joining the conversation, she was already on her feet, making her way over.

Doc crouched down to be face to face with Teague. "I'm not gonna lie to you," he said. "I did what I could. It's up to him from here on."

"What does that mean?" asked Cash.

"It means," explained Doc. "That his body is stitched up. We damn near drained Shane to give it all to Finn. Right now, everything is working the way it's supposed to. Whether he heals or survives, the trauma is another thing." He paused, taking the time to make eye contact with everyone. "He's unconscious, and he's gonna stay that way for a while," he said. "At least until the drugs wear off, which is gonna be quite some time."

"But after that, he'll be okay, right?" asked Zac.

Doc sighed and shook his head. "I just don't have an answer for that," he replied. "Like I told Shane, we'll just have to wait and see." He stepped back and signaled for one of his nurses. "Rose is going to take you back to him." He turned his attention to Beth. "It's your turn, young lady," he said. "Let's get you taken care of."

The nurse led them down a narrow corridor. River remembered this place from the last time they were there, back when it was Cash who was in mortal danger. The scent of bleach hung heavy in the air as the cold light splashed onto the white walls and floor. A faint beeping sound bounced off the sterile walls.

River let out an audible gasp as she walked into the room. Finn was lying in the bed, looking clean but alarmingly pale. He had an oxygen mask over his mouth and nose. A monitor beside him beeped and flashed, keeping track of his pulse and heartbeat. River's heart sank as she took it all in. She tried to reassure herself that it was just the lighting that made Finn look so close to death.

Teague took a seat next to the bed and picked up Finn's hand in his. With tears streaming down his cheeks, he rested his lips on Finn's hand and whispered something, then he put his head down, hiding his face.

They sat there silently, listening to the soothing sound of the monitors.

River needed to do something with herself. If she had to sit in that room listening to the steady beep, waiting for who knows what, she would lose her damn mind. Beth. Beth needed someone with her.

She wandered out into the hallway where she found a nurse. "Excuse me," she said. "Where'd they take Beth?"

The woman smiled and pointed. "Back that way, turn left and down the hall."

Confident that the others would get her if necessary, River left them to wait while she set her focus on the one family member she knew she could comfort. Following the nurse's directions, she made her way to a small room where Beth sat alone. As soon as she saw River, her eyes lit up. She reached her arm out and River took hold of her hand immediately, then sat down beside Beth and waited for Doc to read the x-ray.

Chapter Thirty-Five

Cash was seated next to the bed, his gaze fixed on the figure lying before him—the lifeless husk of one of his best friends. The incessant beeping of the monitor, which had irritated the hell out of him at first, had now faded into the background, drowned out by the persistent hum of the oxygen machine.

Was he still in there? How would they even know if they were merely keeping a lifeless body alive? If that were so, would Finn even want this?

He looked over at Teague who hadn't lifted his head or even moved since entering the room. It was clear he was not doing okay. If Finn didn't make it, how was Teague going to handle it? Come to think of it; How the hell was he going to handle it? Or any of the others for that matter?

Zac was sitting on the chilly tile floor at the opposite end of the room, lost in thought, with a look on his face that conveyed the same emotions as Cash. Mari was seated next to him, even though she didn't have a reason to be there since she didn't know Finn that well. However, she was there, sharing the same sorrow as everyone else. It was admirable that she was true to her word when she said that Finn was family to her.

Family. Jesus. What a roller coaster. They came to El Paso to get a peek at Finn's bio dad, and they ended up hanging out in his bar and having drinks with the man. Without even knowing it, they ended up meeting Finn's entire family. If Cash didn't believe in the Fates before, he would be a full convert now.

Thinking of family, the rest of their misfit clan would want to know what was going on. He pulled his phone from his pocket and carefully crafted a post, giving the pertinent details.

Cash: OK, all, I have some bad news to post. I don't know where to start, so, I'm just gonna give the big details. I'll fill in anything I can when you ask. So here goes.

We're at Stoney's doctor's clinic outside of Las Cruces. Turns out Finn's bio dad knows him too. Small world.

We found Beth, she's currently being looked at by the doctor. River's with her. I'll let you know about that when I get an update.

From what I have gathered, Daniel was the reason for Beth's disappearance. He used her to get to Finn. It worked. We're not really sure what happened, because Beth was beat up pretty bad, I think her jaw is broken. Like I said, Doc is stitching her up right now. As for Finn, it's bad. Daniel did a number on him. He's currently hooked up to machines, and unconscious. Doc did what he could, we're all in the clinic with Finn, waiting. We don't have any idea how this is gonna go.

. . .

He hit send and stared down at the screen. Seeing those words written out clearly triggered a torrent of sorrow. Cash pinched the tears from his eyes and breathed. There was so much he wanted to tell everyone, but his mind went blank. He sighed and waited for their responses.

The server came to life immediately. One alert after the other, the messages popped up on his screen. He glanced over at Zac who had pulled out his own phone and was reading along. Teague, however, still hadn't moved.

Cash turned his focus back to the screen and readied himself to answer all the questions.

```
Tripp: WTH? How?
    Porter: Dear Lord.
    Bella: Send us your address.
    Stoney: I got it. Cash, tell the others we're
on our way.
    Gunner: Be honest. How bad is it?
    Ben: Jesus!
    Spinner: How's everyone else?
    Mara: Is Beth gonna be okay?
    Max: What the hell happened?
    D. B.: Where the hell are you?
    Sam: Yeah, give us the address.
```

Stoney shared an image of the clinic on a map, which included the street address. This led to a surge of posts from people requesting train information from Porter.

. . .

Cash: I don't know the full extent of the damage,
but apparently Daniel gutted Finn. He almost bled
to death.
 Gunner: I thought Daniel was dead.
 Zac: I fucked up. He survived.
 Gunner: Don't take the blame for that son. None
of this is on you.
 River: He's right Zac, you didn't do any of
this.

Cash peered up from the screen. "He's right," he said, aloud to Zac.
"None of this is on you."

Zac wiped his eyes and nodded.

Cash: There's so much to tell you. It's too much
to type.
 Bella: You can fill us in on everything when we
get there. In the meantime, you tell Zac that he
is in no way responsible for any of this. You
tell Finn he is not allowed to give up. And give
Teague a hug. We'll be there soon.

Porter began posting train details for everyone.

Gunner: Stoney's ready to head out. I'm riding
with him along with Spinner and Bella. We'll be
there in a couple of hours.
 Porter: As soon as I get everyone situated,
I'll be heading out as well. Be there as soon as
I can.

· · ·

Everyone chimed in with their estimated times of arrival. Seeing this ragtag family of misfits drop everything to come running for one of their loved ones gave Cash a much-needed boost.

The messages stopped coming in. Once again, they were alone in the sterile room with the artificial sound of the monitors. Teague remained motionless and unresponsive. Throughout the conversation with the others, he never lifted his gaze. He didn't even flinch. Cash wondered if he had fallen asleep. He didn't want to risk waking him up. If Teague was indeed sleeping, it would be a gift right now.

From across the room, a chime from Zac's phone broke the silence. It was most likely a text from Cole, checking in on his brother. While Zac was busy typing away, Cash stood up and stretched. He felt the urge to move around, so he decided to check up on Beth and River—he needed a change of mood.

Cash stepped out into the hall. On a busy day, filled with people, hospitals creeped him out. Standing alone, in one that was empty, was far creepier than he ever imagined. The only good thing about how silent the whole place was, was the fact that it made it easy for him to hear River's soft voice.

His first reaction upon entering the room was to gasp in horror at the state of poor Beth's face. Not wanting to upset her, he kept his reaction hidden.

"How's she doing?" he asked River, as he sidled up alongside her and planted a kiss on her head.

"She's pretty beat up," she replied. "But she'll be okay." She squeezed Beth's hand. "Ain't that right?"

Beth nodded and tried what appeared to be a smile, but all it did was make her bloated and purple face even more monstrous.

"What's the damage?" he asked.

"They just finished wiring her jaw closed," said River. "I was just teasing her, saying that means she can't argue with me anymore. So, she has to do what I tell her to do." She sighed. "Other than that, she got a few butterfly bandages here along with a couple of stitches there, she'll be okay."

"Finally, some good news," said Cash. He grinned. "Beth can't be a smartass."

Beth furrowed her eyebrows and shook her finger at him.

Cash chuckled. The energy in this room was so much lighter than the other one. He didn't want to leave it.

A nurse came in, pushing a bed on wheels in front of her. "Hop on," she said to Beth.

"Just in time," said River. "We're on our way to Finn's room. Beth needs to get some bed rest, so we all figured it would be best if she did that in the same room as everyone else. That way we can keep an eye on her and Finn at the same time."

So much for a reprieve. Cash waited until the nurse got Beth situated, then he pushed the bed down the hall, to Finn's room, setting her bed right alongside his. River was right, at least this way they could all be together.

Chapter Thirty-Six

As Zac sat there, time seemed to drag at an agonizingly slow pace. Each time he stole a glance at the clock, he could have sworn it was either stopped or even ticking backward. The incessant beeping of the machines served only to exacerbate his restlessness. Every now and then, a conversation would spring up, only to be quickly stifled. It was as though everyone was afraid to smile or show even the slightest bit of happiness.

The chill of the tile floor was getting to him. His back muscles grew tighter by the minute, yet he refused to budge, holding onto the hope that Finn would wake up any second now, and he didn't want to miss it. For that reason, he stayed put.

It was good to see Beth, even though it was hardly under the best circumstances, he was glad to see she pulled through. Watching her and River connect again was like watching family reunite. It made his heart happy to witness.

Teague hadn't moved since taking his seat beside Finn. He sat there, looking like an extra in a horror movie, covered in blood that crusted and flaked off, leaving tiny flecks on the white hospital blanket, like crimson, colored salt.

As for Finn, Zac was unable to bring himself to look squarely at him. The few times he tried when they first settled into the room sent him into a tailspin of heartache. As long as he didn't look at Finn, he could believe his brother would awaken soon and everything would be okay. That fleeting hope would be dashed the moment he laid eyes on the pale, lifeless creature splayed out on the bed, hooked up to all those machines.

Next to him, Mari moved closer and placed a gentle hand on his arm. His skin tingled with electricity at her slightest touch. She slid her hand down his arm and intertwined her fingers with his, making his hand seem gigantic in comparison. Leaning her chin on his arm, she looked up at him with her big, beautiful, brown eyes. Eyes he could get lost in.

"Come with me," she whispered.

After a brief internal struggle, he allowed her to tug him to his feet. As they slipped out the door, Zac glanced back to find Cash, smiling at him with that knowing grin of his, giving a quick nod of approval.

The clinic appeared to be deserted, devoid of any human presence. Mari ushered him into a dimly lit, unoccupied room and quietly closed the door.

"We needed a little break," she breathed, as she wrapped her arms around his neck.

Mari's soft lips met his, igniting a fiery sensation that spread throughout his body. He surrendered himself to the moment. Mari was right; they needed this break.

His phone buzzed in his pocket. At first, he thought the buzzing was coming from his own body, until he realized it was from the device. Someone was texting him. It could be serious!

Zac retrieved his phone from his pocket and noticed it was another message from Cole, who was simply checking up on him. He smiled, it felt good to have regular contact with his little brother. So many things had happened over the past few months—wonderful things. Things he would never have allowed himself to dream about.

"It's my brother, Cole," he said. He typed a quick response, then shoved the phone in his pocket and turned his attention back to Mari, the other wonderful thing that had happened.

"You're fine," she said. "You don't have to stop messaging with him for me." She smiled. "I'm not going anywhere."

Zac wrapped his arms around her waist and pulled her close. "He's a big boy," he said, then kissed her on the forehead. "He was just checking in. I told him I'll let him know when something changes or give him an update in a few hours."

"You're a good brother," she said. "Family's important."

"Yes, it's everything."

"That's what makes you so adorable," she said. She reached up and kissed him on the neck. "You understand what's important. That's why we've been looking for Finn." She kissed him again, letting her hand slide down the front of his jeans where she undid the buttons.

Zac wasn't in the right state of mind for that. As much as he hated to do it, he took hold of her hand, pulled back, then sat down on the edge of the bed. "It's still blowing my mind that you're his sister."

"Is that good or bad?"

He raked his fingers through his hair. "I don't even know." He shook his head. "I mean, I don't even know how he'll take it."

"Does it make it any better that I'm not related by blood to him?"

Zac chuckled. "Family is so much more than blood," he said, tapping his chest. "It's here. And you already know that. In here, he's your brother."

"Besides," he continued. "I beat up your dad. Finn's dad." Saying those words aloud hurt. Of all the ways he imagined how the meeting would go with Finn and his bio dad, never once did he dream, he would end up punching the man in the face. He exhaled loudly.

"Shane's been in fights before," she replied.

"What if he hates me now?"

Mari sighed and ran her fingers through his hair. "He won't."

"He might."

She shook her head. "Not possible. The Shane I know is a badass, an outlaw and capable of doing all sorts of horrible things when needed." She smiled. "But when it comes to his family, he's a teddy bear."

"I ain't exactly family."

"You are," she countered. "In every way that's important, you are family. You were defending a brother. He, of all people, can respect that."

Zac wanted so badly to believe her. "What if he never forgives me?"

"Give him time," she said. "He just found his son, then damn near lost him again. He needs to adjust." She grinned. "After all, he is an old man."

"I hope you're right," said Zac.

"I am," she replied, then leaned in to kiss him. Once again, she slid her hand down to the buttons on his jeans. This time, he didn't stop her.

Chapter Thirty-Seven

Shane jolted awake and looked around the room in bewilderment. His confusion dissipated when he saw Catalina sitting peacefully beside him. He let out a long exhale, wiped his face, and gazed up at the white, tiled ceiling.

"Any word?" he asked.

"Not yet. He's still hanging in there though, so that's good."

She was right, at the moment, no news was good news. "How about Manny?"

"He texted an hour ago," replied Cat. "They cleaned up the mess. Everything's good. They're stopping for some coffee, then coming over. And Gabby's with my mom, blissfully unaware of all of this."

He sat upright and then swung his legs over the edge of the bed.

"Take it slow," warned Cat. "You gave a lot of blood, so you might find yourself a little weak."

"Weak my ass," he grunted, as he moved to stand up. The room swirled around him; his body felt as though he had just stepped into a deep hole and he was still falling.

"Next time, listen to me," admonished Cat, as she scooted under his arm, giving him support. "Where are we going?"

"There's only one place to go, isn't there?" he asked. He kissed her on the head. "Thank you, but I think I can make it on my own."

Shane's legs felt unsteady, but he reassured himself that he would be alright. The hallway was deserted, the hum of medical equipment creating an eerie echo. Every stride demanded more effort than he anticipated. Shane hated weakness. He pushed himself to find the necessary reserves or whatever his body needed to do to stop being so pathetic.

Halfway down the hall, a door to one of the rooms opened. Mari bounced out. She turned and flashed one of the biggest smiles Shane had ever seen on her face. He followed her gaze only to find the big redhead behind her. Mari startled momentarily when she saw Shane and Cat standing nearby, then shrugged and reached a hand out for Zac.

Shane took a step forward, halting just a few inches from the towering redhead. His gaze drifted down to the unbuttoned pants of Zac before returning to meet his eyes with a grunt of disapproval.

Shuffling his body nervously, the boy quickly buttoned his pants. Luckily for him, Mari was ready. With a soft tug, she gently pulled the kid away.

"How long are you gonna ride that boy?" asked Cat.

Shane watched Zac and Mari disappear inside Finn's room. "Until it ain't funny anymore," he replied, with a sly grin.

She slapped him playfully and scoffed. "Don't push him too hard," she said. "He's a good boy."

"They all are," he replied. "But after the way that one beat my ass, I have to ride him for a while. It's a matter of pride."

"Come on," prodded Cat. "Let's go see the kids."

The room was quite crowded, with the added bed and all. Shane's first stop was Beth. "How are you feeling now?" he asked. He didn't expect much of an answer, the poor girl had been through the wringer. Her face was swollen and littered with yellow and deep purple bruises. It was a miracle she was alive. The fact that a grown man would do such a thing to a woman made his blood boil.

Cat touched Beth's arm. "Mija, you should be sleeping. Rest is what your body needs to heal."

Tears welled up in the girl's eyes as she stared up at Cat. She slowly nodded, then allowed the older woman to fluff her pillow so she could settle down.

Cash was seated on one side of Finn, with Teague on the other, both still covered in dried and crusty blood. Shane looked down at himself and noticed that he was also covered in the same way. He walked over to the bed and Cash stood up, motioning for him to take his seat. Shane readily accepted, grateful that he didn't have to ask.

"How's he doing?" he asked, staring at the unmoving, blond-haired mess across the bed from him.

"Nothing's changed," replied Cash. He nodded toward Teague. "Neither of them."

Shane studied the monitors, all the important signs were stable, which was a good thing. At least the boy wasn't on a ventilator. That meant he was breathing on his own, albeit with some help from the oxygen.

Cat placed a gentle hand on Teague. "Mijo," she whispered. "You should come with us to get cleaned up."

Teague kept his head down, but the tension in his body when Cat touched him made Shane think of a feral animal in pain, ready to lash out.

Unfazed, Cat continued, "Why don't you come back to our place, get cleaned up and then come back?"

Nothing.

This time River joined in, "Teague, baby," she said softly, making her way over to him. "She's right, you need to clean up."

"I ain't leavin'," he replied, with his head still down.

"They have a point, Brother," added Cash.

"We'll be here the whole time," said Zac, standing at the foot of the bed. "We got him."

Teague raised his head and surveyed the group with red, swollen eyes. The misery he was feeling was painfully obvious. He fixed his gaze on Shane, wearing a mournful expression, before directing it toward Finn. "He'll be waking up soon," he uttered, in a quavering voice.

"Doc said he's got a few hours before that can happen," said River.

"Our home is about forty minutes away," explained Catalina. "You can come with us, get cleaned up, and be back here in no time." She nodded toward Shane. "He's not going to stay away long, either. But both of you need to get that blood off of you and eat something hearty."

"I ain't goin'," replied Teague. "I'm stayin' right here 'till he wakes up."

"That's going to be several hours from now," said Doc, as he entered the room. He skirted around the bed to examine Beth. "You need to sleep, young lady," he said. "Do I have to have Linda give you something to make that happen?"

Beth shook her head and laid back against the pillows.

He waded around everyone to get to Finn. After listening to his lungs and making sure everything was recording properly, he turned to Shane. "He's doing exactly how I want him to be doing right now. All his vitals are strong." He glanced over at Teague. "There's no better time for you to run and get cleaned up. He's going to be out for several more hours."

Teague opened his mouth to say something only to be interrupted by Doc, "Seriously. When he wakes up, we don't know how he's going to be feeling. He might need you. If you go clean up now, you can guarantee you'll be here when he does need you." He locked eyes with Shane. "That goes for both of you. And while you're at it, eat a thick steak. We might need some more blood."

"Go on, baby," said River. "We can keep an eye on him while you're gone."

Teague shifted, leaving a crusty path of dried blood on the blanket. In his attempt to clear it away, he only managed to smear more of it around.

"See what I mean?" said, River. She touched his hair and pulled away crusted blood. "You look like an extra in a horror movie."

A pathetic attempt at a smile spread across his face. He turned to Cat. "How far?" he asked.

"Forty minutes," she replied.

He glanced around at the others, then down to Finn.

"He'll be okay," said River. "We're all gonna be here the whole time."

Teague gazed at his hands and flexed his fingers. A shower of crimson flakes drifted down onto the white blanket. He spoke in a hushed tone. "Alright, let's go."

Cat guided him around the bed toward the door. As soon as she realized Shane hadn't moved, she turned around. "You too," she said, less delicately. "Come on."

The look in her eyes told him she wasn't taking no for an answer, so Shane climbed to his feet and followed. Before he left the room, he called over his shoulder, "If anything changes, you send us a text right away."

After a round of agreements, he turned and left the room, following Cat and Teague to her vehicle; there was no way he was using his truck any time soon.

Chapter Thirty-Eight

River trailed behind them as they made their way to the parking lot, ensuring that Teague wouldn't have a change of heart. She watched as Cat's car disappeared into the distance, its red taillights fading away. Initially, she had contemplated going with them or sending Cash instead when the idea first came up. However, she eventually realized that Teague and Shane needed some alone time to get to know each other. After all, their mutual love for Finn was a significant bond they shared, and it was best for them to sort out their emotions on their own.

As she made her way back through the clinic, she stopped at a cart to grab some clean blankets. One was for Beth to keep her warm, and the other was for Finn to replace the blood-encrusted one Teague had left behind.

After Beth had been tucked in, River leaned over and planted a gentle kiss on the top of her head. "You need to get some sleep," she said sternly. "When you wake up, we'll all be right here waiting for you."

Beth nodded and closed her eyes.

River watched her for a moment. The poor thing was a mess. The bruises would heal, and the jaw would mend, but she worried about Beth's emotions. Living through such a traumatic experience can change a person forever.

Moving over to Finn's bed, she swiftly changed the blanket and paused by Cash to plant a kiss on his cheek. Turning to Mari, she expressed her gratitude, "Thank you for staying back to assist. It wasn't necessary, but I appreciate it."

Mari smiled at her. "He's my baby brother," she replied. "I have to."

Upon hearing someone refer to Finn as a baby brother, River couldn't help but smile. She pondered how Finn would react upon hearing the title for the first time, and she was willing to wager that he would not take kindly to it.

As River walked out, a sudden flurry of activity erupted in the hall. It was then that she caught sight of Stoney, Gunner, Spinner, and Bella walking down the hallway.

"Baby girl," cooed Bella, with arms open wide. She pulled River in for a firm hug. "Where is everyone?"

Zac and Cash appeared in the doorway and waved hello.

"Is he in there?" asked Gunner. Without waiting for a response, he brushed past them and made his way into the room, vanishing from sight.

After everyone said their hellos, once again, the room was full of people.

River and Cash dedicated some time to update everyone on Finn's condition. The explanation of all that had occurred took quite a while. Fortunately, Mari was present to provide additional details from her perspective, which was helpful because River realized she was unaware of Shane and his group.

"How are you doing, sweetheart?" Bella asked Beth.

The younger girl nodded and gave a thumbs up.

"Doc gave her some strong painkillers," added River.

Bella gently brushed aside a strand of hair that had fallen across Beth's face. "We're relieved to see you're alright," she said softly, tucking Beth into bed. "Take some time to rest now. It's time to begin the healing process."

"What did Doc say about him?" asked Gunner, staring down at Finn.

River shrugged. "Just that he's doing as good as he hoped, and that now we wait until he wakes up."

"Any idea when that's supposed to be?" he asked.

Cash shook his head. "Doc says it'll be hours. That's why we were able to convince Teague to leave with Shane and Cat to get cleaned up."

Gunner nodded. "I'm surprised he left."

"He wasn't going to at first," replied River. "But he finally agreed when Doc told him that Finn was doing as well as he expected and that it would be a while before he woke up."

A sharp whistle erupted from the hallway, followed by a familiar voice, calling out, "Where's everybody at?"

Gunner stormed out of the room. "Keep it down," he said to Max. "This isn't a place to get loud and stupid. People are resting."

"It's okay," said River. "We're the only ones here."

"I was talking about Beth," said Gunner. "That girl's been through a lot. She should rest."

He was right; they needed to keep the noise down somewhat.

Gunner scanned the area. "Where's the doctor now?" he asked.

River shrugged.

"I'm gonna go find him and ask a few questions," he said. He nodded once, then wandered off with Spinner and Stoney in search of Doc.

"How's everyone doing?" asked Bells, in a part whisper.

"As best as can be," replied River. "Teague left with Shane and Cat. They'll be back soon."

D. B. raised an eyebrow. "He left Finn alone?"

"Not really," replied River. "We're here. Besides, he was a mess. He needed to clean up." She glanced over at Tripp, then Sam. "Where'd y'all meet up?"

"We crossed paths in Odessa," replied Tripp, with a shrug. He gave River a peck on the cheek, then looked around. "Where's your man at?"

She smiled. "He's inside the room, keeping an eye on Finn."

Without any more conversation, the group walked into the room where they huddled around the two beds. Beth was sitting up, smiling and seeming to enjoy the company. River didn't have the heart to usher everyone out, Beth seemed as though she needed the time among friends. The room was so crowded; she had to move sideways to get around.

After some time, Gunner returned with Spinner, Stoney, and one of the nurses.

Looking at everyone in confusion, she weaved her way through the crowd to Finn's bedside where she proceeded to check all the machines. Reaching over Finn, she startled and stepped back. "Um," she said aloud. "That bag just growled at me." She pointed to Gunner's backpack sitting on the bed beside Finn. "Is there a dog in there?"

Gunner lifted the pack and positioned it on Beth's bed before partially unzipping the pocket, giving Gypsy a chance to peek out.

Beth let out a high-pitched sound of delight as she embraced the small dog and pulled her in for a tight hug.

The nurse stared disapprovingly. "Okay, I'm going to allow the animal to stay with her." She smiled warmly at Beth. "But he needs to stay off this bed," she said, pointing to Finn with a stern hand. She waited for Gunner to acknowledge her orders, then with a curt nod of her head, she made her way over to the door, bumping into D.B.

A small, black paw with sharp claws swiped out from his hoodie pocket and hissed. She stepped back in shock. "Did your hoodie just hiss at me?" she snarled.

D. B. quickly stuffed the paw, tiny knives and all, back into the pocket. Spyder responded with a low, ominous moan.

The nurse stared at him long and hard. "Just keep that one out of trouble," she said, with a shake of her head, she stepped near the door and turned around. "Are there any more creatures I need to know about?" She moved her gaze around the room, taking time to look everyone in the eyes. "Any rats? Or some sort of reptile?"

Everyone stood silent, shaking their heads.

"Good. I meant it, keep the animals off of his bed," said the nurse. She stared at Gunner and D. B. "All of them." She turned to Beth and said, once again with a softer tone, "And you, young lady, you should be sleeping right now. Your body needs rest to heal." On her way out of the room, the nurse bumped into Gunner who she eyed up and down then huffed and stalked away.

"Okay, everyone," said Bella. "The stern woman has a point. Maybe we're being too loud."

"Pshh," replied Stoney, waving dismissively. "Finn needs to know we're all here."

Bella sighed. "Okay, then," she said. "Let's pull up some chairs and dim the lights."

Chapter Thirty-Nine

Teague remained silent throughout the entire ride, lost in a flurry of memories, hopes, questions and every so often, nothing at all.

The vehicle came to a halt in front of an iron gate made of some of the thickest barbed wire he had ever laid eyes on. Upon closer inspection, he realized that the barbed wire was actually rebar that had been twisted to look like barbed wire. The gate seemed extremely sturdy and heavy.

Cat typed the code, and the gate silently slid open. A moment later, they were driving down a long and winding gravel driveway past a small, cozy cottage with a forest of metal whirly gigs in the front garden. Warm lights glowed from the windows.

A little farther up stood an impressive farmhouse, fashioned in the old style. Teague wondered if it was as old as it appeared. A large barn stood off to the side, dark and foreboding, its giant, wooden doors left open.

The vehicle rolled into a two-story garage that was much larger than it first appeared.

"Okay," said Cat, as she pulled the keys from the ignition. "Let's get you two cleaned up." She flashed a friendly smile at Teague and climbed out of the vehicle.

He stepped out and took his time, checking out his surroundings. The garage was clean and well organized. He strolled past a workbench laden with tools. An image of Finn hung by a thumbtack on a corkboard above the workbench.

"Come on," prodded Cat.

Teague hung back and watched as Shane moved past Cat toward the house, then he followed.

They entered through the laundry room. Bright light accosted his eyes, as his senses were overpowered by the scent of laundry soap and cleaning chemicals. Following Cat, she led him into the kitchen. Aside from the architecture outside, the interior of the home was anything but old. Shane pulled off his jacket and disappeared down a hallway, leaving Teague to follow Cat over to a bathroom near the kitchen.

She held open the door and gestured with her hand. "Right in here," she said.

He slowly stepped closer.

Cat sighed and placed a hand on her hip. "Mijo, you have to relax. You're as tense as a barn cat in a pen full of dogs. You're among family here. Consider this your home." She smiled, then eyed him up and down. "Do you have any clean clothes? I'm sure Shane has some old things that might fit. You could wear those and I can clean the ones you have on."

He shook his head and dropped his pack on the floor. "I got some. No need," he replied. "But thank you," he quickly added.

"Okay," replied Cat, with a bright smile.

Teague felt guilty for his silence. The woman was trying to help him, and he could sense that she genuinely cared for his well-being. He didn't have much experience with mothers; he wasn't entirely sure how he was supposed to act around her. "What's it short for?" he inquired.

"What's that?"

"Cat," he continued. "What's it short for?"

Her eyes lit up. "Catalina," she replied proudly.

"It's pretty," he said. Seeing the smile that spread across her face made him feel good. "I'm sorry for being like this," he explained. "It's been a rough few days, and I'm not so sure how to act right now."

"It's okay, Mijo," she replied, placing a gentle hand on his arm. "You have a lot to process. Take your time." She glanced around the room. "In the meantime, you can clean up and maybe feel a little more like yourself." Gesturing with her hands, she said, "Soap is in the shower and clean towels are in here. Just put your dirty clothes on the floor, I'll gather them when you're done to wash them. Feel free to add any other clothes in your pack that you might want washed." She moved toward the door. "If you need anything, just call, I'll be in the kitchen making some food for you before we head back." With a quick wink and a caring smile, she closed the door behind her, leaving him alone.

Teague stood motionless before the mirror, his eyes fixed on his reflection. The scarlet stains on his clothes had dried up, leaving behind a musty smell in the air. His hair was matted with coagulated blood, making it feel sticky and heavy. The sight of himself was enough to make him cringe, as he couldn't help but feel the rough texture of the crusty substance on his skin.

He reached into the giant shower and turned on the water. Steam rolled up from the floor, a warm cloud of mist billowed around the room, filling the air. He stripped his clothes off, both the shirt and jeans feeling like cardboard. Every so often, flakes of dried blood would fall to the floor like tiny grains of sand.

As he stepped into the steamy shower, the sound of water cascading down his body filled his ears. Closing his eyes, he basked in the warmth of the water as it enveloped him from head to toe, washing away the blood that stained his skin. At his feet, red swirls disappeared down the drain, taking the metallic scent with it. As he stood there, every emotion that he had suppressed came crashing down on him with a fierce intensity. Teague tilted his head back, feeling the warm droplets crashing onto his face, mixing with his tears and washing away the blood that belonged to Finn.

He took several minutes to gather himself before finally picking up the soap and beginning to scrub away the filth that clung to his skin.

When he was finished, he felt a lot better, the energy in his body was returning and his skin no longer felt like it was covered in sand. He opened the door from the bathroom. A gust of cool air sent the steam roiling around like a low-hanging cloud. Teague stepped into the kitchen, to the savory aroma of sausage browning in a cast iron pan on the stove.

As soon as she laid eyes on him, Catalina's face lit up. "Come, come," she said, guiding him over to the table where she pulled out a chair. "Sit down. I'll bring you a plate."

A moment later, she slid a plate filled with eggs, sausage, and biscuits covered in gravy in front of him. His mouth watered; his stomach grumbled. The aroma was intoxicating.

"Go ahead," she prodded. "Eat. There's plenty. You'll need your strength. Our boy is going to need all of our attention in the coming weeks."

Our boy. Hearing those words roll off her lips triggered a deep sense of protectionism. These people didn't even know Finn, yet here they were, speaking of him as though he was already a part of their family. Teague wasn't sure if this made him angry or wary. The tantalizing aroma of warm food wafted into his nostrils, pushing aside all other thoughts or feelings. He dug in and devoured the meal hungrily, amazed by his own appetite.

Catalina slid into the chair beside him, cradling a steamy cup of coffee between her hands. "Are you feeling better?" she asked.

"I am," he replied. "Thank you. For everything."

"We're your family," said Cat. "There's no need to be thankful. Like I said, this is home." Her face became serious. "It's not just Finn's. It's yours as well."

Wariness descended on his heart like an opaque shroud. He

studied Cat's face for any sign of deceit and was unable to find any. This woman meant every word that rolled from her lips. He was being foolish. "I'm sorry for being this way," he said. "We don't have much reason to trust anyone outside of our own group."

"There's no need for apologies," replied Cat. "This is all new. I understand. Take your time to adjust, we're not going anywhere."

Teague nodded and allowed himself to relax.

"You said it's been a rough few days," said Cat. "Care to expand?"

"We went to Gainesville," he said. "That was a whole thing all of its own."

Cat nodded. "That place seems to have that effect on members of this family. The last time Shane went there, he found out about Finn. Those people up there are marinated in secrets and lies."

"This is true," replied Teague. He continued, "As if that all wasn't bad enough, we hit that storm and got separated. So, we've been traveling in two groups." He swallowed. "Me with Zac and River. Finn with Cash. They were a couple of days behind us." He sighed. "Finn's not too good at keeping his phone charged." He smiled sadly.

"Ah, yes," said Cat. "Shane has the same problem. It must be genetic."

Teague chuckled.

"You and me have something in common," she continued.

"What's that?"

"We're fools who have the misfortune of loving a Ryan boy deeply." She shook her head and sighed. "They certainly don't make it easy. Sometimes, it's a lot like trying to save a feral kitten. If you move too quick, you get the claws."

He laughed out loud. "That's exactly what it's like."

"It just means you and I have to stick together." She smiled and winked.

Shane wandered into the kitchen, regarding Cat and Teague with a suspicious eye. "Good to see you two are bonding," he said. He wandered over to the stove and set himself a plate then joined them at the table. He looked at Teague. "You look a lot better all cleaned up."

Seeing the older man regarding him, one blue eye and one amber brown, was startling. Teague realized that the man before him was essentially an older and more masculine version of Finn, causing him to wonder why he hadn't noticed the resemblance earlier. Shane shoveled a forkful of eggs into his mouth. His mannerisms were identical to Finn's, minus the messiness.

"What?" asked Shane.

"I see him in you," replied Teague. "And it's strange."

Shane twitched his nose and grunted in approval. He peered up at Catalina. "Any word?"

She shook her head.

"Well," said Shane. "No news is good news right now." He locked eyes with Teague. "You look like a man who has a lot of questions."

Teague nodded.

"We got some time now," said Shane.

"How long have you known about him?" asked Teague.

"Just under a year now," sighed Shane. "Ever since the day the old man told me he was alive, I've been looking for him."

Cat carried two cups of coffee to the table and served them to the two men, placing each cup in front of them.

Teague wrapped his fingers around the mug, letting the warmth course through his hands. "You mentioned the old man," he said. "That would be Melody's father, right?"

Shane nodded solemnly. "If I could've killed him several times over, I would've."

"So, it was you who burned the house down," said Teague.

"Someone's been doin' some research," said Shane. "Margaret?"

Teague nodded.

"It's a wonder she's still alive," said Shane.

"She looks like she's got a few years left to her."

"You know," said Shane. "As soon as I found out he was alive, I got a friend of mine to search." He grinned. "Y'all might remember him. An older man, reeks of ex-cop. He made the unfortunate mistake of running into y'all and found himself zip-tied to the ass end of a train."

"That was your man?" asked Teague, laughing. "We thought he was a pervert."

Shane nodded. "Between you and me, you're not entirely wrong."

The laughter felt good. Teague finally let his guard down. "What was she like?"

"Melody?" asked Shane. His eyes took on a dreamy look. "She was the first person in my life who treated me like a human being." He took Cat's hand in his and squeezed. "When she died, it left a mountain-sized void in my soul. One that I thought would never be filled." He stared into Cat's eyes. "But life has a way of changing when you least expect it."

Shane scooted his chair back and climbed to his feet. "Be right back," he said. Then he disappeared down the hall, returning a moment later carrying an ornate, wooden box. He placed it down atop the table and flipped open the lid.

"She was about six months' pregnant here," said Shane, pushing a photo in front of Teague.

He stared down at the beautiful woman in the image. It would be cliché to say she was glowing, but she really was. Her face, a face that had an uncanny resemblance to Finn, had the most sublime smile Teague had ever seen. Her hand rested lovingly on her belly.

"I can see her in his face," said Teague. He glanced up at Shane. "He's got her features, but your eyes and mannerisms."

Shane smiled proudly.

"Let's hope his head ain't so thick," teased Cat.

Next came a black-and-white ultrasound image. Teague studied the baby in the picture, the tiny arms and legs and, of course, the fist shoved in the mouth. Finn had that fixation from the moment of creation. Teague smiled as he recalled something his mawmaw once said, "We come into this world exactly who we are."

The next picture was of a young, handsome Marine, standing beside his beautiful bride. The couple was absolutely beaming.

Teague's heart broke with the knowledge of all that took place after this picture was taken. "How did she die?" he asked.

"It was a car accident," said Shane. "Or, between you and me, it was made to look like an accident." His face became like stone, his eyes had a look that was all too familiar. "I don't know exactly what happened, but I know in my soul that her demonic cousin had a lot to do with it."

"Tricia?" asked Teague.

Shane nodded. "The real story about what happened that night is a mystery," he said. "One that I'm still lookin' to find out. Tricia seems to have disappeared. Until I can find her, I've got nothin' more to go on than my gut. And that tells me she had a lot to do with the accident."

"Shortly after we ran into your guy," said Teague. "Daniel caught up with us. That was when he told me that he wasn't Finn's father. He also said something about Tricia." He scoured his memory. "He said he had already taken care of her."

"Well, damn," sighed Shane. "That explains why Derrick couldn't find anything on the woman. Looks like I ain't gonna get a chance to deal with her myself." He dug around in the box and pulled out a photo strip. "I believe this belongs to you," he said, sliding it across the table.

Teague stared down at the strip in shock and surprise. He had forgotten about this little snapshot of a precious moment in time. He ran his finger across the tape that had been carefully applied to piece it back together. A violent swarm of memories rushed forward in his mind, bringing a barrage of emotions, many of which were not good. "How?" he croaked.

"I told you," replied Shane. "I've been searching for him ever since I found out the truth. It just so happens, Father Killoran is an old friend of mine."

"Finn told me about him," said Teague.

"By the time we got to San Francisco," continued Shane. "Everyone was gone. That strip was the only tangible thing that was left. From what I heard of Finn's state when he was there, I can only imagine your state of mind when you ripped it up."

Teague had so many questions. How did he know he was the one who tore it up? He had never met the priest. So how did Shane come to have this strip? Confusion joined the circus of emotions that roiled inside. "It was a dark moment," he said. "I was so sure that was the end."

"From what I heard from Father K," said Shane. "Finn was at war with himself. Oddly enough, I'm well acquainted with that feeling." He stared at Teague for an uncomfortably long period of time. "Was that who messed you up so bad?"

"He wasn't himself," replied Teague. "The confrontation with Daniel pushed him into a breakdown."

Shane nodded in understanding. "So, was it Daniel who shot Cash?"

"Finn had nothing to do with that," replied Teague, startled by the force behind his own voice.

The silence around the table was deafening. Teague stared down at the photo strip, so much had happened since that day. He peered up at Shane. "What's your intention here?" he asked.

"My intention?" asked Shane.

Teague nodded. "What are you trying to do here? You said you've been searching for Finn. Why?"

"He's my son."

"He's not something that you can claim ownership of," replied Teague.

Shane's eyes narrowed as he flexed his jaw in an all too familiar way.

Teague had seen this stance many times before, the older man was clearly struggling with rising anger, doing his best to find the right words to use in response.

"Look, Son," said Shane, in a measured tone. "I am not trying to claim ownership of anyone. He's my son. My flesh and blood. I've loved him since before he was born."

"Yet, you forgot about him," seethed Teague. He watched the older man struggle internally against the anger that was brewing inside. A not-so-small part of him was enjoying the spectacle. For some irrational reason, he wanted to see the man blow up.

"That's where you're wrong," replied Shane. "I may have left that town, those people and that hope behind, but I never once—not even for a moment, forgot my son. I mourned him every waking hour of every day." He locked eyes with Teague. "You have no idea what it's like burying your life. When I saw those graves for the first time, I wanted nothing more than to lie down and crawl into the dirt with them."

Seeing Shane's raw emotional reaction, brought forth a deep sense of shame in Teague. He was being needlessly cruel. This man was every bit as much a victim of the whole mess as Finn. His hatred should be centered where it belonged, squarely on the shoulders of those who lied. The ones who played god with the lives of three people, out of nothing more than malice and envy. "That's why you buried the dog tag," said Teague. "Isn't it?"

Shane nodded.

"And it was you who knocked over the gravestone, wasn't it?" asked Teague.

The older man didn't respond; he didn't have to.

"The time we lost together can't be taken back," said Shane. "I'm angry as hell at that wicked, old man and that skeevy witch, for what they did to us—mostly to Finn. I'm also plenty angry at myself for believing them all those years. For falling for their lies."

Teague realized he was angry at Shane for the same thing. This man knew the hate those people had for him, yet he believed them. He didn't even bother to question the narrative. A tiny, inner voice broke through Teague's thoughts. There was no logic or sense in being angry at the other victim of all of this. Still, Finn was the true victim, he was the one who suffered the most. He was the one who didn't deserve yet another messed up situation. Teague studied Shane, still struck at how similar the man was to Finn. "What if he doesn't want you in his life?" he asked.

"Do you think that's a possibility?" asked Shane, with a trembling voice.

The look on the older man's face shattered every bit of enmity that Teague held in his heart toward him, leaving behind nothing but empathy, followed by regret for uttering those words.

"I don't know," he replied, honestly. "He's suffered so much at the hands of so many. He's slow to warm up to new people. I don't know how he's gonna react." Teague stared down at the photo strip. "Give him time. He might just come around to the idea." He peered up at Shane. "You have no idea what he's been through. The world is full of vile people, and he's met more than his fair share of them. It ain't my place to tell you the details, so we'll have to leave it at that."

A look of understanding spread across Shane's face. "I just want to be a part of his life. To watch him and help him grow into the man he was meant to be. I'll settle for anything he's willing to allow."

"Well, that might be fine with you," interjected Cat. "But I want to hug him, to fatten him up and get all up into his life. I want to smother him in love and food and protect him from any more pain." She wiped her face and sniffled. "And I will seriously cut the next bitch who tries to harm him in any way."

Both Teague and Shane chuckled.

The laughter felt good. He smiled at Cat, knowing she meant every word she just said.

There was an eruption of activity at the front door, followed by a gush of fresh air and the unmistakable sound of a little girl's voice. Teague glanced up just in time to see a young girl with long, brown hair bounding down the hall, heading straight for them.

"What are you doing up at this hour?" asked Cat.

The little girl ignored her, choosing instead to climb up on Shane's lap. "I saw you come home," she replied.

An old woman appeared, slightly out of breath. "I am getting too old for this," she said playfully. "I'm sorry. She saw you come home, and she just couldn't wait. I didn't think you would mind." She strolled over to the sink, on her way, taking the time to pat Teague on the shoulder as though she expected to see him there.

"How come you weren't sleeping like you were supposed to?" asked Shane.

The little girl smiled lovingly up at him, then turned her head and locked eyes with Teague.

He let out a sudden and sharp gasp.

"Teague," said Shane. "This is Gabby."

His heart raced in his chest. Teague swallowed against the lump in his throat. The little girl had the same eyes as Shane—as Finn. He knew it was possible that Shane had other children, it just never felt like a real possibility, or at least he just never considered what that meant.

"Hi, Teague," said Gabby. She smiled at him.

"Hello," he choked.

The little girl raised her eyes in a painfully familiar way, then asked, "Is Finn with you?"

Teague was startled. He didn't know how to respond. All he could do was stare at Gabby—Finn's little sister. He wondered how Finn was going to take this news.

"Okay, that's enough visiting for this late hour," said Shane. He scooted the little girl off his lap and lifted her onto his back. "You can visit more tomorrow. Right now, it's bedtime for you."

Gabby sighed and slumped her head and shoulders, then turned her head and smiled as she waved goodbye to Teague.

He watched in shock as Shane carried her up the stairs.

"She knows about Finn?" he asked.

Cat nodded. "We told her about him a while back. As you can tell, she's excited to meet her big brother."

"How do you think he'll take the news that he has a little sister?" she asked.

"I don't even know," replied Teague, still staring at the staircase. "I don't even know how I feel about it." He turned to Cat. "This is a lot to take in.

Chapter Forty

The small and cramped room felt cozy and comfortable, especially after dimming the lights. River's heart was filled with joy as she listened to her eccentric family's banter. Despite the uncomfortable, hospital chairs, she leaned toward Cash as much as possible, and he reciprocated with a smile and a contented sigh. Finally, after hours of worry, things were starting to feel better. River allowed herself to feel a glimmer of hope that everything would turn out alright.

Beth had eventually drifted off to sleep, which was a much-needed relief for the poor girl. She had put up a strong resistance to it, endeavoring to keep her eyes open to relish the sensation of being in the company of her friends.

In a way, it was a good thing she stayed awake for a while, otherwise, they wouldn't have known what happened out there with Daniel. It was Max's idea to give Beth a notepad and a pen, River still found it hard to believe that simple thought hadn't occurred to her earlier.

Pen in hand, Beth was able to give a full description of the way things went down. How Daniel grabbed her at the beach one night.

His insane rantings about Tricia and Finn and his deep-seated hatred for both.

She explained how Finn saved her life by releasing her from the seatbelt, only to run straight into a battle with Daniel.

River was amazed by Beth's explanation and that she didn't run away when Finn was in danger. Instead of obeying his orders, she chose to stay and fight for his life. Although she could have fled and forgotten about him, Beth's resolve saved his life.

And Daniel was dead.

It was still difficult to wrap her brain around the knowledge that Beth, of all people, killed the most violent monster River had ever come across, with nothing more than a crowbar, and a whole lot of rage. She'd never felt so proud of Beth as she did at that moment. Even the others sat in awe of the whole event, as it was described by Beth. The girl had truly grown in the months she was on her own. On the outside, she looked like the old Beth, albeit a purple and swollen version, but on the inside, she was a completely different person— mature, strong-willed and fully confident in her ability to take care of herself. She even seemed to have a newfound admiration for family and close friends.

The silence was interrupted by the sound of everyone's phones chiming at the same time.

River pulled hers out to see a message from Mara announcing their arrival. She shoved the device in her pocket and followed the others out of the room, through the clinic and out into the parking lot.

An older-model class-C motor home sat parked close to Shane's truck. Standing outside, were Nate, Tanner, Ben and Mara. As soon as she laid eyes on River, she ran toward her with arms open wide, slamming so hard against her that River feared they might topple over.

"What are you doing here?" asked River. "You should be home, resting with Zephyr."

Mara smiled. "Now, you know, there's no way in hell we wouldn't be here." She stepped back. "Speaking of Zephyr. I'll go get him from his car seat." Mara turned and disappeared inside the RV.

"What's this?" asked Spinner, gesturing to the motorhome.

"Mara's uncle let us borrow it for the trip down here," answered Ben. "As soon as we heard, I made plans to head down. Mara wasn't gonna let me go alone." He shook his head. "She was ready to hop with us."

"Please tell me you weren't on board with that," said Stoney.

Tanner chuckled. "Have you ever tried to convince that woman that something she's determined to do is not going to happen?"

"I told her no," said Ben. "She challenged me to try and stop her. Rather than sit back and watch the fight happen, Mara's uncle offered this." He waved his arm to show the RV.

"Given the opportunity to ride in comfort," explained Tanner. "Nate and I opted to travel with them." He grinned and rubbed his back end. "But our boy here sucks at driving," he said. "Damn near hit every pothole he could find and don't even get me started on how he takes turns. Out of fear for my life, I actually had to put my seatbelt on."

Nate chuckled. "I was getting nauseous. It was the worst ride I've ever had."

"My boy is a road hazard," teased Tanner.

"Hey," said Ben. "Gimme a break. It's been a long time since I drove, let alone something this big. I think I did an excellent job." He grinned. "I got us here in one piece, didn't I?"

"Well, thank goodness for her uncle," said Bella. Her face lit up as she peered up at the door of the vehicle.

Mara stood in the opening, wearing a wrap that held the tiniest of babies River had ever seen.

An audible gasp escaped Bella's lips as she approached slowly. She reached out a gentle hand, cradling the back of the baby's head. "Hello there, sweet one," she cooed.

River stood back, afraid to get closer. She'd never been this close to a newborn before, she didn't know how to act.

"Well, I'll be," sighed Gunner. "He's even cuter in real life." He turned to Ben. "Congratulations, Dad, you and Mama did good."

Mara glanced around. "How's Beth? Is she inside?"

River nodded. "She just fell asleep."

"Is she doing okay?"

"She is," replied River, with a nod. "She's been through a lot, but she's strong and she'll heal."

"What about Finn?" asked Mara. "Any change?"

River shook her head. "Doc says he'll be out for several hours."

A look of concern swept across Mara's face. "Where's Teague? Is he still inside with him?"

"He left with Shane to get cleaned up," replied River.

"Shane," repeated Mara. "That's Finn's bio dad, right?"

"He is," replied River.

"I'm surprised he agreed to leave," said Mara. "Or did y'all have to tie him up and drag him away?"

"I was worried we might," said River. "But he went of his own free will. It was a good thing for him to get some fresh air and clean up. He was covered in Finn's blood, not to mention, his clothes were still slightly damp from the rain over the past couple of days."

"Ah, yes," said Mara, with a slow nod of her head. "I don't miss those rides at all." She glanced over at Zac and Mari, standing off to the side.

"Are you gonna introduce me to your lady, or do I have to do it myself?" she asked Zac.

River had to suppress a giggle while Mari greeted them both. What surprised her was that Mari seemed completely at ease around the baby, unlike River, who felt uncomfortable.

"Our boy seems infatuated," said Ben.

"He's been that way since he met her," said River. "For what it's worth, she seems just as enthralled by him as he is by her. It's kind of cute to see."

"Who is she?"

"You won't believe it," explained River. "She's Shane's step-daughter, or as we've all come to think of her, Finn's older sister." She chuckled.

Ben laughed out loud. "So, our boy is a baby brother?"

River nodded. "He doesn't know yet, though."

"Well, now I'm even more glad we came," he said. "I can hardly wait to see the shock when he finds out." A serious look swept over Ben's face. "How is he really doing?"

"He's hanging in there," replied River. "Which is all we can hope for right now. Doc says he's doing good, but the rest of us will buy into that prognosis when we see him sitting up and smiling."

"I hear ya," replied Ben. "Can we go inside and see him?"

"Absolutely," River called out, to the others. "We're about to go inside, anyone else coming?"

With hardly a word between them, the group moved as one toward the clinic.

As they crossed the parking lot, Mara wrapped her arms with River's. "I like her," she said.

"Mari?" asked River. "I do too." She glanced over at Zac, taking note of the way he looked at the girl. "He's happy right now and with everything going on, that seems like a win."

Mara nodded in agreement.

As they entered the tiny room, Mara gasped in shock at the sight of Finn lying death-like in the bed.

Even though it had been a few hours, River had already become accustomed to it, so she was slightly shocked to see Mara's reaction.

Beth's eyes fluttered open.

"Here," said Mara, as she pulled Zephyr from the wrap. "Hold him so I can go hug Beth." Saying nothing else, she lifted the baby and placed him softly in River's arms. Mara smiled up at her and said, "You're a natural." Then she spun around and fell into Beth's arms for a long hug.

River was frozen in fear, unable to move or even take a breath. She gazed down at the small human nestled in her arms, feeling his warmth and softness. Whenever he stretched, he emitted tiny sounds that tugged at her heartstrings. She held him close, rocking back and forth while humming a gentle melody.

It took her a moment to notice the sudden silence in the room. Looking around, she realized that everyone had fixed their gaze on her, sporting a mix of facial expressions that consisted of amusement, surprise and weird grins. "What's up?" she asked, still swaying to and fro.

"Nothing, nothing," muttered Max, as he quickly glanced away.

She peered over at Gunner who had the strangest smile on his face, as did Bella, Stoney and even Spinner.

Her face suddenly felt warm as she turned to see Zac, his wide grin reaching from ear to ear. Cash was standing next to him, wearing an unusual expression.

"Psh," scoffed River. "Y'all are ridiculous. Haven't you ever seen a woman hold a baby before?"

"I've seen lots of women do that before," said Tripp. "However, it occurs to me that I've never seen you hold a baby." He flashed a playful grin and turned to Cash.

Ben clapped a firm hand on Cash's shoulder. "Watch out, my man," he said. "Once baby-itis sets in, it's all over." He sighed and shook his head. "I should know."

"Go ahead, buttheads," said River. "Yuck it up all you want." She spun around and swayed over to the doorway. "I'm taking my little buddy here out of the room. Y'all are a bad influence," she said, before walking out into the hallway. As she gazed down at the small baby, she couldn't help but notice how perfect he was in every way, from his dainty hands to his sweet coos. She leaned in and placed a tender kiss on his soft, fuzzy head, and he responded by curling his fingers around hers and drifting off to sleep. For the first time in her entire life, River wondered what it would be like to be a mom.

Chapter Forty-One

Nah, nah, nah," said Cyrus, shaking his head. "Why you always gotta bring out the bullshit?"

"It's not bullshit," protested Craig. "Finn, back me up."

Finn shook his head. "I didn't see anything."

Cyrus snickered. "That's because there wasn't anything to see."

A fluffy, billowy cloud of sweet, strawberry-scented vapor floated above Finn's head, shimmering with a bright, white hue in the warm, early morning sun. He looked up and gazed at the clear, pristine, baby-blue sky stretching out as far as the eye could see. The faint chirping of birds echoed in the distance, and a gentle breeze brushed against his skin, creating a soothing sensation. It was a picture-perfect day.

"Pshh," scoffed Craig, with a dismissive wave of his hand. "You two can go ahead and not believe me if you want. But I know the truth." He held his hands in front of him a foot apart. "That fish was huge. And I woulda caught it if the line didn't break."

"You go on and keep believing that," teased Cyrus.

Finn gazed at the still water, so tranquil it looked like a mirror.

He felt a refreshing breeze brush against his skin, sending a shiver down his spine. He wondered how the water could remain smooth as glass despite the gentle wind. Finn shifted his gaze to the trees surrounding him, their leaves swaying softly in the breeze. He took a deep breath, inhaling the crisp aroma of pine and cedar that filled the air, and sighed contentedly. As he looked around, he noticed that the trees were not the evergreens he had expected but rather aspen trees.

A soft, fluffy plume of white mist enveloped his head, gently swirling around him. He inhaled, expecting to smell the aroma of strawberries, but was met with a complex mixture of scents. The pungent smell of pine and cedar mixed with an unusual, metallic tang, with an underlying aroma he struggled to put into words, almost like the scent of plastic.

The sun felt like a gentle caress on his skin, warming him from head to toe. Finn closed his eyes, letting out a contented sigh as he tilted his chin up toward the bright, blue sky. Cyrus and Craig's laughter blended with the soothing sounds of nature, creating a comforting background noise. Finn was completely at peace, as if time had stood still in this tranquil forest. He could stay here forever.

"But you can't," said Cyrus.

Finn startled and opened his eyes. He looked at Cyrus. "What?"

"You heard me," said Cyrus. "You can't stay here."

"But I didn't say I wanted to," said Finn.

"You didn't have to," said Craig. "We heard you thinking it." He tapped the side of his head, reminding Finn of Teague.

Another plume of smoke wafted by. Finn turned to Cyrus. "Think you could blow that the other way?"

"Blow what?"

"Your vape," said Finn. "It keeps blowing in my face."

Cyrus held up his hands, showing they were empty. "You're trippin'," he said. "I ain't smoking anything."

Confusion roiled in Finn's mind. He scanned the water; it was still as smooth as glass. That ain't normal. Another plume of mist.

What the hell was going on? He peered up to the sky. Where the hell was the sun?

"You feelin' okay?" asked Cyrus.

Finn slowly nodded his head.

"You sure?" asked Craig. He gestured down at Finn's body. "Because you don't look too good."

Finn followed his gaze. His hands were sticky with blood. He held them up into the air, watching as the crimson liquid dripped down onto the boulder he was sitting on. A stab of pain erupted in his belly. He reached down, feeling a gaping hole where his insides should be.

He tried to jump up, but his legs wouldn't move. Blood covered the entire lower half of his body. A scream was trapped in his throat, all he could do was emit a pathetic moan.

Gunner's voice floated into his ears. Finn struggled to understand what he was saying, but he may as well have been speaking a foreign language.

The forest seemed to be moving rapidly in and out of his view. The pleasant aroma of pine and cedar soon vanished, giving way to the sharp odor of blood and the unfamiliar smell of plastic.

Finn peered up at Cyrus. "What's happening?"

"Time to wake up, buddy," said his old friend, clapping a solid hand on Finn's shoulder and smiling.

Confusion overwhelmed Finn. His mouth was dry, his body ached in ways he had never felt before. He tried to call out for Teague, but his throat would not comply. He reached out for Cyrus, only to have his hand go right through the man as though he were a ghost. The forest spun out around him, falling away, leaving nothing but blackness in its place. Both Cyrus and Craig were gone. For the first time, Finn wondered if they had ever really been there. I have to be in a nightmare he thought. He struggled to wake up—to open his damn eyes, but his lids were heavy as lead blankets. Any movement sent a shock of searing pain throughout his entire body. The sound around him cleared, allowing him, for the first time, to hear the voices.

"Yeah," said Cash. "What are the odds that we'd stumble into that exact bar?"

"It was meant to be," said Bella.

"So, Shane is his father?" asked Gunner.

"He is," replied Cash. "Same eyes and everything. When we first met him, he was wearing contacts to hide his eyes. It's weird because we spent hours in that bar, hanging out, playing pool without knowing he was the man we came to find. He's Finn's father."

Finn's mind was reeling. His lips moved, spitting out the words, "He's my what?"

A gentle hand touched his chest. The blackness fell away, leaving a white, tiled ceiling in its place. He reached up and pulled a mask away from his face and inhaled. The chemical smell of bleach assaulted his nostrils. He glanced around at all the familiar faces standing around him. "We played pool with my father?" he asked.

"Oh my god!" shouted River. She flew around the side of the bed and wrapped her arms around him.

The pain was immediate. Finn cried out as his whole body screamed for mercy.

"I'm so sorry," she said. Tears flowed down her cheeks. She sniffled and adjusted his blanket. "I can't believe you're awake!"

"Doc said you'd be out for a long time," said Cash.

"He probably never came across someone as bullheaded as Finn before," joked Tripp.

Finn glanced around the room, taking in all the faces, half expecting to see Cyrus and Craig in the crowd. It seemed as though everyone was there—everyone except one person. "Where's Teague?" he asked.

"Just texted him," replied Zac. His phone chimed. "He's almost here."

As a plume of vape mist, smelling of sweet strawberries, filled the air, Finn momentarily wondered if he had slipped into another dream.

"Max!" barked Gunner. "I am not gonna tell you again, put that damn thing away or take it outside."

"Sorry," replied Max, sheepishly. "I forgot."

The big man peered down at Finn. "I cannot tell you how good it is to see you awake." He clasped Finn's hand in his giant paw. "You had us all worried."

Finn moved his attention to the other bed in the room. "How are you doin?" he asked Beth.

She nodded and attempted to smile, but her face was far too swollen to do the expression justice.

A deep chill ran through Finn's body, causing his muscles to shudder uncontrollably.

"I'll get more blankets," said River. She took off into the hall, only to reappear a moment later with a stern-faced woman in scrubs trailing behind her.

The woman weaved her way through the crowd, making a point to glare disapprovingly at anyone who had the misfortune of making eye contact with her. Behind her, a slight man followed, wearing a white lab coat. He passed the nurse and leaned over Finn, placing a stethoscope against his chest.

"It's not often I like being proven wrong by my patients," said the doctor. "But I have to say, I'm happy to see you do it." He smiled and studied the monitor, then sighed. "Everything looks good. You are a strong, young man."

Finn's body shook uncontrollably as he nodded in agreement. He attempted to express his gratitude, but all that escaped his lips was the sound of his teeth chattering together.

"Let's give him some pain meds," said Doc.

"No!" shouted Finn, startled by the force of his own voice. "It'll put me out. I wanna stay awake until Teague gets here."

Doc sighed and shook his head. "Okay," he said. But as soon as he gets here, we're putting you out again. You need to rest and you're not going to do it if your body isn't comfortable."

Finn let out a deep exhale of relief before resting his head on the soft pillow.

"The apple didn't fall far from the tree," sighed Doc. "He's just as tough as his father."

The words from Finn's dream snapped into his mind. He grabbed the doctor's arm before he could move away. "Who?"

Doc blinked and glanced around the room. "Shane, your father."

The room was silent as Finn grappled with this new knowledge.

"Looks like we've got some explaining to do," said Cash.

"He didn't know?" asked Doc, incredulous. He peered down at Finn. "Well, then, I suppose now would be a good time for me to leave you with your friends." He moved toward the door, stopping at the threshold. "I'll be out here waiting." With a final nod, the doctor left the room.

"Does he know Shane?" asked Finn.

Mari stepped to the foot of the bed. She smiled down at him. "Yes, he does," she said. "And so do I." She smiled. "You met him earlier while sitting at the bar. He was too scared to say anything, so he kept it a secret."

Questions swirled in Finn's mind. He hardly knew where to begin.

"You wouldn't be here right now if it wasn't for Shane," said River. "He damn near drained his blood dry to save your life."

Words evaded him. His thoughts roiled in a storm of images.

A flurry of activity erupted at the door. Finn glanced over just in time to see Teague rush across the room toward him, his eyes filled with tears.

Finn smiled. "What gives?" he asked, in a feeble attempt to lighten the mood. "You act like I just about died or something."

"Couillion," said Teague, then he kissed him.

The room cleared out, leaving Finn alone with Teague and a lone, tall figure. The older man that everyone called Boss stood silently by the door as though he was unsure if he should stay or leave the room with all the others.

Finn reached out his hand to Shane. "I hear I owe you my life," he said. "More than once." He tried to smile, but the best he could pull off was a halfhearted grin, followed by a full-body shiver.

They clasped hands. Shane smiled, peering down at him with tear-filled eyes—eyes that were just like his own. "When you're better, we've got a lot to talk about."

Finn nodded. "I can see we do," he replied. "I'd like that."

The nurse appeared at the side of the bed. Without another word, she inserted a needle into the tube attached to the back of his hand. "Time for you to rest," she said, in a tone much softer than expected.

A rush of warmth spread throughout Finn's body; the pain was melting away. His eyelids grew heavy. Unable to keep his head up any longer, he leaned back and let himself go.

Chapter Forty-Two

The ride through the desert was a welcome change. For the past three weeks, the only sights Finn was able to see were inside the clinic. He was tired of the sterile air and the deep chill from being encased in a manmade environment for days on end. He longed to feel the warm sun on his skin.

He rolled his window down, letting the dry, desert breeze rush over his face. The vast landscape stretched out before him, the rocky hills rolling like waves in the distance. He leaned his head as far as possible toward the window, taking in the scent of sagebrush and juniper trees that filled the air. He closed his eyes, feeling the sun's warmth on his skin and the gentle vibration of the truck as it rolled along the highway.

The truck slowed, rolling to a slow stop in front of a heavy iron gate. Finn peered out at the surrounding area, noting that there wasn't much around. A bird called out overhead. He tilted his chin toward the clear, blue sky, watching the raptor coast effortlessly on the wind current.

In the driver's seat, Shane punched in the security code, and the massive gate slid open silently. Finn found this impressive, based on its size, he was expecting the gears to whine in protest of the heavy weight.

A horn sounded twice behind them, he swiveled his head back, smiling as he saw River's face smiling back at him from the front seat of Manny's truck. Sitting behind her, just barely visible, was Cash. The vehicle behind them was driven by Catalina, that was where Zac, Mari and Beth were riding. He couldn't see them, due to the dark tint on the windows.

The truck bumped and jostled as they rolled across the cattle grate. The pain was immediate. Finn's face twisted in agony as he tightly gripped his stomach, feeling the sharp pain radiating through his body. He wondered how long it would be before his guts stopped feeling as though they were free floating around in his abdomen.

Finn set his focus on things outside of his body, scanning the area as they rolled slowly along the long, winding gravel driveway. A small, cozy home appeared to his right. Metal whirligigs spun in the soft breeze, their blades glinting in the early, afternoon sunlight. He smiled, remembering Violet and her big, old dog, Gus.

A large barn loomed up ahead. Finn shifted his gaze over to the impressive farmhouse that sat to the side. A cozy porch surrounded the building, offering perfect views of the landscape no matter what side of the house you were on. A colorful banner hung from hooks above a set of white rocking chairs. It swayed gently in the soft breeze, displaying the words "Welcome Home Finn!"

Tears pooled up in his eyes as he read the words he never thought he would read, even in his wildest imagination. For the first time since leaving the clinic, he wondered if he was awake. This was the sort of thing his mind would conjure up in a fever dream.

They rolled past the house, coming to a stop just outside of a big, two-story garage.

He stepped out of the truck, his gaze fixated on the banner as if unable to look away. The words seared into his brain.

Welcome Home Finn.

The door suddenly swung open, and a young girl with long, dark hair burst out. She leaped down the steps two at a time and ran at full speed toward Finn. Although they hadn't met in person yet, he knew who this was, Shane had already filled him in. She crashed into him, sending another round of searing pain through his body. He howled in pain.

"Gabby!" shouted Cat. "No!"

Finn held up his hand. "It's okay," he gasped, through clenched teeth. He took a step back and peered down, wanting to get a good look at her. She stared up at him with tears streaming down her cheeks from eyes that were just like his own.

"Hello, Gabby," he said softly.

The little girl wiped her cheeks with both hands and sniffled. She waved her arm behind her, gesturing toward the front porch. "Do you like it?" she asked. "I made it myself."

Finn peered up at the sign and swallowed against the lump in his throat. "I think it's the best sign I've ever seen," he replied.

She flashed a smile and took his hand, pulling him gently toward the house.

"Be gentle," warned Shane, his tone soft. "He's not ready to go running around."

Gabby nodded and slowed her pace, all the while still guiding him forward.

Shane quickly climbed the steps to the porch, coming to a stop in front of the door. "You and Teague are staying in a room in the house," he said. "No stairs to climb. It'll make it easier to keep an eye on you until you're healed." He nodded toward the garage. "The others'll stay in the apartment above the garage. Once you're ready, we can sort out a more permanent arrangement." He turned the hammered-metal handle and let the door swing open.

The delicious scent of freshly cooked food drifted toward Finn's nose. His mouth watered in anticipation—his stomach grumbled. It had been a hot minute since he had any sort of food he could consider tasty. Based on the mouthwatering aroma alone, he could hardly wait to feast on a plateful of whatever was cooking; he was certain it would be a vast improvement over anything he had eaten in the past few weeks.

In the entryway, an elderly woman emerged and began wiping her hands on her apron. She locked eyes with Finn and said, "Nieto." She approached and gently wrapped her arms around him, pulling him in for a hug. "Welcome home," she said.

Finn didn't know what to say or how to act, he had never had an old person refer to him as family before. Much to his surprise, it felt good. She smelled of spices, the same spices that were cooking in the kitchen.

She stepped back and took a good look at him. "You're too skinny," she said, with a twinkle in her eye. "No worries, I can fix that." She turned her gaze over to Teague. "You too," she said, then held out her arms, waiting for a hug from him.

"This way," said Cat. She led him through the living room and down a hallway.

The walls were lined with photographs. Shane, Catalina, Manny, Pillar and Odie smiled out at him from their frozen moments in time. Farther down, there were several images of Mari and Gabby, depicting them as infants and toddlers. He came to an abrupt halt and stared at the wall in disbelief. Certain he was seeing things, Finn blinked and rubbed his eyes. His own face peered out at him from a cluster of pictures that included images of Mari and Gabby. Never in his life had he seen his own image on a wall like this. A wave of emotions crashed over him; he didn't know if he wanted to smile or cry.

Cat smiled gently. "Now that you're here, we can get a better one." She leaned close. "Maybe even a family portrait with all of us."

Teague moved past him, carrying his pack.

Finn followed him into a bedroom. The fresh scent of laundry soap hung heavy in the air; it was a nice change from the smell of disinfectant in the clinic. The room was large, with its own bathroom and even a small sitting area with a television. Finn sat heavily on the edge of the bed, completely drained from the physical effort of walking and overwhelmed by a flood of emotions.

"We'll let you two get settled," said Cat, as she strolled over to the door. "If you want to get cleaned up, the shower has everything you need. I'll come get you when it's time to eat." She locked eyes with Finn. "This is your home, Mijo," she said. "Both of you." She stepped into the hall. "Oh!" she said quickly. "I went ahead and bought you some new clothes. Your style is very similar to Shane's, so I think I got things you'd like. They're in the dresser drawers and hanging in the closet." She paused, smiled softly, "Welcome home." Without another word, she pulled the door closed behind her, leaving Finn alone in the room with Teague.

His body was weak from the exertion, his mind and emotions threatened to overwhelm him. Finn laid back on the soft bed and peered up at the ceiling, watching the fan spin.

"Ça va?" asked Teague, sitting down beside him.

Finn held back his tears and let out a sigh. He asked, unsure if he really wanted to know the answer, "Is this a dream?"

Teague's face hovered above him. "Mais non," he said, with a slow nod. "It's all real." He flashed an impish grin. "Want me to pinch you to prove it?" He raised his hand as if he was about to do it.

Finn chuckled and took hold of Teague's hand; this time he didn't mind the pain.

The door burst open. "Wow!" exclaimed River. "You two waste no time. Do you?" she teased.

Cash strolled in behind her. "Leave the kids alone," he said.

Beth strolled in. Her face still had a yellow hue to it, but the bruises were gone. There were still a few weeks left before the wires would be taken out, which meant that she couldn't talk much during that time. The group took advantage of that every moment they could. Naturally, their teasing was all good-natured fun. She was, after all, part of the family.

Finn sat upright and gave a gentle tap on the bed beside him, inviting her to take a seat.

She sat down and looked around the room, giving a nod of approval while gesturing with her hand.

Mari sauntered in, followed by Zac. Seeing them together made Finn smile. By no means was he an expert on relationships, but he knew the face of a smitten man when he saw one. It was good to see Zac so happy. As for Marisol, he liked her, though he could do without all the little-brother stuff.

"The others are on their way," said River. "They wanted to wait until you had settled in before coming by," she said, strolling over to a nearby window and peering out through the curtains. "They'll be here in time for the bar-b-q." She spun around and walked over to the bed, plopping herself down between Finn and Teague. "How does it feel to have a big celebration just for you?" she asked.

He glanced around the room. "I was just telling Teague, it doesn't feel real yet," he said, shaking his head. "It feels like I'm still dreaming."

"Want me to pinch you so you can see it's real?" she asked, with a mischievous grin. With a soft chuckle, she planted kisses on the sides of both of their heads before springing to her feet. Reaching a hand out for Beth, she said, "Okay, we just wanted to check on you. We're gonna go get cleaned up." She pointed to him and Teague sternly. "You two should do the same. And no messing around; dinners about ready and I'm dying to dig in." She smiled. "The smell of all that food out there is making my mouth water."

A flurry of activity ensued as she ushered everyone out, and then the door shut, leaving him and Teague alone once more.

He slowly rose to his feet, wincing at the tug of his muscles.

"You want a pain pill?" asked Teague.

Finn shook his head. "Nah, I hate how they make me numb," he replied. "I wanna feel everything." He staggered toward the bathroom, breathing slowly with each step.

Teague scooted under his arm and helped him the rest of the way.

He didn't say it out loud, but Finn was thankful for the help. It had been a few weeks since he had a real shower; he was looking forward to feeling the warm water wash over his skin. He intended to take one of the longest hot showers he had ever taken.

Staring at his own reflection in the mirror, he was stunned by the angry, red scar that ran across his abdomen. The sight of it made his stomach churn. He could still feel the sickening sensation of the knife piercing his skin, the sharp pain that shot through his body, and the warm, sticky feeling of his own blood as it flowed out, draining from his body. He ran his fingers over the rough, raised flesh, wincing as he felt the jagged edges of the scar. He wondered if it would ever fade, or if it would always be so vivid?

"Looks like you win the scar competition," quipped Teague, standing behind him.

Finn chuckled softly. "I'm a disfigured man," he replied. "You might wanna rethink this whole thing." He grinned.

"Mais non," replied Teague. "The most important parts are just fine." He winked. "Your face is still pretty." He planted a kiss on the side of Finn's head, then spun around to set his focus on the shower. "Let's get you cleaned up," he said. "There's a small army out there waiting on you so they can dig into some of that food. Abuela has her heart set on fattening us up. I, for one, am more than willing to let her do her worst."

After Teague helped him shower, he guided him over to the bed, where Finn could rest while Teague took his own shower.

Finn didn't intend to fall asleep, but that was exactly what happened. The sudden crash of the door opening jolted him awake.

With a rush of air, Gabby burst into the room, jumping on the bed beside Finn. "You ready?" she asked.

"Gabby!" scolded Cat, as she ran into the room after the girl. "I told you that you cannot go running into their room unannounced."

The little girl gave a playful pout then stared up at Finn. "You don't mind. Do you?" she asked.

Finn wasn't sure he was ever going to get used to seeing his eyes on so many faces. He smiled. "You're welcome anytime," he said.

She giggled and snuggled up to him.

Cat smiled and shook her head slowly. "I see she has successfully wrapped you around her little finger too. Okay," she said. "There's a bunch of starving people outside waiting. If we don't get out there soon, my poor mother is going to have to fight them off with her wooden spoon." She chuckled. "Not that she wouldn't be able to, she's a force to be reckoned with, with that spoon of hers." She held out her hand. "Come on, Gabrielle, time to let him up."

Finn wasn't prepared for the pain he felt when he rose to his feet. For the first time since leaving the clinic, he wondered if he shouldn't take something to dull his senses. Based on the look on Teague's face, he was wondering the same thing. In the end, he decided to forgo any pain meds. He was sure all he needed was to move, his body would get used to it in no time.

All the same, he was thankful that Teague was there, giving him a strong body to lean against.

They made their way down the hall and into the living room where a set of large sliding glass doors stood open.

He stepped off the porch into the warm and inviting glow of string lights that hung overhead. Soft music could be heard playing from hidden speakers. The spicy, sweet scent of barbecue floated on the air, emanating from the outdoor kitchen area complete with grill, oven, refrigerator and a sink. A roaring fire blazed in the center of a stone pit, casting flickering shadows across the patio. The old woman stood in front of the table, a wooden spoon in her hand. When she saw Finn, her face lit up with love.

Everyone he knew and loved, as well as many new faces he was looking forward to getting to know better, peered up at him with happy smiles. Shane rushed up and helped Teague as he guided Finn over to a comfortable seat by the fire. Once settled, the old woman appeared with a warm plate in hand. She placed a napkin on his lap and handed him a fork. "You eat," she commanded, then turned and strolled over to the table where she made sure everyone had a full plate.

The horizon was painted in a bright, red hue as the sun slowly set behind the mountains. As Finn sat in the company of his friends and family, a sense of well-being washed over him, threatening to overwhelm him. This was all too good to be true. Once again, he found himself wondering if this was real or not.

Plate in hand, Gabby ran up and sat on the edge of his chair, he moved over to make more room for her. "I'm glad you're here," she said, then leaned close to whisper, "Maybe Marcus will leave me alone now."

"Who's Marcus?" he asked.

"He's a boy in my class," she replied. "He likes to make fun of my eyes."

A wave of anger rushed forward at the thought that some little creep was making Gabby upset. "As soon as I'm up for it," Finn said, with a wink. "I'll make sure he ain't a problem for you anymore."

She beamed up at him and shoved a forkful of refried beans into her mouth.

His stomach grumbled. He set his focus on his own plate, devouring it in record time, only to have a fresh one, filled with even more food, handed over to him. The old woman wasn't joking, she intended to fatten him up.

As the sun slowly vanished, the sky turned dark and the desert sky twinkled with a blanket of billions of tiny stars.

"You look a little overwhelmed," said Shane, as he took a seat. He lit a cigarette and took a long drag, then handed it over to Manny.

"Yeah, you're looking a little pale," agreed Manny. "How's it feel to be home?"

Finn let the words roll around in his head—home. He locked eyes with Shane. "It's almost like this is all a dream," he said.

"Here," said Manny. "Let your Tio help you out." Sporting a wicked grin, he reached out and pinched Finn's ear.

Finn pulled away, rubbing the side of his head.

"There, now you know it's real." Manny nodded toward the collection of misfits and outcasts gathered around. "Besides, if this is what you would dream about, I'm a little disappointed." He winked at Finn, then sauntered away.

"I guess that answered your question," said Teague, grinning wildly.

Shane laughed. "Better heal up," he said. "There's a lot more of that in your future." He stood up and stretched, then turned, one more time to Finn. "Take your time, Son. It's a lot to take in," he said, with a brief nod before turning away.

Finn watched Shane saunter over to Cat and wrap his arms around her waist, pulling her in for a kiss.

Son.

He let the word bounce off the walls of his mind. Growing up, he would cringe every time he heard it coming from Daniel, but for some reason, hearing it uttered from Shane's lips made him feel happy. He glanced around, taking in the scene before him. His close friends, laughing and talking with one another, mingling with all the new people.

Zac was off to the side with Mari, the two of them lost in their own little world. River was busy holding little Zephyr, swaying back and forth as she hummed, while Cash sat nearby, watching her, occasionally adding to the conversation with Ben and Tanner.

Shifting his eyes toward Beth, he noticed her sitting with a notepad atop the table, jotting things down while engaged in an animated conversation with Nate.

He reached out and took hold of Teague's hand then relaxed against the chair basking in the deep sense of well-being that washed over him. As difficult as it was to wrap his brain around, he was home.

Chapter Forty-Three

Two Years Later

Finn peered up at the clear, blue sky, watching a group of swallows flutter about. Some were busy catching bugs in the air, while others swooped down to skim water off the pond's surface to build their nests on the wood structure that Teague insisted they built. As promised, the structure attracted the birds, who in turn kept the mosquito population to a minimum.

Shane placed his fishing pole down and leaned forward to light a cigarette. "You know," he said, exhaling a plume of smoke. "When you said you wanted to put a bayou cabin on this pond, I sure as hell didn't imagine this." He leaned back against his chair and cast his gaze out over the area. "Using that old container for the building was sheer genius."

"Yeah, man," said Manny. "I'm a little jealous." He took the cigarette from Shane. "If I'd've known this was an option in life, I'd have made some different decisions." He exhaled and handed the smoke back.

Finn watched the two men with a humorous eye. "You know, I gotta ask," he said. "Why is it that you two are always doin' that?"

"Doing what?"

"Passin' a smoke between you," replied Finn. "It occurred to me just now that in two years, I've never seen you smoke alone. Either he lights up, or you do. It doesn't matter, 'cause you're always passin' it back and forth. Why?"

Shane glanced down at the cigarette in his hand, then up to Manny. The two men laughed. "Old habits die hard, I suppose."

"When we were young," explained Manny. "We were always broke. So, we'd share smokes." He shrugged.

"That's it, huh?" asked Finn. "That simple?"

"What can I say," replied Shane. "We're simple men." He flashed a smile.

Finn nodded, knowing damn well that Shane and his guys were anything but simple men. In fact, they were some of the most cunning men he had ever come across. His respect for them had swelled over the past two years, making him more than a little proud to be considered a part of their family.

"Goddammit!" cursed Pillar, as he pulled his line from the water. "He did it again!"

"I think he likes you," teased Manny.

Pillar held the line in the air so everyone could see there was no longer a hook or bait attached. "I swear to god," said the big man. "If that turtle snaps at my line one more time, I'm gonna stop fishing and make me some turtle soup." He turned to Finn. "Why? Why did you bring him here? Who the hell puts a giant, snapping turtle in his fishing pond?"

"It was either Hector or Walter," replied Teague. "And believe me, we're all a lot better off with Walter in Louisiana where he belongs."

Manny leaned back against his chair and rested his feet on the porch railing. "I like how you used these old boat seats," he said. "It's a lot better than sitting in a regular chair."

"It'd be a whole lot better if I could catch a fish," added Pillar.

Odie hollered and pulled on his fishing rod. "Maybe it's not the fish, so much as it's the fisher," he laughed.

"It's that damn turtle," said Pillar. "He's got it in for me."

"Whatever you gotta convince yourself of," said Odie.

"I gotta do this at my place," said Manny. "We could blow out a bigger pond in that far corner where nothing grows."

"If we do it," said Odie. "I'm the one in charge of the explosives this time."

"Still salty, I see," teased Finn.

"Until you came along, explosives were always my gig," said Odie. "I have no intention of stepping down." He glared playfully at Finn. "No matter how much you whine about it."

Finn laughed, recalling the day they blasted the hole in the ground that would become their private pond. Odie was so upset that he didn't get to push the button, it was comical.

Two years had passed since that fateful night. It took Finn almost no time to adjust to the new dynamic—which, in hindsight, was quite a surprise. He never imagined what life would be like when they stopped moving around and found a place to settle down. For sure, he never thought that he and Teague would end up building a container cabin, complete with a deep pond and a great view of the rolling hills.

Shane was more than happy to set them up on the back end of his property, he wanted them to be nearby.

From his earliest memory, Finn used to imagine what a good father would be like. His childish mind conjured up a man with strength, resolve, and inner calm. One who understood how to control his anger, but also knew there were times when a man had to fight for what he wanted. Shane was that man. The older man always liked to say he was far from perfect, but in Finn's eyes, he was exactly that.

Gabby, Cat, Abuela and Mari were all a bonus he could have never conjured up in his wildest imagination. It didn't take long at all for him to come to love them all.

Cat was like the mom he never had. Fierce and protective, she reminded him more of a lioness. Her face wore a ready smile for those she loved, but she had nothing but pure malice for anyone who went against her family—even Manny.

Abuela was absolutely hell-bent on fattening him up. It didn't help that her food was always so delicious. Teague loved the old woman. The two of them would sit for hours talking about everything from spice to family to the general state of the world.

As for Gabby, that was a surprisingly easy adjustment for Finn. He'd never had someone look up to him like that. At first, it made him nervous, after all, he didn't want to do anything that would taint the little girl's perception of him. Come to think of it, Cat was right that first night, Gabby had him wrapped around her little finger the moment he laid eyes on her.

The most difficult transition was with Marisol. Witty and confident, the woman knew how to maneuver in the world. He admired her for that; however, he could have done without all the big sister stuff. Finn couldn't quite explain why, but for some reason, hearing her refer to him as her baby brother made him cringe every time. Even now, two years later, he still bristled a little over it. Was it irrational for him to feel this way? Sure. Was he working toward changing his feelings? No. Even with all the banter between them, Finn knew they loved one another. Shane would sometimes comment, saying that Finn and Mari reminded him a lot of Cat and Manny. Whenever he would do this, both Mari and Finn would pass a knowing glance between them. They were more than okay with the comparison.

His phone chimed in his pocket. Finn didn't have to pull it out to see what was up, Teague was already on it.

"Zac and Cole are about an hour away," announced Teague.

"Well," sighed Shane, reeling in his fishing line. "That's my cue. I'm sure Cat and Mari have things I need to do before they arrive." He climbed to his feet and stretched. "We'll see you at the house for dinner," he said, glancing back and forth to Finn and Teague.

Odie, Manny and Pillar packed up and left with Shane, leaving

Finn alone with Teague, sitting on their porch, listening to the chirping of the swallows.

Tonight was going to be a big deal. This was the day Zac had waited for, the day he and his little brother were back together, ready to build a new life together.

Zac and Mari's wedding was in two days. He wanted to wait until Cole could be there, and Mari agreed wholeheartedly.

If you asked Finn what he envisioned for the future, Zac's wedding would have never come to mind. Though, in hindsight, Zac was always destined to find a beautiful woman and settle down with lots of kids and a ranch of his own.

Come to think of it, weddings seemed to be happening every twelve months—the last one being Cash and River.

That one was hardly a surprise for anyone, that is, aside from River and Cash themselves. Their celebration was held at Stoney's with all the Nomads present, including the new additions to the family—Shane and his crew.

So much change had taken place among the entire Nomad crew.

Cash opened his own tattoo shop in the studio space above Shane's bar. The money was steady enough that he and River moved into their own apartment in town. It wasn't much, but they made it their own.

Gunner and Gypsy had stopped riding, according to him, it was because the little dog was getting too old to hop on and off all the time. Everyone knew better, but no one even dared to point out what was obvious. It was good to see the older man settled and content. He still had his job as a bartender in Terlingua, as well as helping Stoney build out his compound which now had a total of ten units, not including Gunner or Stoney's homes.

Spinner and Bella had finally found their dream home in Belize and were living it up on the soft, sandy beaches.

As for Ben, Mara, and little Zephyr, they were busy making plans to relocate down to El Paso. They wanted to be closer to friends.

Beth was riding with Tanner and Nate, though from what they

all heard, she and Nate were ready to split off on their own—young love would do that to you.

According to Ben, Tanner was planning on moving to El Paso as soon as he and Mara were there.

Of course, Tripp and Sam were still doing their thing, though even they began to ponder life off the rails. It seemed as though everyone was moving forward with their lives. Even Bells, Max and D. B. had been pondering whether it was time to stop.

"Whatcha thinkin' about?" asked Teague.

Finn shrugged. "Just processing all the changes."

Teague nodded. "Oui," he replied. "I think about that too from time to time. It all seems good; everyone's happy."

Finn could hear a vehicle roll up on the gravel. It honked its horn twice, then Cash called out, "Yo! Where's everybody at?" A moment later, both Cash and River wandered up onto the porch. Something was off. Their facial expressions were strange. Finn shot a worried glance over at Teague.

Cash disappeared inside the cabin and came out with a bottle of whiskey, which he promptly opened and downed a huge gulp.

"What's up?" asked Teague, apprehensively.

River plopped down into a chair and put her feet up on the rail. "You tell them," she said.

Cash took another gulp and wiped his mouth. "We just got back from the doctor. River's pregnant."

Finn gasped in unison with Teague. Unable to think of anything to say, he stared in stunned silence at River.

"Yep," she said happily. "Looks like Cash is gonna be a dad."

"And River's about to be a mom," said Cash, smiling.

Something wasn't fitting. They both seemed happy with the news. So why did they arrive with such stunned looks on their faces?

"What are you not telling us?" asked Teague.

River chuckled and placed her hand softly against her belly. "Apparently, we can't do things like normal people," she said. "It seems as though twins run in one of our families." She held up two fingers for emphasis. "Who knew?"

Finn turned in shock to Cash who was staring into space with an almost green look to him.

"Merde!" exclaimed Teague.

"Wow!" said Finn. He took the bottle of whiskey from Cash. Upon further reflection, he handed it back. "You know, you're only supposed to do this one at a time," he teased.

Cash's only response was a nervous chuckle.

"So, do you know if they're boys or girls?" asked Teague.

"Too soon to tell," said River. "All we know so far is that there are two of them in here." Once again, she rubbed her belly in that unconscious way, expecting moms do.

"I have about six months to get things together before they arrive," said Cash. He took another swig, then screwed the cap back on the bottle and handed it over to Finn. "Looks like you two are gonna be uncles." He sauntered over to River and wrapped his arm around her.

Teague leaned back in his chair. "Looks like we got some baby proofing to do around here," he said, to Finn.

"Hell, naw!" replied Finn. "As uncles, it's our job to teach the kids to live life on the edge." He grinned. "And to kick some ass when someone's bothering them. Just ask Manny."

The sound of everyone's phones chiming at once echoed off the metal wall of the cabin. This time Finn pulled his phone out and read the message. Zac had arrived with Cole. They were waiting for them at the main house.

"Welp," announced Cash, shoving his phone in his pocket. "That's our cue." He took River by the hand. "We'll see you guys up there."

"We'll be right behind you," replied Teague.

After a brief hug, once again, Teague and Finn were alone.

"Come on," said Teague, slapping Finn on the arm. "Let's get packed up and head on over. There's a whole bunch of people waiting to visit."

They went inside and put on clean clothes. On his way toward the door, Finn stopped by the wall of photos. In the center hung a lone image of Melody when she was pregnant with him. Surrounding her were pictures of all the people Finn loved, including one with his entire family.

A sublime smile spread across his face. Life was good, and the future looked bright.

The End

Acknowledgments

If you enjoyed this book, please take a moment and leave a review or rating. It doesn't have to be anything super in depth, a simple five-star rating will be just fine.

First of all, I want to thank all of you who have come along for the roller coaster ride. It's been one hell of a journey and I appreciate y'all more than you know.

I wanna take a moment to call out a few folks for their undying support for the Nomads. First, Vic Willette – this woman is a never-ending source of enthusiasm and emotional support for me. If y'all have a friend like her in your lives, you are truly blessed.

Samantha Dayton – Believe me when I say this woman has been there from the beginning. Her encouragement and feedback are things I honestly wouldn't be here without.

My kids, Brenna, Connor, Meagan, Shannon & Rory and the two significant others, aka my bonus sons, Cody and Logan. I spent two decades supporting and cheering them on to pursue their dreams and now these wonderful human beings are doing the same for me. From feedback, to shouts of support to artwork and design help... seriously y'all I have the best kids.

And of course, we cannot forget, Robert McLaughlin, my partner —my rock—my best friend. He listens to my rants and ravings, all the while, offering input "whenever he can. He is my road trip partner— my sounding board—my anchor. He will always be the love of my life.

Afterword

Whew! We made it! I'm both overjoyed to be here and more than a little sad. This little band of misfits has been such a personal part of my life for so long, it feels strange to let them go. I'm gonna miss them. Who knows, maybe someday I'll be drawn back into their world to reconnect and see where they are in their journeys. It's not too far-fetched, I mean, after all, it only makes sense that they would be a perfect addition to Shane and his crew.

When I originally set out to write the story of these hapless misfits, I didn't do so with the intent to write a mainstream, commercial hit. After all, writing a story based around a group of normal, non-magical young hobos, is hardly mainstream fodder. Could I have made the Nomads vampires? Sure. They would have taken the world by storm. But that was never my intention with this story.

This was a labor of love. These characters had been trolling around in my head for years and they needed to be brought to life on the page. They needed to be very real people with very real issues that needed to be overcome. It's been an absolute joy to see the mix of readers who have been drawn into this little world. Even now, the story and the characters gain new fans every day, it's amazing to see and it makes my heart sing.

Now, that's not to say there won't soon be a story based around a young, trainhopping vampire. I mean, why not? Anything's possible.

I do still have some Nomad origin stories to post. The story, Melody, on the next page is indeed one of these. Originally written as a part of book four, it simply didn't make the final cut. However, it is an important and heart wrenching story, so it needed to be shared. Be sure to keep some tissues on hand.

If you are on Inkitt you can follow me there.

https://www.inkitt.com/nlmclaughlin

Or simply follow me on my website, as they will be posted there as well. Link below.

Here's a link to my website...

https://www.nancylmclaughlin.com/

So, what's next you ask? Lots of writing.

My shapeshifter horror, Tricksters, will be released in July of 2024. I am including the first chapter at the end of this book, just as a teaser of what is to come. Be sure to give it a read.

Popular Monsters—If the Pied Piper was a three-man metalcore band, set on a mission to turn their fans into minions who do their evil bidding. This one was originally supposed to be a quick write, but, like the Nomads, it has taken on a life of its own. It's become a much deeper story. I'm slowing down to give this one all the time it needs to come to life. It'll be worth it.

And finally, Feral—this has now become a sequel to Tricksters. I can't tell you exactly what it's about, because I don't want to give any spoilers for Tricksters. But suffice to say, you're gonna love it.

I have a few other ideas bouncing around in my head, but I'm trying to get these out before jumping into anything new. I know, I know, good luck with that.

So, that is all I have to share for now. Thank you so much for giving my creations a chance. As always, feedback or input is always appreciated. If you want to keep up with what's going on, give me a follow on any of the Social Media platforms—I think I'm on all of them.

Until next time, peace to y'all.

Nancy

Melody

Twenty years ago–Gainesville, TX

RED LIGHTS FLASHED, casting an eerie glow on everything in view, as the piercing siren blared, cutting through the quiet night. The ambulance accelerated, its tires screeching against the asphalt as it navigated the city streets, cloaked in darkness.

All around her people spoke in technical terms with professional tones. She rubbed her hand across her belly, feeling the baby inside move against her touch. "It's gonna be okay, little one. Just hang on," she whispered.

Electronic machines beeped in time with both her heartbeat and the baby's. Whoosh, whoosh, whoosh, was the sound coming from the monitor on the child. Beep, beep, beep was the sound of her own.

The paramedic leaned close, a gentle smile on her face that didn't quite reach up to her eyes. "We're almost there mama, everything's gonna be okay." The scent of antiseptic lingered, mingling with a faint metallic tang.

"How's my baby? Is he okay?"

The woman glanced at the monitor that was tracking the baby's heartbeat. She nodded her head. "He sounds just fine mama."

Melody wanted to believe her, but between the look in the paramedic's eyes and the glance she shared with her partner, trust was hard to come by. She placed her hand on her distended belly, feeling a tiny foot press against the inside. She traced the outline of the tiny heel. The pain meds had dulled the pain, but she could still feel the alien sensation of another life struggling to break free from inside her body. The baby stretched. Melody ran her hand along her abdomen, noting the position of the baby. His feet were just under her sternum, his head facing down toward her pelvis. This was exactly where he needed to be. She breathed a sigh of relief.

She inhaled; her lungs didn't seem to take in enough air. She breathed in again, only this time deeper. Dizziness washed over her, the cabin of the ambulance spun around in her vision. In her chest, she could feel her heart race—no it was more of a flutter. She closed her eyes and inhaled, trying to catch her breath. A mask was placed over her face, cool air rushed past her lips into her struggling lungs. The beep of her own heartbeat slowed, the pause between each thump grew longer. The paramedic turned the dial down low; so low, Melody could no longer hear it.

Inside her belly, the baby lashed out with a violent kick, then another much harder than the last, followed by yet another. *He's struggling.*

Melody focused on the sound of his heartbeat. At first normal, whoosh, whoosh, whoosh, it slowed ever so slightly with each beat, whoosh... whoosh... whoosh.

In a swift motion, the paramedic dove for the controls, turning the dial all the way down.

Melody could no longer hear the heartbeats. "What's wrong?" she asked with rising concern.

"Shh, shh," replied the paramedic. "It's okay."

"It's not okay!" shouted Melody. She tried to pull her mask off, but the paramedic forced her hands down along her sides and secured them to the gurney. Panic exploded in her chest. The baby thrashed in her belly. Tears burst from her eyes, streaming down the sides of her face, dampening her hair. Each breath was a struggle.

Her baby writhed inside her. *"Please save him," she begged.*

The ambulance came to a halt, and the door swung open. A flurry of activity erupted around her. Medical lingo, most of which she could barely understand flew around her. The gurney was removed from the ambulance and rolled into the hospital. A gauntlet of people in scrubs passed by in a stream of greens and blues. They wheeled her into a brightly lit room, lifted her from the gurney, and placed her onto a table.

A man with pale hair and scrubs removed the mask from her face and raised another as a replacement.

"Please save my baby!" pleaded Melody. She grabbed hold of his arm and looked him directly in the eyes. "Don't let him die."

The man responded with a solemn nod, then gently swept an errant lock of dark brown hair away from her eyes. He smiled, yet another one of those smiles that never made it to the eyes, then he placed the mask against Melody's face.

The air was filled with the sound of beeping machines, the soft hiss of oxygen escaping through tubes, and the faint buzz of fluorescent lights above.

A blue fabric shield was placed just above her abdomen, making it impossible to see anything but the overhead lights. The only face she could focus on was that of the pale haired man.

Inside her belly, the baby's movement slowed. Instinctively, she moved to hold her belly, but her hands were restrained. *"Momma loves you, baby. Hold on," she muttered under her mask.*

Medicine dulled the pain, but she could feel every tug and pull. The movement reminded her of the sensation of being dressed by someone else. Tugging and pulling, her body moved around by the hands of strangers. The baby writhed in her belly. A quick tug nearly lifted her body from the table, then suddenly the baby was no longer there. For the first time in months, she could no longer feel his presence. Her body was her own, like it had been her entire life, a deep feeling of emptiness settled deep inside her soul. She had grown accustomed to sharing her body with him, now suddenly, that was no more. Darkness closed in around the edges of her vision; her eyelids grew heavy.

In the room's corner, a baby wailed. Her baby.

"Let me have my baby!" she yelled. "Please," she begged. "Bring him here."

The doors to the room swung open, and her parents entered. Her mom sat down on the edge of the bed. Her dad stood several feet away, tears streaming down his red, blotchy face.

"Mom, please tell them to give me my baby," she said, with tears streaming down her cheeks.

"It's okay baby girl," cooed her mom. "The nurse is bringing him."

Something about her tone struck Melody as odd. She studied her mother's face, noting the blotchy redness and puffy eyes. When she smiled, her lips quivered; when she spoke, her voice trembled as though the words were stuck in her throat. She looked around the room. The monitors were all turned off, and the medical staff had left. Something wasn't right, she struggled to make sense.

The baby wailed, pushing out every ounce of breath from his tiny lungs.

"Shh, shh," cooed the nurse as she stepped near, holding the swaddled baby in her arms. "Here's mama." She placed him against Melody's chest, then stepped back.

The baby immediately stopped screaming. Tremors ran through his tiny body with every breath he took. He stared up at Melody with one blue eye and one amber brown. *Just like daddy.* She brushed a gentle finger across his cheek and under his chin. "Hello there, little man," she whispered.

The baby yawned then shoved his tiny fist into his mouth, his body now completely relaxed in his momma's warm embrace.

Melody stared down at the beautiful, tiny human being in her arms. Never in her life had she ever seen a more beautiful sight. She kissed the top of his fuzzy head, breathing in his scent. The world dropped away; it was just her and her sweet baby boy.

"Finnegan Shane Ryan," she hummed in sing-song notes. "Your daddy's gonna be so happy to meet you."

The nurse lifted her blanket, removing a blood-soaked pad that lay beneath Melody's body, replacing it with a clean pad.

Melody hardly noticed the activity or the general mood around the room. The only thing she cared about was the precious baby boy, nestled in her arms. She breathed in deep, relishing the soft scent of her precious baby boy. She grew sleepy. With each passing second, her eyelids grew heavier. She didn't want to close them; she wanted to stare at her baby boy forever.

He stared up at her, alert yet calm. "You're perfect," she whispered. She kissed the top of his fuzzy head one more time.

Sleepiness came on strong, she struggled to keep her eyes open but to no avail. *Maybe just a little rest.* Her body relaxed and her arm slipped. Before she could correct herself, the nurse swooped in and scooped the baby away. The woman stood close, swaying back and forth as the baby, once again, broke into crying.

"It's okay baby boy," sighed Melody, her eyes closed, her breathing slowed. "Momma's gotta rest. Just for a little while."

The baby wailed, a flurry of movement erupted around the room, but Melody didn't care. She let herself fall into the heavy darkness that swallowed everything.

Tricksters

Coming July 2024

CHAPTER ONE

Surrounded by a blanket of sparkling stars, the full moon hung heavy in the midnight sky. On the ground, delicate shadows danced like specters between the skeletal limbs of desert plants. The earthy fragrance of wild sagebrush permeated the air.

Accompanied by the sound of gravel crunching beneath his boots, the young man made his way toward the small, back country gas station. Tonight was an important night. It was his chance to prove, for once and for all, that he was a grown member of the pack. To finally show his older brother Caleb that he was an equal. Two years had passed since his first turning, his acceptance as an adult member was long overdue. Forever relegated to the rear, under the watchful eyes of the others, he longed for a time when the pack trusted him enough to carry out important tasks. The gravity of this opportunity could not be overstated. What happened this night would dictate how the pack—how Caleb viewed him going forward.

Pax halted and surveyed his surroundings. Born and raised in the west Texas mountains, he could hardly imagine a more beautiful place to call home. As far as he was concerned, people could keep their cities to themselves. He much preferred the freedom of the open desert. Only two visits to the city in nineteen years were sufficient for him to realize it wasn't a place for someone like him. The overwhelming smells and commotion made it unbearable.

He leaned forward to light a cigarette. As he exhaled a cloud of smoke and gazed down at the lighter, he ran his thumb over the emblem sculpted into the shell of polished bone. A perfect circle of ancient runes surrounding four coyote paws. Of all his possessions, this was the most cherished. Pax was never much of a collector or keeper of things, but this small trinket held great importance to him. This was the only item he kept that belonged to his father.

A lone coyote called out; Caleb was letting him know he was nearby. Pax grinned and let out a howl, releasing a cloud of cigarette smoke at the same time. A round of coyote chatter answered in kind.

He took another long drag from his cigarette, then pocketed the lighter. It was time to stop fooling around and get down to business. He picked up his pace and made his way to the gas station.

Standing in the shadows on the corner, he took a moment to adjust to the blinding lights above and survey his surroundings.

Because of the late hour, all was quiet and calm. A blue SUV was parked alongside a pump. The driver, a big, bearded man was smoking a cigarette while holding the nozzle. He nodded his head toward Pax, who reciprocated.

Pax rounded the corner of the building hoping for better options, and was met with the sight of a red sports car sitting idle in a parking slip. The owners of the vehicle were nowhere in sight, they must be inside. The sound of a vehicle engine rumbling to life startled him. He glanced over just in time to see the blue SUV pull out onto the highway. As he watched the taillights disappear into the dark, Pax finished his cigarette.

The double glass doors opened with a whoosh, blowing a gust of artificial cold air into the night. Two young women stepped out, nearly crashing into him, their arms laden with bags heavy with junk food. A pretty redhead paused in front of him and gave him a once-over. "Hello," she said with a smile.

Pax ran his fingers through his sandy blond hair and flashed his most charming smile. He cleared his throat and took a single step forward.

Once again, the doors slid open and out came another young woman, not as pretty as the other two, but still quite attractive. She rolled her eyes in disgust and sighed at her friends. "What did I tell you about picking up strays in the desert?" she scolded as she shoved the other two women toward the vehicle. "Do you wanna get murdered by a serial killer? Because this is how you get murdered by a serial killer."

"Come on, Nikki, don't be like that," said the redhead. "He's cute."

The one named Nikki eyed Pax. "Sorry Mr. Serial killer, I'm sure you're a lovely person, but you're gonna have to find other victims tonight," she said.

The redhead turned to Pax and made a pouty face. "Sorry, cutie, mom says no." She gave a shrug then climbed into the car.

"You're pathetic, Sarah," said the driver as she, too, climbed inside the vehicle.

The sound of laughter could be heard as the car backed out of the parking slip. Before the vehicle drove away, Sarah leaned out of the window. "Maybe next time," she called out, then blew a kiss at Pax. The women's laughter echoed as they sped away in a cloud of dust, leaving him alone under the bright fluorescent lights.

For the first time all night, doubt, followed by anxiety, crept into his thoughts. What if those girls were his only opportunity for the night? Why hadn't he spoken up sooner? Or at all? How was he going to explain this to Caleb? He couldn't stand the thought of seeing the look of disappointment on his brother's face.

As though the universe had heard his despair, a pair of headlights became visible on the horizon. Too small to be an eighteen-wheeler, and too large to be a regular passenger vehicle; it coasted along the highway, then slowly down the offramp and along the side road, heading toward the gas station.

Game on, thought Pax, as he prepared himself to put on a good show. This time, he would get it right.

As the vehicle approached, he could make out that it was an old model RV. The vehicle lumbered into the gas station, pulling up alongside a pump with the sound of squeaking brakes that reverberated throughout the hills.

A man climbed out of the driver's seat and stretched. Clean shaven and muscular, he surveyed the area, pausing briefly to study Pax. In the passenger seat, there was a woman digging through a bag on her lap.

With no other opportunities in sight, and eager to move forward with the night, Pax stepped off the curb and approached the man. A thousand conversation starters played out in his mind.

"Evenin'," he said in a friendly tone.

"Evenin'," replied the man. He shot a quick glance around the gas station. "Need a ride?"

Right to the chase, this made things a lot easier. He put on his best trustworthy country boy act, and replied, "That obvious, huh?"

The man's lips curved upward in a smile. "Not much else you could want out here."

Pax nodded. "I don't need to go far. Just a few miles up the road."

He studied the man, noting his muscular build and the way he carried himself with quiet confidence. Everything about his mannerisms screamed military. Moving closer to the vehicle, Pax peered inside at the passenger. The woman with long, dark hair and trusting eyes rolled down her window and smiled at him. An infant cried from the back of the RV, followed by a slightly older child asking, "Who is it, momma?"

Pax's face broke into a sly grin. He returned his focus to the man.

"How'd you get all the way out here?" asked the man, his eyes darting around the barren landscape.

"I live about ten miles that way," replied Pax, pointing toward the hills.

A look of confusion swept across the man's face. "Then what are you doing here at this hour?"

"I had a little disagreement with my girl, sir," said Pax, doing his best to sound convincing. He smiled innocently. "She kicked me out of my truck and took off, and well, here I am." He bowed his head.

The woman let out a small chuckle. "You must have done something real bad to make her that angry," she said.

Pax peered up at the woman with his best impression of an innocent teen, and replied, "In all honesty, Ma'am, she knew what she was getting into when she hooked up with me." He winked at the man. "And for the record, I am an absolute gentleman."

The man let out a laugh. "I bet you are," he replied.

"My dad taught me to always be a gentleman," said Pax. "Lord rest his soul." He stared down at his boots for emphasis. "I wouldn't do anything to sully his memory."

The man's eyes grew soft. "Well, why don't you hop on in? We'll give you a ride home. As a dad myself, I wouldn't want my son out here alone at this hour. You can sort things out with your girl tomorrow."

"Thank you very much, sir," replied Pax, trying hard to stay in character. He strolled over to the side door and waited.

A moment later, the latch clicked, and the woman stood in the open doorway. She greeted him with a soft smile and said, "Come on in. Make yourself comfortable." She gestured for Pax to sit in the passenger's seat, then settled in beside the infant.

"Who's he momma?" asked a little girl sitting in a booster seat, her hair tied up in two pigtails. Clasped in her arms was a small brown rabbit that looked like it had seen better days. With a wary eye, she stared at Pax while twisting a soft ear in her tiny fingers.

The baby, who was strapped into the car seat, fussed, and arched its back.

"My name's Sherry," said the mom.

"I'm Chris," said the man as he climbed into the driver's seat and nodded in greeting.

"Pax," he replied with a big smile. "Nice to meet y'all." He nodded toward the little girl. "And you too, miss."

The little girl stared suspiciously.

"That's Ella," said Sherry. "She doesn't take easily to new people. Don't worry about her. She'll warm up soon enough."

Pax winked at the girl, then set his focus to the infant in the car seat. "And who's this?"

With a smile on her face, Sherry picked up the child. "This little man is Colter." She settled him down on her lap and offered her breast.

"Pax," said Chris. "That's a good, honest name." He leaned forward and turned the key. The engine rumbled to life. "Alright son," he said. "Where am I going?"

"Head up the highway a few miles. I'll let you know where to turn off."

Chris nodded and pulled away from the station. "It sure is peaceful out here," he said.

"That's the way we like it," replied Pax.

"What is it you do for work all the way out here?"

"My family owns a ranch," replied Pax. "What about you folks? Y'all on vacation?"

"Chris is reporting for recruiting duty," said Sherry. Her words dripping with pride.

She took the baby from her breast, settled him on her shoulder and rubbed his back.

"Is that so?" asked Pax. "What branch?"

Chris cleared his throat and sat up straight. "Army. I'm heading to Midland to take on a recruiting position. You ever consider serving?"

"Me? Nah, my people ain't really a good fit for the military."

"That's too bad. There're a lot of perks to serving." Chris peered up at the night sky through the windshield. "There's an entire world filled with exotic places and interesting people to see."

"You mean besides all the women?" quipped Pax.

Sherry giggled in the back and shook her head.

"Turn off here," said Pax, pointing out the window.

Chris pulled off the highway and turned down the gravel road. "You mentioned your father passed. Does your mother run the ranch?"

"No sir, she died with my father. My older brother and I run it all now, my sister's a little too young to do much." A sense of melancholy settled in at the thought of his parents. Pax preferred not to think about his mom and dad, it only made him feel bad. He commanded himself to focus on the task at hand. They were almost there.

They drove in silence for three miles before Chris showed signs of suspicion. "You sure this is the way? It looks like there's nothing down here."

"Yes sir, I'm sure. We're comin' up on the gate now," replied Pax calmly.

At the gate, Chris parked the RV. "Wow! This really is in the middle of nowhere," he said. "It's pretty though." He scanned the darkness. "I'm curious. What is it that your family does out here on the ranch?"

"Cattle," said Pax. He leaned back in the seat, taking in the final moments of calm in Chris's life. Too bad the foolish man had no idea what was about to happen.

"Well," said Chris. "It was nice meeting you, Pax. If you ever change your mind about serving, give me a shout." He held out a business card.

"That's not gonna happen," replied Pax, his tone serious. He stretched his jaw, revealing a mouthful of long, sharp, white teeth. His eyes shined with an icy blue glow.

Realization slowly dawned on Chris; his facial expression changed from apprehension to fear.

Pax didn't move, savoring the moment as they stared at one

another in silence. The blissful ignorance of the innocents in the back of the RV ignited a rush of adrenaline that coursed throughout his body, his limbs twitched in anticipation.

When Chris attempted to move, Pax immediately lunged forward and wrapped a clawed hand around the man's throat, holding him in his chair and inhibiting his breathing.

"Don't struggle," he hissed.

The trickster's strength and power were overwhelming for Chris. Despite the warning, he struggled against Pax's grip, his face turning red from the lack of oxygen.

As soon as Sherry realized what was happening, she screamed, causing her children to respond with equal terror. When she moved to intervene on her husband's behalf, Pax lashed out with his free hand, knocking her to the floor.

"Try it again and I'll rip his throat out, then hang you with your children's entrails," he growled with a vicious sneer.

Sherry obeyed with tears falling down her cheeks, choosing to curl up on the floor, close to the children, and cry. Restrained in their car seats, the children wailed.

"Please," begged Chris, tears pooling in his eyes. "Take me—just let my family go." His throat constricting with each word.

Pax let up some of the pressure on the man's throat. He leaned close enough to smell the fear emanating from his pores. "Whether they live or die is up to you," he said. "So, listen carefully."

Chris swallowed and gave a curt nod.

"Good man," said Pax. He released his grip and tapped Chris on the side of his face. "We're gonna play a little game. In a minute, I'm gonna let you and your family go." A wicked smile played across his lips. "If you can get to the next town, you'll live to see another day. There's only one caveat." He reached down and pulled the keys from the ignition. "You're gonna have to do it on foot."

"Why?" stammered Chris. "Why are you doing this?"

A coyote's howl carried through the air.

"Because we prefer to hunt our meat," replied Pax. "Enhances the flavor. You know?" He reached over to the glove box and flipped it open, exposing a handgun. "I figured you'd have one of these." He gave the gun to Chris, who refused to take it at first, remaining motionless. "Go on, you can take it," said Pax. "I want you to use it. It's best if you learn now that your toy won't do you much good."

With trembling hands, Chris took the gun.

The stunned silence was shattered by the deafening sound of a gunshot.

A searing pain erupted in Pax's shoulder; his ears rung. Hardly phased, he stretched his neck and popped his jaw, making room for his growing teeth. He raised a hand to his chest and retrieved the round, then held it high. The tiny metal object glinted in the moonlight. "Like I said," he warned. "It ain't gonna do you much good." He dropped the bullet to the floor and rose to his feet. "If you head out that way," he said, pointing. "You'll come to the next town in about thirty miles."

Pax strolled over to the door, pausing in front of the sobbing woman. He stared down at her, breathing in her scent. The fear was intoxicating. He turned and swung the door open, allowing it to slam against the RV wall, then stepped out onto the ground. Banging his fist twice on the side of the vehicle, he bellowed, "Come on out. And make it quick."

With the toddler in his arms, Chris appeared in the doorway, while Sherry stood behind him, holding the baby closely.

"Well, stop dawdling," said Pax. "We ain't got all night. Get down here."

The couple did as they were told.

"Well, well, well," came a voice from the shadows. First to appear was Ezra, his wide grin and glistening teeth illuminated by the moonlight. Not far behind him were Bass, Izzy, and finally Caleb.

"I was beginning to think this night would be a bust," said Ezra.

"You and me both," teased Bass. He grinned and locked eyes with Pax. "What do we have tonight?"

"A family pack," quipped Pax.

Caleb stepped forward and placed a hand on the teen's shoulder. "You did good, little brother."

Reveling in the compliment, Pax smiled. "Well," he said. "What are we waiting for?" He turned his attention to the terrified family.

The little girl buried her face against her father's chest, dropping her bunny as she whimpered.

Pax retrieved the toy and tucked it under the arm of the cowering child, then leaned close to Chris. "Run," he growled.

Without another word or prompt, the family took off running into the desert, leaving the pack behind.

While they waited, Izzy's soft, melodic voice counted down as she danced in anticipation. "Twenty-two, twenty-three, twenty-four, twenty-five." When she reached sixty, she turned to the group and smiled. "Ding, ding. Dinner time," she said.

The sound of shedding skin echoed around Pax as he and the others transformed. He was ready for the hunt. His excitement mounting, he let out a bone-chilling howl that pierced the stillness of the night. With a chorus of yips and howls, the others responded, then took off in a frenzy of excitement, following the scent of their prey.

To Be Continued... July 2024

www.ingramcontent.com/pod-product-compliance
Lightning Source LLC
Chambersburg PA
CBHW061646190726
48289CB00006B/1768